Hidden Ties

A DARK MAFIA ROMANCE

CARMEN ROSALES

Erotic Quill Publishing, LLC

Manufactured in the United States of America
First Edition February 2023

Also by Carmen Rosales

Hillside Kings Series

Hidden Scars

Hidden Lies

Hidden Truths- (Leo & Katalia)-April 1st, 2023

Hidden Scion-(Alex & Alina)-Coming Soon

A Dark Duet

Giselle

Briana

Standalone's

He Loves Me Not- Coming Soon

Dirty Little Secrets-Coming Soon

Dearly Beloved-Coming Soon

Vows Written in Blood-Coming Soon

The Prey Series

Thirst

Lust

Appetite-May 20, 2023

Forgive Me For I Have Sinned

Steamy Romance

Changing the Game-

Until Her

Until Now

Hidden Ties is part of the Hillside King's world and is a standalone tying it together. The original title was the Elysium Trilogy. It has been rewritten and reedited. There are new scenes and events.

Dear Reader,

The triggers include death, acts of violence, and acts of bullying. All sex is for the enjoyment of all characters involved. This series touches themes that might be triggering for some readers.

After finishing her degree at NYU, Selena Tenaka is having trouble finding her identity. When her closest friend Mia offers her a dream job in Seattle after she graduates, she accepts, but she never expects to fall for the dangerously attractive billionaire Relic King. The push and pull she feels for the first time are both powerful and forbidden.

But she can't deny that Relic's dark and dangerously good looks are what draws her to him. He comes from a dark world, and to him, she's simply another woman who falls for his charms but pushes his true feelings for her away and breaks Selena's heart because she is not from his world.

So he thought.

When Selena's childhood friend Jiro comes to take her after she is heartbroken, she is forced into a world where she is destined to rule. Her grandfather's legacy is hers to claim, even if she thought she looked like an outsider when she would visit Japan when she was younger.

Jiro helps her find herself and reminds her of all they shared when they were kids. She never thought she would fall in love all over again. When she is required to go back to Seattle and take her place, her past and present collide. Hidden ties are revealed.

Enemies want to destroy her.

Her safety is a priority.

Old feelings that were buried resurface.

Two powerful men vow to protect her, they both want her, but her heart is split in two.

She can't choose one over the other.

My phone alarm jolts me awake, like someone breaking into a window with a hammer. I groan as I turn it off, but it's replaced by knocking on my bedroom door.

"Selena! Are you awake?" Mia, my best friend, asks, her loud voice coming through the door. "You don't want to be late on your first day of work."

"I'm up! I'll be right out."

I drag myself out of bed and get ready to begin my new life as a business analyst for King Enterprises, one of the most prestigious corporations in the world. My first "real" job since I graduated from NYU and moved to Seattle. King Enterprises is a family business passed down to Mia's boyfriend, Deacon, and his two brothers. According to Forbes and the media, they are the youngest to inherit a billion-dollar fortune.

Thankfully, Mia works in accounting at the company and pulled some strings to get me hired. She informed me that getting a position at King Enterprises without a significant amount of expertise in the field is practically unheard of, so it's temporary for six months until I can prove I am a good fit. Hopefully, I do, considering I direly need a job to provide for myself. I barely have any money left after paying for student loans.

After I shower, I go through my closet and realize I don't have shit to wear. The job requires professional attire, so I dress in a pair of black slacks and a button-down top I purchased from a thrift shop. I'm not used to wearing clothes like this, so it's a bit like a woman wearing high heels for the first time and wobbling like Bambi. I might as well walk around with a gigantic sign that reads, *this is my first grown-up outfit!*

I'm winding my black, waist-length hair into a bun when Mia knocks again.

"Selena, are you ready?"

I heave a sigh and reassure her, "I'm coming!"

When I leave the bedroom, I am greeted with the sight of Mia waiting expectantly at the kitchen island.

"I can't wait to show you off on your first day!" She gives me a frowning face as she examines my clothes. "Um, whatever the hell you have on is at least one size too large for you. Why didn't you take something from my closet and try it on?"

As I walk to retrieve my bag from the counter, I give her a hesitant grin. "No way, Mia. You have helped me enough. You got me a dream job, and you also gave me a place to live. I can't borrow your clothes too."

At NYU, I was fortunate enough to room with Mia in the dorm, and we have had a close friendship since then. I struggled to find a place to live when I moved from New York to Seattle, but Mia offered to let me stay with her for free until I landed on my feet. While I insisted on paying the rent out of what little money I had saved, she urged me not to worry about the money issue.

At twenty-three, the last thing I wanted to do was go back to my parents' house. They refuse to let me grow up, and I put in a lot of effort to get a full scholarship at NYU to show them I can fend for myself in the world, so going back home is not an option.

"Whatever," she replies, rolling her eyes at me. "It's not a big deal. Will you at least put on makeup?"

"Mia, I'm sorry, but I'm trying to make a good impression, and if I get all dolled up, it will make me feel like I'm trying too hard."

"Okay. Fine, I got it. Ready to go?"

I nod, relieved she doesn't push. She must see that I'm nervous as hell. She was kind enough to offer to drive me to work in the mornings; however, I'll take an Uber home since I'll be working in a different department and will need to remain two hours later than her.

We head out and take off toward her G-Wagon, a gift from Deacon on her birthday. When I saw him pick her up from NYU occasionally, he seemed to be a nice guy who was in love with his girlfriend. Hopefully, my new boss, Relic, will be just as nice.

We arrive at the enormous structure that houses King Enterprises. She drives into the parking garage, where she has a designated spot. It doesn't surprise me because Deacon treats her like gold. We enter the building through an employee door and make our way into the luxurious lobby, which has cream marble flooring and chrome furniture. Since they conducted the employment interview online, I have never set foot inside the building, and I admire the magnificent architecture as I follow Mia to the elevator.

My mind is slowly coming to terms with the fact I will see my boss in person soon, and my hands tremble when the elevator doors slide open.

"Don't worry, Selena, you've got this," Mia assures me as we step inside the elevator.

"I know," I mumble in a low voice. "I'm just so nervous."

"You have nothing to worry about; they will like you no matter what." She takes my hand and squeezes. "I know they will offer you the job permanently."

As I hold her hand tightly, tears well up in my eyes. "Thank you, Mia. You are the best friend a girl could have." My vision blurs with moisture as I blink repeatedly.

She looks over at me and grins. "Thank god you're not wearing any mascara, or you would look like shit."

I laugh as I wipe away the tears that slip from my eyes. "Just so the record is clear, you're not just a best friend. You are a sister to me."

"Same. And if someone messes with you, I will kick their ass," she says, and we both burst out laughing at her statement.

The elevator stops, and before she steps out onto her floor, she turns around. "Remember, you'll find Walter on the thirty-fifth floor, and you'll need to tell the receptionist who you are. He is looking forward to seeing you."

"Okay, thank you, Mia. I'll see you later."

I wait for the doors to shut before pressing the button that will take me to the thirty-fifth floor. The elevator signals it has arrived and the doors open to a large modern space designed for comfort. I cross the marble floor and approach the receptionist's desk. A young brunette wearing a stunning outfit that makes me feel underdressed and unsophisticated looks up at me. Her perfectly made-up face and hair let me know why Mia fussed about my appearance.

"Hello, how can I help you?" she greets me.

I give her my most professional smile. "Hello, my name is Selena Tenaka. I'm the temp for the business analyst position. I was informed Walter was waiting for me."

She gives me a once-over, and I can tell she is wondering how I got the position dressed like I am. Her clothes look designer, whereas mine are not, and I'm sure everyone that works here dresses the same way. She can hide it in her tone and body language, but there is something in the way someone's eyes wander over a person. Like they're writing a message for you with their eyes instead of telling you with words.

"Oh, absolutely. Walter is looking forward to meeting with you. You arrived just in time." She gives me a grin before dialing an extension to let Walter know that I've arrived.

After two minutes, the doors to my left side open, and an attractive man emerges. To my relief, he's dressed in khaki pants, a dress shirt with long sleeves, and a blazer. He greets me with a kind grin that immediately puts me at ease.

"You must be Selena. Please follow me. I'll give you a tour and show you to your office."

I let out the trembling breath I had been holding while he constantly talks. He also introduces me to everyone in the business department and tells me all the perks the firm offers if I am picked permanently for the role. The fact I could get free admission to Elite Gym piques my interest even as a temp. It will give me something to do after work or on my days off.

After the office tour, Walter escorts me to the human resources department, where I'm greeted by an elderly woman in an elegant chignon wearing a fitted suit. "Good morning, Selena. I'm Claire, from your interview."

I can't help but grin. "Good morning. It is a pleasure to meet you in person."

She smiles, and I glance at the pictures on her glass desk of her with small children and then similar faces as they grow up like a time capsule. She seems like a really nice lady that loves her family. I hope to have a family one day and a husband that loves me and our children.

"I have all your documentation that you filled out online. All I need is your signature, and Walter will take you to your office."

"Thank you." I use the pen that has been placed for me on her glass desk to sign the paperwork. I'm excited, and I can't wait to get started.

She reviews each signature and flashes a grin. "Perfect. Everything is in order, and I've already noted your credentials."

"Okay. Thank you."

"My pleasure, Selena."

I walk out of her office and find Walter waiting for me outside the door. "I'll take you to your office now."

He leads me down the hallway, past offices with doors made of clear glass and tinted glass in others, until we reach an office in the corner.

"Here you are. Your computer should include all the necessary materials and a planner. The corporate directory's contacts section contains all of our coworkers' names and contact information.

I inhale deeply and then gently exhale the air out of my lungs. "Yes, and I am grateful for your help, Walter."

"Welcome aboard, Selena," he says, giving me a kind grin before leaving me in my new office.

I take in the surroundings of the average-sized office with a contemporary glass desk, turning to gaze at the landscape outside and then placing my things on the desk.

While sitting in the ergonomic chair at my desk, waiting for the computer to power up, I look around and appreciate the Scandinavian design of the furniture.

After logging on, I immediately get to work on the responsibilities specified by the analyst who was here before me. Mia informed me that the person who had my previous position had retired.

During the day, I spend time gaining knowledge, finding my way through the company's data, and offering suggestions. I must provide Diane, the director of the business department, with weekly reports and report to her regularly. Email and the electronic submission of papers that are then validated by an internal software system are the foundation upon which they manage the business.

It's not a terrible way to have things set up. It puts an end to workplace chitchat, but I noticed a break room where everyone was conversing and genuinely taking a break.

Software systems run the entire company. To become familiar with all the systems in my first week, I have to watch many training videos and manage everything via email or on the work phone. Therefore, there is little paperwork, but one thing that stood out to me was that I have yet to meet my boss, Deacon's older brother.

T he next morning, I'm at the office bright and early, carrying a duffel bag. I can't wait for the day to end to try out the gym. After lunch, I remind Mia of my plans.

Me: Hey. I'm going to the gym at six o'clock, and I won't be back until about eight.

Mia: I knew you would end up finding something to do to escape and avoid going out. I thought you would be back earlier. I'll let it slide for now. ;) Send me a text if you need me, and I will pick you up.

Selena: Okay. I'll talk to you later.

Mia has been trying to get me to go out and celebrate with her, but I need to save the money I have for Ubers and food until I get my first paycheck. If I go hang out with her, she will insist on paying for drinks because I'll just sit there with a glass of free water.

When I get to the gym, I stand in line to sign up for a membership. I scan the area behind the information desk and gaze at the cutting-edge fitness center. It seems more like a health resort than a fitness center from the outside and it's kind of fancy.

When it's finally my time, I show the young girl at the desk my employment identification from the firm and she registers me as a member. She hands me a map that details the amenities found in the fitness center, and I head to the locker room to get dressed in red leggings and my most comfortable sports bra.

Once I'm changed, I undo the bun I've been wearing and pull my hair back into a ponytail, tying it tightly, before heading out to the treadmills.

The gym has a zen atmosphere and the spotless facility is quite calming to the senses. On my right, rows of exercise machines hide behind a sparring ring and punching bags. The second level houses private rooms that may be used to work out in groups.

I pick a treadmill, and as soon as I plug in my headphones, a remixed song, "Eyes on Fire" by Blue Foundation, starts playing on my playlist. As I begin the first thirty minutes of my warm-up on the treadmill, I look up and see two tall men, both well over six feet, working out on the punching bag.

One guy is holding the bag while the other punches it in various combinations, his enormous biceps straining with each jab. After a minute of me staring, the dark-haired one striking the bag pauses and looks my way with piercing amber eyes. They remind me of a lion that has found its prey.

He's shirtless, and tattoos cover his upper body, even the tops of his hands. When he tilts his head, releasing the tension in his shoulders, I see a massive crown that spans the breadth of his throat.

The guy holding the punching bag glances in my direction, probably curious about what is capturing his friend's attention. He offers me a wink, to which I react by averting my gaze. But I can't help myself when I peek over again and admire the one with the crown on his throat as they resume their exercise on the bag. I look over to the one that gave me a wink and notice they both have the same crown tattoo on their throats.

Odd.

When he glanced at me on the treadmill, there was something in his eyes that caused my feet to stutter for a fraction of a second. The irony of it all is the lyrics playing in my headphones matched when I looked into his eyes.

He hits the bag with more force, and a sheen of perspiration runs down his toned muscles to his sculpted abs. I stop admiring him, not wanting him to think I'm ogling him. Even if I am. How could I not? The man is utterly gorgeous, but he gives the impression that he is arrogant and full of himself.

I focus on my workout and scan the surrounding environment, taking note of where various equipment is situated. But the pull of the men hitting the bag has me gazing over again.

This time, he strikes the bag with increasing force, causing his muscles to tense and bulge in protest like he's killing his opponent. If he unleashed that fury on someone, they wouldn't be breathing.

As soon as I complete my run, I head toward the unoccupied side of the gym that has free weights and avoid staring over at them. I keep walking in the opposite direction and don't look back, making a point of staying away. The danger from those two comes in waves, and it's better not to be around guys like that.

After I've finished my exercise, I make my way to the showers at the rear of the gym, and on my way there, I open the app to request a ride. I'm looking down at my phone, checking the available times, when it feels like I run into a brick wall.

When I glance up, a pair of piercing golden eyes stare down at me. He must have just gotten out of the shower because his dark hair is wet and combed back.

The powerful aroma of his recently applied cologne assaults my sense of smell, and his muscular chest stretching a black V-neck T-shirt draws my attention to the fact I am still in sweaty gym clothes.

I can't help myself. My eyes eat him up until I reach the band of his sweatpants, sitting low on his hips, where his designer brand underwear peeks just above the strings that keep them in place.

I am about to apologize, but he interrupts me and says in a grating voice, "You need to pay attention and stop glancing at your phone."

Even with the serious attitude he is sporting on his face, he is stunning up close. I am left speechless for a minute after comprehending his comment has an abrasive edge, as if he is reprimanding me like I'm a kid.

Even though it was an accident, and I had no intention of running into him, he had no right to be such a dick about it.

I eventually find my words and retort, "If you had been paying attention to where you were going, you wouldn't have bumped into me. It should go without saying that I am standing in front of you. Something more interesting was on my phone, and I was looking down, but what's your excuse?"

I understand I am acting like a bitch, but he is so arrogant, and apologizing to him-- *not gonna happen*. He seems annoyed as he stares down at me from his towering height.

Since I am just five feet three inches tall, he towers over me by about a foot. He inhales deeply and then exhales all of his air, lifting his upper lip like he smells something foul.

While sidestepping and walking around me, he says in a condescending tone, "How about you worry about taking that shower?"

Embarrassed, I turn away and hurriedly make my way inside the women's locker area, where the private showers are located. Before I exercise, I use body splash with a fruity scent and apply deodorant. I'm almost positive I don't smell *that* bad.

I take my time in the shower, and when I'm done, I check the time for my ride to arrive, hoping I won't see him when I come out of the locker room.

I finally make it to Mia's apartment, grateful I didn't run into him again on my way out and tell her what happened as I fumble around in the kitchen, searching for something to eat.

Mia jumps on the island and says, "He is probably some wealthy snob who doesn't know how to behave around a beautiful woman." She settles herself on the island, watching me pop a frozen dinner in the microwave as her feet swing back and forth. "Oh, I almost forgot. On Friday, we are heading to a club owned by the Kings called Mayhem. I have been dying for you to hang out with us since you moved here from New York. Deacon thinks it would be great for you to come out and celebrate the new move and the new job. He made reservations for a VIP table, and you can finally meet his brothers Relic and Liam outside of the office."

"Mia, you know I do not own a single article of clothing for a night out at a place like that, right?"

She raises her hand, rolling her eyes playfully. "I knew you were going to say that. I've already been shopping and bought you a dress. And I have shoes in my closet that still need to be worn. Our feet are the same size, and I will not accept *no* for an answer."

I stay silent, listening to the microwave hum as it warms my dinner, and watch her expression become more childlike as she implores, "Pretty please?" while blinking like a kid.

The microwave beeps, signaling that my food is ready, and I sigh. "Fine. But that's only because I know you already told them I was going, and I'm thankful for all you've done for me since I graduated," I say, picking up the little plastic tray, trying not to get burned.

Even though I don't want to go, at least I'll get to meet Deacon's brother's, who I have yet to meet at work. One of them must be my direct boss, but which one? Is it Liam or Relic?

My first week goes smoothly, and I get through all the initial training videos and send the completed reports to the CEO. When I look at the name attached to the emails and at the bottom of all the reports I send to Diane, I notice that it's Deacon's brother, Relic. I type a professional email introducing myself as the new hire and click send.

At the end of the day, I check my emails and see he hasn't replied, and I'm suddenly annoyed that he doesn't acknowledge my email or send me a welcome aboard message. *Nothing.*

I shake my head and try to think nothing of it. I should be grateful I work here. I guess he's a busy person who most likely doesn't have the time to reply.

It's Friday and as I send in my last report, my phone buzzes on my desk from an incoming text.

Mia: It's 5:00 on a Friday, bitch. Let's go.

Selena: Meet you in the garage.

Mia: Hurry. I'm dying to leave.

After the drive home and a much-needed shower, we are finally ready and dressed for a night out. I check out my appearance in the full-length mirror in Mia's room. My whole back is exposed thanks to my red dress, which forms a *V* right above my tailbone. My jet-black hair extends a few inches past the opening in the dress's back.

Mia pushed for me to wear it and told me I had to take a risk, even though it is quite short and not something I would ordinarily choose to wear. Since I'm taking a risk, I also put on makeup and used black eyeliner because I wanted my blue eyes to stand out more. Although my eyes may be shaped slightly different, no one believes I have Japanese ancestors. Sometimes people have a hard time guessing my ethnicity because I'm mixed.

My mother was born and raised in North Dakota, and my father was born in Japan. They started dating shortly after meeting while he was still in school in the states, and after he graduated college, he decided to live in North Dakota with my mother. They have been together ever since.

I had a hard time growing up as a kid through high school because I didn't fit in with the Asian kids, nor did I fit in with American kids. The shape of my eyes is in between, like a mix between Kristen Kreuk and Chrissy Teigen.

Mia emerges from her bathroom wearing a white crop top and a tiny matching skirt. Her short blonde hair is styled in an A-line, and she looks stunning. Her silver shoes with red soles are the identical designer pumps I'm wearing, but mine are a beige tint.

"Mia, you look so good in that outfit, but are you sure I should wear this? If I bend even a tiny bit, I'll flash everyone my ass in a thong."

She can't help but giggle. "Yes! You look amazing. Girl, we are going to the most popular club in Seattle. You need to look hot."

I grin. "All right, if I bend down and someone says something about my ass hanging out, then I know who to blame other than myself for agreeing."

"Honey, don't worry about anybody seeing that ass. You are one of the few women I know who can pull off any style and yet look amazing. You ready?"

"Probably not. "

After parking the G-Wagon at Mayhem, Mia and I head inside the nightclub. If the interior design of this building is any indication, the Kings have excellent taste. Velvet curtains border the walkways and entrances to the areas to divide them.

A state-of-the-art lighting system that pulses with the music illuminates the impressive dance floor. The club's curtains, couches, and chairs are all red velvet against black walls. Music pumps at a steady clip, and when I glance up, I see the DJ perched on a platform above the dance floor. It's impressive. Mia takes my hand and leads me to a set of stairs blocked by a red stanchion and a bulky bouncer with his arms crossed.

He turns to Mia and grins, obviously familiar with her. "Hello, Mia."

"What's up, Jack?"

"All good. They're waiting for you upstairs," he adds with a smile when he unhooks the cable to allow us through.

"Thank you, kind sir." She taps him on the shoulder on our way up the stairs.

When we reach the top and pass through the curtains, I stop, almost wobbling in my heels

The man from the gym sits in the middle of a red velvet sofa. Golden eyes that glared at me when I ran into him that day are narrowed, watching me intently as our appearance stops his conversation midsentence. The guy who held the boxing bag is seated next to Deacon. Deacon turns toward us, smiling at Mia.

"Hi," Mia says.

Everyone seated is staring at us, probably wondering who I am.

"Who the fuck is that?" The tone of authority in his voice leads me to believe that he is Relic and that these two men are Deacon's brothers.

"Relic, don't be rude to my best friend. Selena is the one that was hired as a temporary business analyst for your team."

He laughs sarcastically and points in my direction. "So, you're the one that annoys me by bumping into me at the gym and sending pointless emails with reports attached to them," he says in a sarcastic tone.

The last thing I need is to be on bad terms with my boss, so I hide the glare I want to aim at him and say nothing. What bothers me the most is the hard work I have done all week trying to impress my boss is meaningless to him.

I shrug off his remark and squeeze Mia's arm, and she instantly stiffens, realizing he's the same guy from the gym we were talking shit about when I came home.

Mia clears her throat. "Selena, this is Relic and Liam." She points in each of their directions. I smile and give them a silent wave and look over at Liam.

Liam winks at me. "Don't mind my brother. He's nice on most days. You can sit next to me if you want." *Charmer.*

"Good to know. That's okay. I'll stay seated next to Mia."

At first, I just glance at him and notice how different he is from Relic and Deacon, with his light-brown hair and green eyes. He appears cocky, with a sense of humor I didn't expect. The type of friend you hang out with and have a great time with.

When I settle on the sofa next to Mia, I look at Relic in his black designer T-shirt that molds to his broad frame like it was designed for him. He's got a drink in one hand and his red-soled shoe perched on the edge of the table like a king on his throne. The irony, his last name is King, so it's fitting. When his gaze lands on me, his left eyebrow lifts like he is questioning my attention on him.

I try to hold it back, but he makes it really hard to be polite, so I roll my eyes at him and glance at Mia, who smiles at me to ease the tension.

"Alright, look, I didn't come here for us to sit here and stare at one another all night," Mia says. "I invited Selena here to have a good time, so let's kick things off with a few tequila shots." She waves her hand, and a server quickly appears to take Mia's order.

I lean in and whisper loud enough for her to hear, "I can only have two."

She shakes her head and tries to put me at ease. "Relax. We'll get home safe."

The last thing I want to be is buzzed or tipsy around the Kings. But Mia can't be stopped when she sets her mind on something. If she only knew, that really isn't the whole reason.

"What are you two whispering about?" Liam asks.

"Selena isn't a heavy drinker, so she's afraid of being drunk and having to find a way home.," Mia responds.

A waitress approaches the table next to Relic and winks at him before delivering a tray with shot glasses, salt, and lime. Relic hands me the first, and I take it, our fingers brushing during the exchange. Tingles break out over the skin of my fingers, and my stomach somersaults from the contact.

Brazenly grabbing the lime and handing him the second shot, the waitress lightly touches him so that everyone knows they have something going on.

He smirks at me when I ignore him handing me the lime and salt and down the shot. My eyes water, but I prefer to swallow fucking fire before taking anything else from him. While the waitress takes her leave, swaying her ass, he watches her short skirt ride up, showing a glimpse of her garter on her fishnet tights. I toss back a second shot and cough a bit, fanning myself. I hear Relic's chuckle.

I'm about to tell him what I think of him, but Liam stops me from saying something I'm sure I'll regret later. "Want to dance, beautiful?"

I think about it for a moment. My decision is based on the fact I need to leave Relic's presence. I'm not scared or intimidated by him, but I'm afraid I'll do or say something that may jeopardize my position at the company. The last thing I need is to be fired.

"Okay," I say, placing my hand in his. He gives me a relieved smile, probably because I didn't turn him down.

Relic glances at me and his brother with a bored expression, downing his drink and placing the glass on the table in front of him. He reaches for a blunt on the table and lights it with the Zippo that was next to it. The red tip glows as he inhales. A cloud of marijuana smoke fills the room as he rises from the velvet sofa.

Everyone's eyes are drawn to him when he announces, "I'll be in the back room with Sophia."

I look at Mia, Relic, Deacon, and Liam, pinching my brows in confusion when they have these knowing looks on their faces.

"What's in the back room?"

Liam answers, "It's a private room the VIP customers use to fuck."

My eyes widen at how naive my train of thought was when they mentioned a back room. Of course, Relic would announce he is taking whomever Sophia is to go fuck.

I nod in understanding and glance at Relic, quirking my brow.

"Good luck with that."

Liam chuckles and places his hand on my lower back as Relic's eyes watch his brother's hand land on my skin. Liam grins as he guides me to the dance floor with "RAPSTAR" by Polo G playing in the background.

Chapter Four

SELENA

Liam pulls me close, my arms wrapping around his neck as his hands move to my waist. "Has anyone told you that you look beautiful tonight, Selena?"

"Yeah, Mia," I tease, looking up and finding his green eyes caressing my face. "Thank you," I say shyly.

Liam seems nice, and I feel comfortable dancing with him. He doesn't make my heart speed up, give me tingles on my skin when he touches me, or ignite my insides on fire. But a guy like that breaks your heart or, worse, steals it after he breaks it and leaves you with a small piece to survive.

I can't shake the feeling of someone's eyes slicing me in half, heating me up. The song shifts in beat, and Liam turns my body so that my back is to his front as we dance.

Thankfully, he isn't the type of guy to just rub his cock on my ass. He lowers his lips near the crook of my neck, and the feeling of someone watching me has me looking up where there is a catwalk. I spot Relic watching me and Liam dance with his hands on my waist. I can't see his expression, but suddenly, Relic storms off. *Weird.*

Two songs later, the effects of the shots course through me, and I suddenly need to use the bathroom.

I turn and rise on my heels so I can whisper in Liam's ear. "I need to use the restroom."

"Don't get lost," he says, joking. "Follow the signs for the restrooms."

"Right," I say with a smile, reminding myself about the back rooms.

"I'll meet you back at the table."

I nod and weave through the sweaty throng of bodies in the direction of the sign that reads restroom. I try to steady myself and curse these six-inch-high heels, but I have to give Mia credit. They make me feel sexy.

I come to a stop when there is no sign to tell me which way to go and look around. After debating whether to go left or right on the following turn, I take a risk and turn left along a corridor lined with crimson velvet curtains. I can hear the deep bass from the music playing on the opposite side of the club, but this area has no clubgoers in sight, making it seem like nobody uses this part of the club.

I open the first door to check whether I'm really lost and should turn around, but I immediately freeze when I catch sight of Relic sitting in a leather chair with his T-shirt raised, showing his chiseled, muscled chest. His pants are unzipped and a blonde is sliding his rock-hard cock into her mouth. The girth of his cock is wide, glistening after being sucked. My eyes train on the woman's lips as she struggles to take him inside her mouth.

I tighten my grip on the door handle, and he glances at me. He doesn't ask me to leave or what I'm doing at the door. His stare lowers to my braless nipples with hunger in his eyes.

My black lace thong is see-through and probably on display because my hand is grasping the hem of my dress, raising it, and I know he can see it because I can feel the air on my hot flesh.

My heart rate increases and I bite my lower lip and squeeze my thighs. His huge cock is a piece of art, making me want to straddle him and impale my pussy on it.

His nostrils flare as he grabs the blonde by the hair and pushes her face lower so she can take all of him, and I don't know why I stand here watching, but I'm fascinated by the look on his face as pleasure overtakes his beautiful features.

When I look up at the mirror, he smirks at me and angles his head back as he grunts, pushing her head up and down, making her take him faster.

"Faster," he hisses. The woman that must be Sophia moves faster, and I'm transfixed as he grunts, pushing her head down.

He grunts one last time. "Fuck. Mmm... Selena," escapes his lips, but I think I imagined it was my name he uttered. I must have been lost in my head. There is no way he said my name.

His release chokes Sophia, and he looks at me, biting his bottom lip. And it confirms it. I didn't imagine it. He said my name.

I release my dress from my hand, shocked that my name was on his lips as he came in her mouth. For a few seconds, I stare, envying that she knows what he tastes like. When her face shifts slightly, she still isn't aware I'm in the room, but I can see her mascara running and making her look a mess. I notice his eyes are closed. He doesn't look at her like a satisfied man. He doesn't look at her at all.

I back out of the room as fast and quietly as I can, but I slow down when I see people in the hallway. Less than a minute later, I find the women's restroom, panting from my getaway.

I can't believe he said my name while he dumped his load down the blonde's throat. He has balls. I'll give him that.

After I use the restroom, I wash my hands and compose myself to head back to the table. I close my eyes, take a deep breath, and walk out.

I make it to the table and hope I can face him without giving myself away to the others. I just witnessed my boss's cock being sucked by a blonde named Sophia.

Let's not forget he saw me getting turned on watching him come. It must have been the tequila shots. *That's it.* It's the only thing that makes sense. I recently moved and haven't gotten laid.

And apart from Relic's abhorrent attitude, the man is drop-dead gorgeous. He has the bad-boy suit-wearing Mafia thing going on. Watching him and his brothers is like walking onto the set of a Hollywood movie. It was wrong to stand there and watch, but I couldn't help myself. I should have turned around and left.

"Hey, where were you?" Mia asks as I sit down next to her.

I smile and hate to lie, but what choice do I have?

"Sorry, there was a line. Don't worry. I remembered what you said about the signs."

She gives me a knowing look, and I silently promise to share the details with her later. I look around at the other's expressions to see if they found what I said suspicious, but Liam and Deacon are engrossed in a conversation about what they're going to order when the waitress appears.

Sitting on the couch where Relic was seated earlier is the same blonde woman from the back room. She eyes me with disdain as if I'm a threat to her existence. My eyes dart around the VIP area, and Relic is nowhere to be found. Ignoring her, I look away and watch the people dancing below.

"You must be Mia's friend, right?" Sophia asks, causing me to look back in her direction.

"That's right."

She gives me this sarcastic smile that I would love to slap off her face. For some reason, I can't stand her, and it's not because she fucks Relic. He is nothing to me except my boss. *Liar.*

She gives me a sardonic smirk. "Well, congrats on the new temp job. I hope it works out for you. Being the hired help and all."

This bitch.

She leans back and crosses her legs, trying to appear like she is in control, like she's a queen and I'm the peasant. "I don't have that problem. My parents have business with the Kings, and I'm a stakeholder in my father's company."

From looking at the reports and files from work, the Kings run an import-export business, containers of goods from Russia, Japan, and China, to and from Seattle. They own major commercial buildings and real estate. Mia once told me they're into other underground shit, but she doesn't know much about it. Everything I saw in the company's files in their system is all legal.

"That's nice. You're lucky to have wealthy parents who have everything set up for you," I say sweetly, with a fake smile.

Mia looks over at me with a worried frown. She can tell that Sophia is trying to get me pissed off. This bitch is a snob and deserves to be on her knees.

"Yeah, some of us are lucky and born into wealth."

"Oh, come now, Sophia. Sophia is your name, right?"

"That's right."

"You can't honestly tell me you don't get on your knees and do dirty work," I say in a sultry voice with a hint of sarcasm.

Her eyes widen, shooting daggers at me, realizing I know she sucked Relic's cock in the back room. I'm sure she didn't see me. It really was no secret. He practically publicized it to everyone.

"I never do dirty work. I don't have to work a temp job, and I definitely don't need to live with my best friend because I'm broke. I have heard all about you."

I snicker because deep down, I expected her claws to come out. Mia glances at me nervously, knowing I can snap this bitch's head off. I'm not prone to violence unless it's for self-defense, but she wakes up something inside me I will unleash if provoked.

Liam and Deacon raise their brows at our heated exchange.

"Selena, don't," Mia whispers.

Mia recognizes my chuckle as a countdown to getting up and beating her ass, but I calm myself down, realizing it's not worth it. I don't want to make a scene by not keeping my composure. I'll be thrown out of the Kings' kingdom. I'm not Relic's friend, and Sophia has more of a right to be here than I do. I'm no one to these people except to Mia.

"Don't worry, she's not worth it," I tell Mia, talking about Sophia like she isn't in front of me.

I have a keen eye for people sometimes, and Sophia is an evil bitch. She sees me as a threat, and I'll have to watch my back if she is anywhere around.

Relic finally shows up and takes a seat next to Sophia. She places her hand on his thigh as she smirks in my direction.

The alcohol has left my system, and I want to go home. I don't feel comfortable with her here and don't want to lose my temper. I could deal with Relic, but *Sophia* and Relic? That is a hell to the no.

"I'm going to head out," I tell Mia.

"Why?" she asks with a concerned expression.

"I'm tired and just want to go home."

Mia looks at the other guys for help.

"Selena, stay. It was our idea to get you out here," Deacon says.

"I know, but it's okay, really. I'll Uber home."

I'll really feel bad if Mia has to leave Deacon and take me back to the apartment. I know it was their idea, and they were both trying to be nice, but there is no way I can stay. Not with Sophia egging me on.

"She wants to go home. Get her an Uber or whatever. Mia doesn't have to leave. We can all continue to have a good time."

My head snaps at Sophia's comment, and I get up to leave. If I stay one more minute, it will probably take all the men to keep me from clawing her eyes out.

"Where are you going?" Mia asks, frowning.

I give her a comfortable smile. "I'm going home. Trust me, I need to go."

Mia sees the expression in my eyes that if I don't get the fuck out of here and fast, it will not end well.

"I'll call an Uber for you," Relic says.

Mia and I look in Relic's direction.

"Male chivalry at its finest," I say sarcastically, waving my hand at Relic.

Liam chuckles at my sarcasm and says, "I'll take you, beautiful."

I smile at Liam. "Thank you, but you have had too much to drink. I'll take my chances with an Uber. " I turn toward Relic and our eyes lock. "Have a good time, everyone."

I give Mia a tight hug and notice her sad expression, so I whisper in her ear, trying to lighten her mood, "Have a great time with your man tonight. I'll be fine. You know I must leave. We will hang out again some other time, yeah?"

She gives me a halfhearted smile and nods.

I turn with my clutch in hand and walk downstairs toward the valet and wait for the Uber driver to show up.

Chapter Five

SELENA

Waiting patiently outside, I look over at everyone arriving instead of leaving.

A roar of an engine has everyone outside, including me, looking toward the line of cars pulling up. A black Lamborghini Aventador pulls up with a front license plate that reads, *One King*. The valet opens the passenger door upward, and I stay rooted to the spot, waiting for a celebrity or a model to get out.

A bulky guy dressed in a suit walks up to me from my left. "Excuse me."

"Yes?" I ask, furrowing my brow.

He waves his hand toward the black sports car. "He's waiting for you."

"Who?"

He smiles. "Mr. King."

"There must be some mistake. I'm supposed to wait for an Uber."

He shakes his head. "Mr. King said to escort you to his car when it arrived."

My eyes widen as the valet continues to smile, motioning for me to get inside the sleek, black car. Taking a deep, nervous breath, I walk to the car carefully, trying not to show my ass to everyone in line for the club.

The windows on the sports car are all tinted black, so you can't see much of anything. All I can see from where I'm standing is a tattooed, muscled forearm with a Richard Milli watch resting in the center. I recognize it belongs to Relic.

"Thank you," I say softly, sliding in the car as the valet gapes at my low-cut dress.

Relic lowers the window and glares at the young valet. I avert my eyes, trying not to entertain the young guy gawking at me.

Relic's eyes are like a dragon breathing fire with golden flames. His glare is aimed at the valet as he lowers his head to acknowledge Relic when closing the door, but not before gazing up my thighs. Relic reaches over, sliding his hand possessively over my thigh in a soft caress. Goose bumps rise on my flesh at his touch, and the valet closes the door quickly.

I don't remove his hand. I'm too stunned. His hand is like a hot iron on my skin, burning me into ashes in sweet torture. My mind is trying to catch up. He's my boss, and his hand is on my thigh, and I don't want him to remove it.

I want him to slide his fingers between my thighs so he can see how wet I am for him, but the sound of his hard tone snaps me out of my sexual thoughts. "Next time, keep your eyes to yourself."

The young valet's eyes widen. "I-I-I am so sorry, sir."

"Never look at her like that again."

I look at Relic with an eyebrow raised. What is he playing at? He turns up the volume on the car's sound system, and "Invincible" by Pop Smoke plays.

He lifts his hand to caress my face and brushes his thumb on my lower lip. I stay motionless, stunned at his touch, and then he places the car in gear, and it roars forward, speeding down the road.

He glances at my grip on the door handle and slows down, lowering the volume of the music. He raises the windows, stopping my hair from blowing because of the wind.

"Are you okay?"

I smile at him nervously. And not because of the car's speed. I'm still reeling because of the way he touched me like I was his.

"Thank you for the ride home. You didn't have to," I answer, trying to act like he didn't just touch me.

He slows the car to the speed limit and places his left hand on the top of the steering wheel. "I needed to make sure you got home safe. It wouldn't have looked good if something had happened to you at two a.m."

"Right," I say.

Should I feel deflated or relieved?

He's intoxicating, exciting, and the type of man that makes your mind check out and your body check in. He is every woman's dream and every father's nightmare. My body craves him, and I lose all sense of self-preservation.

He continues toward Mia's apartment, obviously knowing where it is. My face and lips still have tingles from where he touched me. But it felt right. Like he was supposed to touch me.

Again, maybe I just need to have sex. My last boyfriend at NYU didn't work out since I was moving to Seattle, and he was offered a job in Boston. We decided to call it quits. And the funny thing is, I wasn't sad or depressed. That was when I knew I was never in love with him.

When Relic touches me, my skin heats on fire. And when I watched him come, I wanted it to be because of me.

He glances at me briefly. "I'm sorry for the way Sophia behaved back there. It ruined your night out with Mia, and she made you uncomfortable. You looked like you were going to snap her neck."

I tilt my head with a wry smile. "You're very observant, but you weren't very nice either."

He sighs. "I agree. We didn't start on the best of terms. Sophia acts jealous when she feels threatened."

I glance at his hands on the steering wheel and admire his strong forearms full of tattoos. I decide to ask him something that is entirely none of my business, but I secretly want to know. "Are you two... together?"

He grins at my assumption. "No. I don't do relationships. I fuck, and that's it. I can't offer commitment. In my line of work, it's not something I can offer."

I wonder what he means by that, but don't ask.

"So, you've never been in a serious relationship with anyone?"

He snorts. "No. Like I said, I fuck."

At least he's honest and doesn't string someone along. Thinking about the waitress, Sophia, and how he touches women and moves on to the next, I believe him.

I Googled him on the internet and found that he is one of the most eligible bachelors alongside his brother Liam. Makes sense, I guess. He's a twenty-eight-year-old CEO of a successful company and has more money than he knows what to do with.

He pulls up in front of Mia's apartment building in an upper-class neighborhood and places the powerful vehicle in park.

Before I exit the car, I face him and say the only thing I can come up with.

"I understand. I get it."

He laughs, resting his head back on the bull stitched into the headrest, and looks at me with his sexy, amber-colored eyes that make my stomach flip. His eyes remind me of a honey trap. Once caught in that sexy stare of his, you're stuck.

"What's so funny? I ask.

"I'm not laughing at you. It's just that you surprise me, Selena. I never expected you to understand and not give a woman's two cents on how I sound heartless."

I frown. "How are you being heartless when you're just being honest?"

He smiles. "I'm glad we understand each other."

He inches closer, and his expensive cologne permeates my personal space. His face is inches from mine, and I sit there speechless, unmoving. Subconsciously, I lick my lips, watching his tattoo move against his throat. Now, I can see it says *King*.

He angles his head and captures my lips with his. I'm lost. His lips softly kiss mine, and he tastes like mint with a hint of whiskey. It's delicious. His hands slide up my face and hold my cheek, and I lean into the kiss, letting him suck my bottom lip. My eyes close, savoring the moment of his deep kiss.

When he pulls away, letting his thumb slide from my cheek to my swollen lip in a soft caress, my eyes flutter open to meet his gold ones laced with desire. My heart beats wildly inside my chest and for the second time tonight, my pussy pools with liquid heat between my thighs, reminding me how much I want him.

"You're beautiful, *preciosa*," he whispers.

I'm stunned speechless by the fact I let my boss kiss me and he just called me beautiful in Spanish.

I open the door. "Good night, Relic," I say softly before closing it and walking up to the apartment building's entrance without looking back.

Once inside the apartment, I head to my room and close the door. I lean against it, breathing fast like I just ran a marathon.

I close my eyes, taking a deep breath, squeezing my thighs at how much my body wants him. He must think I'm stupid for getting out of the car like a scared little kitten. But I know if I had stayed in that car with him, I would have let him do what he wanted, how he wanted.

Chapter Six

SELENA

The next morning, I wake up to the sound of the front door opening and closing. I lie on my bed, waiting to hear Mia's loud voice filter through the closed bedroom door, interrupting one of the best nights of sleep I've had.

"Honey, I'm home!"

The bedroom door suddenly opens, and Mia jumps onto my bed with a giggle. I laugh at her playfulness and try to hide under my sheets.

"What's up, sleepyhead?"

"Trying to forget about last night."

"I'm sorry about last night. That bitch ruins everything. I can't stand her. Total skank."

I pull the covers under my nose, shielding my morning breath. Her brown eyes look at me with laughter. "I'm over that. I'm talking about on my way home," I tell her, sounding muffled.

Her expression changes to a worried frown. "What happened?"

"He took me home, not an Uber."

"Who?"

"Relic," I deadpan.

Her eyes widen. "So that is where he went when you left. He's smooth," she says with a smile.

"Smooth enough to kiss me when he dropped me off," I quip.

"I knew it!" She pulls the sheet down and tickles me, and I giggle. "That's why that bitch was drilling you with the evil eye and smart-ass comments. She noticed how he was checking you out when no one was looking. He thinks you're hot, and that is why he was acting like a total asshole at the gym. Because he saw you noticed him checking you out."

"Yeah, the problem is that he is my boss and not into relationships. Unless it's just fucking."

She waves her hand. "That is what all bad boys with money say. He is not that bad though. He drove you home instead of calling you an Uber."

My expression turns serious. "Don't go thinking he's not full of himself or a nice guy. Before he kissed me, he said he doesn't do relationships. That he only fucks. I give him brownie points for at least being honest, but he is just down for a good time with no strings. So don't get your hopes up for Relic and me."

She takes a deep breath with her eyebrows raised. "Wow, no faith."

"None besides eye candy and a good way to mess up the bed."

She shrugs her shoulders. "It's better than nothing. Who wouldn't want to mess up their bed with Relic King? The man is mysterious, dangerous, good-looking, and must be a good fuck if he has women all over him like that."

I take my hands away from my mouth and roll out of bed before walking toward the bathroom to brush my teeth, trying to forget how his lips and tongue felt.

Changing the subject from Relic, I ask her, "How was your night with Mr. Right?"

She lies flat on my unmade bed, gazing at the ceiling. "Besides you having to leave and then dealing with that bitch and her snobbish attitude, it went great when it was just Deacon and me." She sighs. "I'm so in love, Selena. It hurts."

I smile, leaning on the doorframe of the en suite bathroom with a soft smile at her happiness. "I'm so happy for you, Mia. You can see the love when you two are together. He totally feels the same way about you. I knew it the first time he picked you up at the dorm. He has the same look in his eye when you step out of the room dressed to go out. His eyes are only for you. Even when you told me he didn't want you like that, that he could have any of the women in his circle, I knew it was you he ultimately wanted."

She sighs and throws a pillow at me, laughing. "I guess."

"Is everything okay with the other stuff?"

"I don't bother asking about anything or where he goes. He says not to worry, so I'm not going to worry about it. I have to trust him."

Mia was worried that he was into something with his brothers. She said he would show up with bloody knuckles, and when she would ask what happened, he would tell her not to worry, that everything was fine and that it was safer for her not to know.

The King brothers are well respected in Seattle and practically in the world, being rich heirs to inherit a conglomerate. Some have accused them of being in the Mafia, but no one has linked them with any illegal business activity. It's all speculation and rumors.

"As long as you're safe and it doesn't affect you, it's fine."

She sighs and turns over to look at me. "About Relic, be careful with him. Thinking about it, you were right in me wanting you to be together. You're both headstrong and sparks fly when you're near each other, but I know you, and you have a beautiful heart, and I would fucking hate him for hurting you."

"I love you for saying that, but who said I will fall for him and let him?" She rolls her eyes and throws another pillow at me. "Selena, if you could see your face when you utter his name. You want him."

I throw the pillow right back. "Whatever."

She laughs and places it beside her. "Was it good?"

"Yes, bitch. It was fucking amazing. I hope I can make good on my promise and not take him seriously."

On Monday morning, I'm in the elevator wearing a black pencil skirt, kitten heels, and a sensible blouse on my way to my office. Mia went shopping and bought me a few things for work, and I was so grateful. I'm not going to lie. I secretly want to look good in case I run into Relic.

I touch the Japanese hair clip my grandfather gave me when I was five that's been part of my father's side of the family for generations. My grandfather made sure every summer I would go and learn how to defend myself and learn about my Japanese heritage. It's when I learned I didn't fit in because I didn't look Asian.

My grandfather was adamant about my upbringing being in Japan, but my mother and father convinced him to let me be brought up in America. My mother was not fluent in Japanese and would feel left out living in Japan, but luckily for her, my grandfather understood.

The red kanzashi hair clip is one of the most beautiful pieces I have from Japan, and I have always been afraid to lose it, but I can't help wearing it today. It's one of those days when I need to feel a connection to something. Something that is part of who I am.

The elevator dings and opens, the person I least expected but hoped to see steps inside.

Relic smiles, towering over me. "Good morning, Selena." His eyes sweep over my face.

I look up at his sultry expression. "Good morning, Mr. King," I murmur.

He chuckles. "I think we are past that. If you want to call me Mr. King at work, that's fine, but when we are alone, I would like you to call me Relic. I can align your position with Deacon if it makes you feel better. You will still have to report to me, but for your peace of mind."

"Do as you like. Nothing is going on between us," I say, looking forward, hoping the elevator doors open so he can get off or I reach my floor.

My nipples are already straining under my bra from just hearing his sexy voice insinuating there is something between us that he would suggest having my position aligned under his brother.

He is really sure of himself, but I cannot lie and say I haven't thought of having sex with him a few times since Friday night.

I can see his cocky smile in my peripheral vision. The elevator indicates we have reached a floor, but I'm so lost in my thoughts I don't realize what floor we are on. The doors open, and my hair suddenly cascades down my back. I instinctively place my hand on my head, feeling nothing. My hair clip fell out.

Relic walks out of the elevator in quick strides, his dress shoes echoing on the marble floor.

Before I process what has happened, the elevator doors close and it ascends toward my floor. He took my hair clip. I don't know where his office is, and I can't go around asking where the CEO's office is located.

What am I going to say? *I don't have an appointment, but I need my hair clip back.* That will get the office gossip going to a whole new level.

When the elevator opens, I hurry to my desk and text Mia.

Selena: What floor is Relic's office on?
Mia: Why?
Selena: He took my hair clip in the elevator.

Mia: He what?

Selena: He took my hair clip in the elevator and ran off with it.

Mia: Lol. He really wants you. I've never seen him act like this before. I'm sorry for laughing, but I'm sure he will give it back. I know how important it is to you.

Selena: I hope you're right. I've got to go. See you at home later. If you see him, please tell him I need it back.

Chapter Eight

SELENA

The rest of the week moves quickly, and I don't see or hear from Relic. I went to the gym every day after work, hoping I would run into him, but nothing. I didn't catch him or Liam.

When I make it home, I'm alone. Mia said she was having dinner with Deacon and would be home afterward, so she should be home soon. I'm about to head into the shower but pause when I hear a knock on the door.

Looking through the peephole, I see it's a delivery boy with a box in his hand. I open the door slightly, and the young guy looks at me and then reads a paper slip in his hand.

"Are you Miss Tenaka?"

I frown, not expecting a delivery because I ordered nothing online. *I'm broke.* "Yes."

His mouth lifts in a smile. "Excellent. Can you please sign here?" He hands me a pen and a clipboard with a receipt.

I take it and read the paper, but all it has is my name and address. I sign on the bottom, noticing it's a courier service. I hand him back the clipboard and pen.

He hands me the white box in his other hand.

"Thank you."

"Have a great rest of your evening."

I grin, close the door with one hand, flip the lock, and walk over to the couch, curious to know what is inside the white box.

Sitting on the sofa, I pull open the red bow.

When I lift the lid, a small white card with gold lettering reads *From a King.* This must be a joke. I place the card on the coffee table, pull apart the tissue paper, and gasp...

My red hair clip is sitting delicately on a bed of tissue paper with rows of diamonds mounted in sequence. A huge center stone glitters in a swirl of colors like a rainbow. This must have cost a fortune. I can't even call to ask why he would do this or to thank him. I don't have his personal number, and I can't just thank him via email at work.

It is stunning. I hold it in my hand, admiring the diamonds sparkling in the light. No man has ever gifted me something so beautiful. My stomach has butterflies fluttering inside because of the personal gift.

Not long after, Mia gets home, and I show her the card with the delivered box. She opens the lid and looks inside the tissue paper.

Her eyes light with excitement and she squeals. "It's gorgeous!" Her lips curve in a smile as she turns the clip in her hand, watching it sparkle. "I told you. Relic is into you. I love it, Selena. It is so personal and beautiful."

I sigh. "I know. It really is.".

"If you doubted his intentions before, you know his intentions now."

"Yeah, he expects me to sleep with him."

Mia places the hair clip gently back in the box. "This is a bad thing because..."

I clear my throat. "He is my boss. It's wrong and those types of flings end up in heartache and someone always gets hurt."

"And? Still don't see the issue," she quips.

"Um, it's wrong. It's not like I'm going to marry the man or anything and he was clear he wasn't offering anything other than casual sex, so what's the point?"

She points at me playfully. "You get to sleep with Relic King, one of the hottest bachelors in all of Seattle. Let's not forget the man is loaded and I'll repeat it so you can let it sink in. The man is fine as fuck."

I snort. "Great way to convince me. It's not like my job isn't on the line or anything. Let's not forget my self-esteem and all the other women that he usually screws on the regular."

Like that bitch Sophia.

But I don't tell Mia that. It would mean that I'm jealous and interested in Relic more than I should be. Maybe I am, or maybe I'm not. He makes me feel things, but all guys that look like Relic make women like me feel things. He's gorgeous, rich, and has a body to die for. And let's not forget, beautiful. Wait, I already said that. I'm losing it.

"What are you thinking about?" Mia asks.

I blow a puff of air out of my mouth, plopping my ass on the blue suede couch, causing the yellow linen pillows to almost topple over to the floor. "I'm thinking."

She leans over the back of the couch to look at me. "About?"

I pick up the pillow and playfully hit her on her head with it. "What I shouldn't be thinking about. Relic."

She laughs. "Just fuck him and have a good time doing it. Smile when you arrive at work and have fun. Go home, come back, and do it all over again."

"I wish it was that easy."

"It is," she quips.

Unless your heart wants more than the body, a man like Relic King will break you. He will give you pleasure and make your head spin in the most delicious of ways until he leaves you dizzy and lost. He isn't a man you have sex with and then forget about him like a one-night stand. He is the man you cannot forget after the one-night stand.

Chapter Nine

SELENA

It has been a month since I received the hair clip. I work and go to the gym. The only interaction I have with Relic is the emailed reports at work. He doesn't send me a message other than a specific report or explanation of my analysis, keeping it strictly professional.

I wanted to say thank you for the clip, but only if I see him in person. He never gave me his number, and he never asked for mine.

He could have reached out if he wanted and maybe I could have sent him an email requesting to see him, but I didn't want him to think I was desperate for his attention. So I figured keeping my distance was for the best. My focus should be on my job at his company and not on fucking my boss.

It's Thursday and Sam from accounting invited me to go out for drinks after work. I'm not into drinking or dancing with people at work, but I need to get over this crush I have on Relic. Socializing with other people would be a good idea to get thoughts of Relic out of my head.

Every guy that flirts with me at the gym or downstairs at the lunch café, I catch myself comparing them to Relic. I need to stop. It was just a kiss and I'm reading too much into it. *Into him.*

It is not like he didn't warn me about getting attached. He isn't into relationships. The clip he had made is just another way he gets a woman to fall for his charm, or maybe it was his way to smooth things over. He hasn't invited me to dinner or on a real date. His silence is a red flag. A warning. *Play with me and get hurt.*

I'm shutting down my computer, having submitted my last file for the day, when I hear a knock on the glass. I look up to find a very handsome Sam giving me a smile from the doorway to my office.

"Hey, ready? Are you sure you still want to go?"

Sam looks nervous. I think he still cannot believe that I accepted his invitation. He is the complete opposite of Relic. No visible tattoos, khaki slacks, button-down dress shirt that you can tell is dry cleaned. He has the guy-next-door vibe going—short dirty-blond hair, a straight nose, a cute dimple when he smiles, and gray eyes. He seems like a nice guy. He seems... safe.

I give him my best smile and stand up. "Of course. I agreed, didn't I?"

His eyes follow me as I retrieve my handbag from the bottom drawer of my desk and collect my phone. "I-I wasn't sure. M-maybe you changed your mind," he stammers.

Definitely nervous. Poor guy.

"Oh, I don't have any plans and it's good that I hang out. My best friend is usually with her boyfriend, and I stay in watching movies until it's time to go to sleep."

I know I sound lame, but I don't care. I'm not trying to impress Sam. It's just drinks at a bar three blocks down from the office.

He runs his hand on the back of his neck. "You don't have a boyfriend?"

Is he asking if I'm available?

I slide the loopholes of my handbag onto my wrist, standing in front of him in my gray high-waisted pencil skirt, nude pointed pumps and black body suit I borrowed from Mia. The woman has a closetful of clothes that she doesn't wear.

She wouldn't budge when I told her no and insisted I borrow her clothes until I get nicer ones. She wasn't wrong. Everyone at King Enterprises looks sharp in their office clothes.

"No, I don't. I was seeing someone, but we went our separate ways after I moved from New York."

His mouth lifts in a smile, showing that little dimple. "Oh."

Shit. I hope I didn't give him an invitation to think I want something more.

He isn't a bad-looking guy, but...he isn't Relic. There I go again, thinking about the man.

Sam will just have to do.

"Ready?"

He steps back so I can exit my office. "Yes," he says eagerly. The poor guy looks like he is going to trip over himself.

We took a cab, and I tried to split the fare, but Sam was not having it when I tried to convince him to take my money. He paid before I could argue it further.

When we enter, the bar is full of executives from around the block out for happy hour. Scanning the area, I notice there are basically no available seats. I wait patiently with Sam and notice the brick walls, low lighting, and brown leather couches on one wall with small coffee tables. People are milling about, talking over the music from the juke box.

Sam waves at the bartender and it's obvious they are familiar with each other. The bartender motions him over, signaling to the other side of the bar where there are two chairs leaning forward.

"That's Carl."

"You come here a lot?" I ask, watching his cheeks turn red.

I didn't mean to embarrass him, but it was a normal question. It's obvious he is a regular here, not that I care, and it was just to make conversation to break the awkwardness.

"A few times," he answers, placing a hand on my lower back, causing me to stiffen.

I play it off, not wanting to be rude and ruin the mood. I just walk faster, making his hand fall when we reach the bar. He pulls out the barstool and I take a seat and watch him do the same.

My eyes scan the bar, and I'm thankful I don't see any familiar faces from the office.

"Hey, Sam. What can I get you and your date?" Carl asks, wiping the bar.

I raise my finger. "Oh, I'm not—"

"We're coworkers," Sam interrupts. "Selena just started at King Enterprises and we're just hanging out."

"Oh, I'm sorry. You called ahead for me to save you some seats, and you came in together. I thought you two were together. I guess not."

When Carl's eyes land on me, I sigh in relief and give him a small smile. "I'll have a dry martini."

I can feel Sam shift uncomfortably in his chair next to me, embarrassed, while the bartender eyes me curiously and says, "Sam knew what he was doing. He knows how this place gets and I guess he didn't want to stand after a long day of work."

Sam sags a bit in relief. The bartender places the martini in front of me and a beer for Sam. When I dig in my bag to give him my card, Sam pulls out his wallet, but then a muscular tattooed forearm with rolled-up sleeves reaches above my head with a black card toward the bartender.

"Open a tab, Carl. Put whatever they are having on my card."

I don't want to turn around because I recognize the voice of the man that is standing right behind me. My heel is supporting me from sliding off the barstool in surprise.

Carl looks at the man standing behind me. "Of course, Mr. King," he says before walking away to swipe his card.

Holy shit. He's here paying for our drinks. I look at the martini glass, hoping it can bail me out of this one. I don't even know why I'm nervous. I'm not doing anything wrong. I can have a drink with whomever I want. It's not like I'm taken or anything.

Sam turns in his seat. "Mr. King. You really didn't have to do that."

"I did," he says dryly. As I reach for my drink, Relic leans close to my ear and whispers, *"No te pongas nerviosa, preciosa.* Don't be nervous, beautiful."

I swallow, sliding the glass toward me, lifting it to my lips, taking a sip, trying to swallow the drink down my throat so I can calm the tiny hairs by my neck where his warm breath caused them to stand.

Sam clears his throat. "Selena, how do you like working for King Enterprises?"

I angle my head toward Sam, placing my clammy hands on my lap. Sam must be especially nervous to ask me such a question when the boss is standing right behind me.

"It's great so far. At first, I was worried that my reports weren't good or if I even made valid points based on my analysis. But I guess if I haven't been escorted out of the building yet, they are good enough." I tease about the last part.

The last part was a jab at Relic since he doesn't answer any of my work-related emails. I figured the night he dropped me off was just Relic being Relic and the hair clip was a parting gift.

I hoped he would ask Mia for my number or show up somewhere, but that never happened. He probably forgot I even existed. Which is why courage runs through me and I turn to look at him.

My eyes find a very handsome Relic with his shirt open at the throat, allowing a direct view of the crown on his neck. All three of the King brothers have it. I noticed it on Liam and Deacon, but I never stared or let my eyes linger. But on Relic... I want to stare, and I want my eyes to linger.

My eyes take in his strong jaw, sporting a five-o'clock shadow, and his dark lashes that frame his amber-colored eyes. "Good evening, Mr. King," I say with a smile, trying to get his eyes off Sam. "What brings you here? I would have thought you would still be in the office."

After looking at Sam for a while, he turns his attention back to me with a smile on his face. "Sometimes I come here for business."

"Oh, I wasn't aware you were conducting business. Please, don't let us keep you," I challenge.

We both know he isn't here on business. A man like Relic King would not bring his business into a place that is this busy and crowded.

"I'm here on business right now."

"Oh, what brings you by, Mr. King?" Sam asks with a look of confusion on his face.

"It's personal," he responds while keeping his gaze on me. My stomach flips, and I lick my bottom lip nervously as his eyes zero in on my lips.

"Mr. King, is there anything else you need?" Carl asks. "Can I get you a drink?"

He lifts his eyes to Carl, and then they land on mine again. "I've already found what I need. Close my tab."

"Right away, sir."

I quirk an eyebrow. "They must know you here very well."

He leans close and says loud enough for Sam to hear, "I kind of own the place."

I look around at the people wearing tailored suits and ordering top-shelf drinks. Some are on the patio, smoking cigars, deep in conversation. Of course, he owns this place. What doesn't this man own?

"Wow, I'm impressed," Sam says, probably getting a hard-on. "I have been coming here a lot and I never would have thought--"

"You haven't had dinner, Selena," Relic says, interrupting Sam.

I blink. "No, I haven't. We came straight over." I wonder how he knows I haven't eaten, but he probably knows when I left the office.

"Good. That means it's time for you to have dinner." He glances at Sam. "I'm sure you can find your way home, Sam. I'll see Miss Tenaka home."

Just like that, he dismisses Sam. Feeling bad for Sam, I give him an apologetic smile. "I'll see you at the office tomorrow?"

Sam swallows and glances at Relic nervously. "Y-yeah, of course."

"Thanks for the invite, even if it was short."

Sam stands. Poor guy.

"Anytime."

Chapter Ten

SELENA

We walk out of Relic's bar and there is a black Rolls waiting out front with a driver holding the door open. I get inside the luxury vehicle, and Relic follows, sliding beside me on the seat. He presses the button on the divider while the driver closes the driver's side door like it's final.

I'm alone inside the back seat of a quarter of a million-dollar car with Relic King.

"Why?" I ask as we drive away. I reach down to massage my aching feet. Heels are lethal on a woman's feet. I'm usually barefoot at home or wearing sneakers at the gym.

His gaze follows my hands, massaging my ankles. "Take them off," he demands.

Not wanting to argue the point further and needing relief, I slide my feet out of the heels, almost groaning in relief at my feet being released from the offending shoes. *Fuck yes.*

He reaches with his hand to grip my calf gently, causing my pencil skirt to ride up my thighs. I let him lift both legs over his thighs and his hands begin massaging my feet.

"Oh my god. That feels so good," I breathe out while he rubs the arch of my left foot and then the right. The fact he is the one doing it makes me want it more. It makes me feel hot and wet all over.

His eyes glide over my thigh-high stockings. "Do you want to take them off?" He asks.

If he only knew. I want him to take them off and take me right here, but I can't. I won't. It's probably what he is used to. A man that massages a woman's feet and is not interested in a relationship or marriage is dangerous.

Dangerous to the wetness pooling between my thighs. I hope I'm not making a mess in my panties. The inner part of my thighs feels hot and I'm hoping––no praying—I don't make a fool of myself. If he notices that I'm wet just from him rubbing my feet, I'm in big trouble.

He would know.

That I want him.

That all he has to do is make a move and I'll open my legs and let him have me. I haven't had sex in four months, but I know he must have had sex since the night of our kiss.

There is no way he hasn't, and that has me pulling my feet away from his hands. It is what has me adjusting my skirt and sliding my feet back into my shoes.

I shake my head. "No, that is all right. Thank you."

"You're welcome."

The car stops. I hear the door slam from the driver exiting the car. When the back passenger door opens, I see we are in front of a Mexican restaurant. It is not fancy. It's welcoming. And I like it.

We are seated in a booth, and I look around, noticing that we are overdressed. But it's refreshing and laid back, painted in vibrant colors that are customary in Mexican restaurants with the Day of the Dead skulls on the walls.

I like it and I feel comfortable. I don't feel like everyone's eyes are watching me. It is like we are just two people having dinner after work and not an employee having dinner with her billionaire boss.

A server places two glasses of water, tortilla chips, and salsa in the center of the table. Relic grabs the saltshaker and sprinkles some over the basket.

"Why did you show up at the bar?"

He gives me a grin, takes a chip, and places it inside his mouth, forcing me to wait for his answer while I listen to the crunch of the chip as he chews.

I lean back in the seat, grinning as he observes me from across the table. A waiter walks by our table and the smell of freshly cooked fajitas sizzling hits me, making my stomach groan and my mouth water.

"You know why. You are a very smart woman, Selena."

"How do you know I'm smart?" I remove the paper from both straws and place one in each glass. "You don't respond to my work emails, but you show up at a bar when I leave with a coworker to have a drink. Then you whisk me away to have dinner."

He leans forward and chuckles. It's nice to hear him laugh and when he smiles, showing his straight white teeth, my insides melt like butter.

Before he can answer, an older woman with an apron stops at our table to get our orders. "What would you and your guest like, Mr. King?"

Everywhere he goes, everyone knows him. Or he owns this place, too.

"She will have the steak fajitas. *Yo deseo las enchiladas de queso con crema por favor.*" His eyes meet mine. "Selena, do you want sangria, or would you rather have a Mexican Coke?"

I can't believe he noticed what I wanted, but Relic is always a step ahead. He is always in tune with whoever has his attention. When he isn't sure, he asks, or maybe, he doesn't want to be rude.

"Mexican Coke, please."

He nods at the older woman. "*Dos, por favor.*"

"*Si, patron,*" she answers, walking away.

"Where did you learn to speak Spanish?"

"When I was five. I had tutors teach me Spanish as my second language. I also speak Russian, Japanese, Mandarin, and Portuguese."

I raise my eyebrows. "That's impressive." I pinch my fingers together, leaving a space, and say, "I know a little bit of Spanish I picked up in college, but I'm fluent in Japanese."

"I was going to ask you, but I had your file and checked for myself since I wasn't sure. Your long beautiful hair gives it away." Of course he did. He's Relic King. Did he just say my hair is beautiful? "Your mother was born in North Dakota and your father was born in Japan, but they have lived all your life in the US. You graduated top of your class at NYU and that's why I told my brother it was okay to hire you when Mia asked if you could apply."

"Do you hand select all your employees?"

"On my team, yes. Especially for your position. I apologize for not responding to you. I don't need to. Your analysis is perfect. I prefer to respond to you in other ways."

The food is placed in front of us, and the smell of fajitas makes me pick up the tortilla and dig in, wanting him to respond to me in all the ways.

After dinner, he has the driver take me to Mia's apartment. I'm surprised he gets out with me and walks me to the door of the apartment. I turn around before inserting the key and his hands slide into my hair. He leans in, brushing his lips over mine.

His lips press firmly against mine. He slides his tongue between the seam of my lips and explores the inside of my mouth. I almost forget where I am until I hear the door behind me open. I freeze, but Relic doesn't care because he doesn't stop. He slides his right hand down my lower back, his left still on the left by my cheek. The tips of his fingers entwine in my hair.

I hear a throat clear, and I break the kiss and land on the back of my heels. I hadn't realized I was still on my tippy-toes. Relic is still taller than me even with my heels on.

I slowly turn around to find Deacon watching us with a knowing expression. Mia is flat out smiling.

Deacon walks around me and taps his brother on the shoulder. "Let her breathe, brother."

He scrapes his teeth over his bottom lip and replies, "I will. I just had to remind her who she prefers dinner and drinks with rather than Sam from the office." He lowers his voice and kisses my cheek. "I'm a better kisser and I don't take women on an empty stomach to a bar to convince her to like me." He pulls back and my eyes dart from Deacon to Relic, talking like I'm not standing here.

"Do we have to have a talk with him?" Deacon asks.

Wait. What? Is he serious? Sam isn't a threat. I get the whole caveman thing, but really?

Relic takes a step back and glances at his brother. "He understood. I promised to look out for Selena. She is fed and back at home safe and sound with Mia."

My stomach drops. That was his reason? My eyes find Mia and

she doesn't look happy. She looks guilty. It was because of Mia and not because he wanted to take me to dinner. She probably wanted to be alone with Deacon.

I'm not mad that she wanted to be alone or that she asked Deacon to have Relic look out for me, but my pride has taken a blow. I thought his interest in me was genuine. The foot massage and now the second kiss. Maybe he kisses all the women he takes to dinner. He didn't propose sex or anything.

At dinner, he was nice and acknowledged that my work was good. He also flirted a bit, but I think he fucks and flirts with every woman he thinks is beautiful. How many women has he told that their hair is beautiful? *A ton, bitch. You're nothing special.*

"Thank you for dinner and babysitting me, Relic. I'll keep that in mind, hopefully you won't have to go through all the trouble again. Have a good night," I say, sidestepping around Mia and walking like a wounded animal to my room where I can lick my wounds in private.

Relic is just a man you fuck and forget. He is the story you tell your kids when you're older about a fling you had that meant nothing but was exciting. The type that would never make it past sunrise.

Chapter Twelve

SELENA

TWO MONTHS LATER

It's Friday, six in the evening, and I'm in my bedroom, turning the TV on to watch Netflix when the door to my bedroom opens. Mia turns off the TV, leaning on my chest of drawers to get my attention.

"Let's go, bitch. We are going to a pool party at Relic's house."

My mouth opens and shuts without a single word being uttered. The sound of Relic's name has me acting like a nervous teenager when someone mentions her crush.

For two months, I have tried to get over what happened. Mia told me she was sorry for asking Deacon to have Relic look after me at work.

She feels guilty.

I know she feels bad about that night Relic dropped me off and they opened the door to find us sucking face. To them, it is normal to see Relic kiss women or fuck around with different females that are around seeking his attention.

It's different when it is me. I don't want to be one of those women that fall for him. Even though that is exactly what was happening.

Sam stopped by my office, asking if I was okay. I have been

keeping to myself. I haven't heard from Relic, and it is best I stay out of everyone's way. I wouldn't want him to have to babysit me again. It is bad enough I live with Mia and don't even pay rent.

When Sam asks if I want to go eat lunch in the break room, I always respond that I'm busy and need to catch up because I have plans. *All lies.* Lies so I can go to the apartment, mope around and convince myself that it is because I'm saving enough to get a place of my own. I guess when I find my own place, I can date and not feel like I'm being watched.

"I can't go with you there. Are you crazy? I wasn't invited."

She places her hand on her hips. "Deacon invited you and you're going."

"Hello, I have nothing to wear!" I shout as she heads out of my room and into the living room. Only to return with a department store bag that is suddenly thrown in my direction.

"You do now. I went shopping with Deacon earlier and bought you a swimsuit and cover-up."

I roll my eyes. "You need to stop buying me clothes. How much do I owe you?"

She doesn't answer, and I don't want to argue with her. I look inside the bag, and there is a red Brazilian bikini that is basically a bunch of strings you tie together with scraps of fabric to cover... basically nothing. I don't want to seem ungrateful and a bad friend, so I fold.

I head into the bathroom and begin to get ready, hoping this is a good idea and I don't make a fool of myself.

I'm ready after showering, having to shave everything off to wear that scrap of fabric. "Are you sure about this?" I ask.

Mia walks in wearing her cover-up, and she looks amazing with her pretty white dress molded to her petite frame.

She smiles. "You look amazing, and if he can't see that, then he is fucking blind."

I put my hands on my hips, looking at my reflection in the mirror. "I am not wearing this for him, and I'm sure he will be there with whoever is the flavor of the week. I'm worried that everyone will think I'm trying too hard."

She snorts. "The girls that are invited are practically nude. You will be overdressed," she says sarcastically.

I opt for my Japanese-inspired kimono from Dubai for a cover-up instead of the transparent minidress cover-up. I have to keep some type of modesty.

We arrive in front of huge metal gates in a neighborhood full of estate homes. Mia presses a button on a call box to the left and the gates immediately open, allowing access to a long circular driveway.

Near the seven-car garage is Relic's black Aventador, a white Ferrari, and a black Nissan GT-R. There are other cars neatly parked on the left side of the driveway. Mia parks next to the GT-R and we gather our bags.

We walk up to the double frosted-glass doors with an intricate iron design in the front, and the door is immediately opened by a tall, muscular guy in a suit. He must be security because he's wearing an earpiece around his ear and talking into a thin microphone in his hand.

The gentleman recognizes Mia and motions us to enter the immaculate home. Once inside, my eyes scan the white walls and Calcutta marble floors. I feel like I'm in a glass of milk.

Even the furniture is white, with only a touch of gray for accents. The living room has a modern sliding door that opens from one wall to the other, allowing the view of the outdoor patio to be seen from inside the house.

I follow Mia through the living room to the outdoor patio. The pool, lit with blue LED lights, is full of bodies and topless girls. "Welcome to the Party" by Pop Smoke plays from the speakers.

When I get a better look, I see a guy playing music next to a bartender serving drinks. Walking closer toward the pool, I see a huge hot tub with steam swirling from the powerful jets. When I inhale a deep breath, taking in the scene, a haze of marijuana hits my nose.

Mia greets Deacon, sitting next to Liam on the edge of the hot tub. When my eyes dart next to Deacon, my eyes meet his golden ones. My eyes slowly follow his chest, displaying all of the ink molded over his chiseled torso.

Relic has both arms spread out like a king, with Sophia on his right and a brunette I have never seen before to his left.

Sophia gives me a murderous glare when she spots me and slides her hand possessively over Relic's chest with a smirk. His eyes never leave mine as she caresses his chest, and my eyes fall to her hand and a wave of jealousy passes through me like ice, but I manage to place a grin on my face.

I grin because I am sick of moping around for a guy that is clearly set in his ways. His interests are everywhere. He is not going to change, and he doesn't deserve me or my time. Not in that way. I need to stop this infatuation I have for him, but like everything, it is easier said than done.

"Hey, Selena. I'm glad you could make it," Deacon says, and I look over to where he is seated with Mia standing directly behind him.

"Thank you for inviting me," I say softly.

A giggle escapes Sophia's mouth as she says sarcastically, "So that's why she's here. Relic didn't invite her. Makes sense."

"I invited her because she's my best friend and has more right to be here than you do," Mia quips.

"It's okay, Mia. She just feels insecure," I reply and glance at Sophia. "Sophia, you can have him. You have nothing to worry about. I'm not into the group thing," I say as the guys, and even the brunette, laugh.

Relic is the only one that doesn't find what I said amusing and eyes me with an annoyed expression on his face. He is probably upset that I insulted Sophia. She can have him; I don't have time for a guy that entertains a woman like that in his house and allows them to insult a guest. She doesn't even live here.

Back in Japan, my grandfather would have thrown her out. It is customary to show respect to your guest and not let others bring negative energy into your home.

"Let's get changed, Selena," Mia says over the laughter as she places her arm through mine.

We walk away, and as we pass the bar, a couple of guys wink at me, but I ignore it. Mia snags me a cocktail and we head through the kitchen into a hallway with many doors on each side.

"Don't pay attention to that bitch, Selena. She just feels threatened because of the way Relic looked at you when we arrived. The look on her face when you told her she just feels insecure was priceless." She laughs.

"Sorry. I just couldn't take it anymore. Every time she is around, it is the same thing with her fighting over Relic. She can have him. He obviously loves to have her around. It's exhausting," I say with a grin.

We enter one of the bedrooms to the left and we take off our cover-ups and place them on the queen-size bed inside what must be one of the many guest rooms. I follow her, trying not to stare at the amazing guest room and we walk back to the party on the patio, stopping at the bar for another drink.

"I'm just going to stay here and dance," I tell Mia over the music. "You go be with your man. I'll be fine."

"Are you sure, Selena?"

"Of course. It's too crowded for me over there," I assure her, giving her a wink.

She smiles in understanding. "One dance, and then I'll go."

She walks over to the guy playing the music and tells him to play a song. "Needed Me" by Rihanna plays and my lips curl into a smile because she knows it is one of my favorite songs.

All the girls in the pool sing along and Mia and I dance to the sultry lyrics, slowly swaying our hips with our red Solo cups in our hand, vibing like we used to in college.

When the song is over, before she leaves to go back to Deacon, she gives me a wink, knowing I love to dance and listen to music.

I walk over and ask the DJ to play "WAP" by Cardi B. He does, and when I begin to dance, all the girls crowd the patio.

They dance along with me as I sway my hips and my hair slides forward like a black curtain.

A cute guy dancing gets directly behind me and loosely places his hands on my hips. Mia cheers from the hot tub, and the guy and I dance in sync when Megan Thee Stallion's verse begins.

A large shadow has people moving to the side as the song changes to "Twerk" by the City Girls.

The guy behind me lets go of my waist when I notice the dark shadow is Relic. My head snaps up when Relic gets in his face. "Get lost before I break your hands and your face," he seethes.

The guy holds his hands up. "My bad, Relic. I didn't know."

He smiles menacingly, tilting his head. "Now you do."

I raise my eyebrows at his reaction. The guy looks at me and I give him an apologetic expression. What the hell is wrong with Relic? I was just dancing, and he was over there with his girlfriends, plural. He pulls me toward his chest, dripping with hot water. The heat radiates from him as my nipples harden under my red bikini top.

He lowers his head and whispers in my ear, "You're staying with me tonight. I want to hear you scream my name as I make you come in my bed all night."

My eyes widen. He is so sure I will just let him decide for me. "If I say no?"

He smiles, whispering loud enough for me to hear. "You're not going to say no because I can guarantee you that if I slide my finger between the lips of your pussy, it will be soaking wet and ready for me, *princessa*. Don't push me because I will do it right now in front of all the guests in my home."

His breath fanning my ear is causing goose bumps to appear on my skin, making me aware that I'm not wet from the drops of water sliding down his perfect body but from between my thighs. I try to not clench my thighs as all eyes are upon us, and I don't want him to notice that he is right.

He places his hands on my ass and pushes me against his wet

Versace swim trunks to feel the hardness of his erection. I'm feeling the heat through the closeness of his body, and my body wants to feel more.

My hands lie flat on his chest, the ends of my hair touching the swell of my ass where his hands are possessively over my red bikini bottoms. His cologne mixed with the pool water permeates my senses as he looks down into my eyes.

The water from his shorts drips down my thighs, pooling under us. His nostrils flare, his eyes darken with desire, and I know I'm truly fucked. I realize I'm not leaving his house without the feel of him deep inside me.

My pussy clenches in anticipation, wanting him, telling me that this is my chance.

I swallow and we just stand there. Our eyes are locked. I feel the smoothness of his skin under my hands and the feel of his wild heartbeat, letting me know that he feels the same way I do. He wants me and he is not hiding it.

He came over to me and he wants me to stay. I know I'm thinking with my body and my mind is on hold, but I decide in this moment that Relic will be my story. The one I can secretly tell someone one day when they ask if I have ever done something spontaneous, knowing it is a one-time thing because Relic doesn't play for keeps. All that will be left is a memory for however long the moment lasts.

Let's just hope my heart can survive it.

"Okay. I'll stay."

Chapter Thirteen

He grins, turning me around so that my ass is to his front, probably to hide his erection from prying eyes. He walks behind me, pushing me forward, guiding me near the towel warmer by the entrance of the house and grabs one to wrap it around his waist.

"Follow me through there." He points to double doors on the other side of the house that must lead to his master bedroom.

We walk over, and I wait patiently until he opens the door to reveal a massive king-size bed, all in white, sitting on a lush gray carpet. The door closes behind me and I watch him lock it, my heart beating wildly in my chest.

I'm nervous, standing in his room in a tiny red bikini, wondering what he has in store for me. He unlocks his phone and is typing when he looks up.

"I'm going to ask you two questions. One, are you on birth control? Two, which song do you want to play?"

He has his phone out, handing it to me. My eyes reach his as I take it in my hands with the music app open on search.

"Answer to your first question is yes, I am on birth control. Answer to your second question will be known shortly, but I have one question."

He crosses his arms over his chest, muscles bulging. His body is dangerously flawless, with ink marring every inch of his skin. "Name it."

He looks down at my stomach, toward the apex of my thighs, and my breathing picks up. "If you're planning on fucking me without a condom, how do I know you're clean? I was tested after my last boyfriend at NYU, and I've never not used protection."

His eyes smolder. "Then I guess it will be a first for both of us, not using protection, and for the record, I get tested regularly. My most recent was last week, and I haven't been with anyone since my results came back."

He walks closer to me, and I raise my chin up. "Okay."

I'm trying to keep my mind shut off.

Imagining the person you want with someone else sucks. *It's just one night.*

I breathe, his scent intoxicating me.

"If you want me to stop, all you have to do is say the word."

I press play on his phone, and "Wicked Games" by The Weeknd plays through invisible speakers in the room. He takes his phone from me and tosses it on a side chair near the dresser.

He reaches behind me, sliding my hair forward over each of my breasts. He undoes the strings of my bikini top, and it drops to the floor. My breasts are visible to his gaze except for my nipples which are covered by my dark hair.

"You're gorgeous, Selena. *Eres, hermosa.*"

He walks me back to the edge of the massive bed until the back of my knees hits the edge, causing me to sit. My head tilts, looking at him as my fingers slide the towel away from his waist.

His eyes watch me as I pull his shorts down over his hard cock. It springs free in all its glory, looking wicked with angry veins and three piercings on the tip.

I slide my hand over its massive length from end to tip, placing my thumb over the precum pooling at the tip, admiring how thick he is.

I lean forward and slide his cock into my mouth to taste him for the first time. My eyes close at the delicious salty and sweet mix of him, stroking my tongue along the underside of his length.

He steps back. "Slide up on the bed, and open your legs for me, *princessa*."

I bite my bottom lip and follow his instructions, removing my bikini bottoms in the process.

I lean back on my elbows, opening my legs, showing him I'm completely shaved. I'm so wet that I'm dripping down the crack of my ass. His breathing picks up as he kneels on the bed, sliding forward, bringing his face to the apex of my thighs. He blows air on my hot throbbing clit and my eyes roll back inside my skull, anticipating his mouth devouring my lips.

He aggressively sucks my pussy, sliding his tongue inside me, fucking me with it. I moan as he continues to suck me harder, sliding his tongue deeper inside me, tasting me. Eating me. *Holy fuck.*

He moans against my clit and pulls his tongue out. "You taste so good," he whispers against my clit. He licks his lips and lowers his mouth on me again.

I moan as I slide my hands through his dark hair as he continues feasting on me. The sensation of his tongue and the suction of his mouth has me coming so hard I scream his name from my lips while my pussy pulsates on his tongue.

He swallows every drop as I shiver from the intense orgasm he has given me. He kisses my pussy before moving up to settle between my thighs with the tip of his hard cock at my entrance. He places his hands on my hips, holding me, and slides balls deep inside my pussy.

I gasp at the intrusion of his massive cock stretching me open. His piercings rubbing on my G-spot have me panting. My chest rising and falling.

"Yes," I mewl.

"Fuck, your pussy is so tight. Are you okay?"

I nod with my bottom lip between my teeth. "Yes."

He waits until I can adjust to his size before he moves in and out of me, our bodies dripping with sweat. The sound of our slick bodies slapping against each other takes me over the edge with nothing between us.

I bite his shoulder as I come all over his cock, milking him while he spills inside me, causing me to release his name on a moan. "Relic."

"Yes, baby, I love when you say my name," he says softly. He kisses me, and I taste myself on his lips.

He slides out of me and picks me up like I weigh nothing, carrying me to his bathroom. He carries me over the threshold and places me on my feet in front of the glass door of the shower.

He opens the door and presses a button to turn on the shower. The jets shoot from different directions, fogging up the glass instantly with steam.

He opens the shower door wider, allowing me to enter and stand under the spray. He steps inside and gently pours soap all over my body, bathing me.

Once all the soap is washed off and he bathes himself, he pulls me close.

My head tilts and our eyes lock. There is something intimate about being in the shower with someone you are attracted to. It's sexy. It's personal.

He slips a finger inside me, and my head tilts back as my want for him builds all over again. His other hand slides between my ass cheeks to my other hole, my eyes widening when he slides his index finger inside, and my knees almost buckle.

My hands hold his shoulders to steady myself. "Relic, please," I plead.

I want him inside me again, possessing me. I'm already addicted to him, my body screaming for more. He slides his fingers out and turns me around to bend me over, the warm water dripping down my body with the smell of his soap filling the enclosed shower.

My hands are flat on the tiles, my ass is in his hands that are spreading me, and he slides his cock inside me. He doesn't take me slowly but begins pounding me hard.

I brace my hands on the white marble shower wall, my hair falling forward in a wet mess, moaning with each of his thrusts. He finds my G-spot and my eyes roll back.

"You're mine," he growls, blocking out all reason and thought of what sex with him means.

The words leaving his lips are what I have deeply wanted to hear since I laid eyes on him for the first time. My thoughts are confusing, mixed with my innermost feelings as he penetrates me further.

My heart beats wildly as another orgasm rides through me like a massive wave crashing, and I know I'll never be the same. He grunts and his hot cum spills deep inside me, making us one while, at the same time, ruining me.

The water, mixed with sweat, runs over my body, and I straighten, my hands holding me steady against the tiles. His cock is still seated deep within me and when I finally get my balance, he slides out of me slowly.

We both pour bodywash and clean our bodies in silence. There is nothing to say because we both know…it was perfect. And words will only complicate what just happened.

Once he is done with himself, he washes my hair, running his fingers through the strands, and when I think it's over, he turns me around and lifts me. My legs wrap around his waist naturally while he presses my back against the shower wall and enters me again.

My eyes roll back at how good he feels inside me. I'm swollen, but the pleasure he gives wins over the soreness he's inflicted.

He gently takes a pink nipple in his mouth and sucks, causing fireworks to explode inside me. He takes the other and bites gently. My hips move in circular motions, riding him into oblivion because he doesn't last long.

He hisses my name as he comes, my arms around his neck, and I kiss him gently. I have no idea how it's possible for me to come so much or how he can keep going.

After our intense shower, we both lie naked in the bed, my head on his chest as I trace the lines of his tattoos with my finger. My fingers feel the contours of his chest muscles, and I swirl my finger over each tattoo as he silently watches me.

"Which one is your favorite?" he asks.

I raise my head slightly, looking at his neck. The first tattoo that drew me to him is the one I favor the most.

"I like all of them, but my favorite is the crown on your neck."

"Really?"

I raise myself up on my elbow and look into his eyes. "It's the one that pulled me to you when I first saw you, and it's the one I get to see no matter what."

He grins. "I would have never thought about it like that."

We talk about our favorite movies, food, and music until we both drift off to sleep. My head is on his chest, and my body is wrapped around his. I feel safe being in his arms, but I know when the impending emptiness of morning knocks, he's not mine to keep.

Chapter Fourteen

SELENA

The light streaming through the bedroom window awakens my perfect world. A world where Relic is mine and I am his. A world where I belong, but when I open my eyes, squinting against the light, waiting for my eyes to adjust, I'm alone.

I slowly wake on a yawn and notice my change of clothes and purse are lying neatly on the chair by the dresser.

At least he was thoughtful enough to have my clothes brought in, so I wouldn't have to walk down the hallway in a bikini. I quickly freshen up, dress, and fix the bed, removing the sheets to have them washed. I unlock my phone and there is only one message from Mia with a wink emoji.

Hopefully, Relic is in the house, and he just didn't want to wake me. I venture out of his room, and as I walk through the hallway, every step I take reminds me of the throb between my legs.

I jolt when a short older woman taps me from behind. "Good morning. You must be Selena."

I turn around in shock, hand against my chest, so lost in my thoughts that I didn't hear her walking behind me. "You scared me."

She frowns for a second. "I'm so sorry. I didn't mean to startle you. I heard you were awake, and Mr. King instructed me to make you breakfast. He had to run to the office and will not be back."

Deep down, I expected he would avoid me, but I thought maybe he would be different with me, at least the next morning. I couldn't have been more wrong.

Taking the hint that he is being polite and offering me breakfast but expecting me to leave, I look at the older lady and smile warmly. "That's okay. I need to get going. Did Mr. King leave me a message?" I know it's a stupid thing to ask, and as soon as the words leave my lips, she frowns.

"I'm sorry. He didn't leave me a message to give you, just instructions. He rarely leaves messages with me."

My eyes lower, and I feel stupid for even asking. Of course, he wouldn't. Taking it for what it's worth, I order an Uber.

I had to leave in the morning for the office. My father requested an important meeting with my brothers, the Kings from Hillside, Arizona, and me. Basically, everyone that is part of my family.

Selena found the problems in her analysis since she came on board, something the previous analyst couldn't even figure out. She has sent me emails so we can go over the discrepancies with the weight of the shipments. I didn't want or need to involve her—and definitely could not keep my hands to myself if she was in my office—so I never responded to her emails.

I am impressed she found the discrepancies. She is incredibly good, and everything she mentioned in her analysis is spot on. I figured the deal that we had with the Polish Mob was too good to be true. The Russian Bratva, Elysium from Japan, the yakuza, and even the other cartel organizations I trust before the Polish Mob. They are shady, and I'm not into their type of business. Human trafficking and the sex trade are not something I agree with nor will I ever be a part of it.

Our organization began with my father and the older cartel kings from Mexico, but our generation, which includes my cousins who are the cartel king's children, wants to legitimize as much as we can in the states to avoid being caught by the government. We can't pay everyone off. It isn't possible but we can have heads turn the other way for the right price.

We became business developers, importing and exporting goods along with rarities that we move under the radar.

There are guns and drugs imported and exported with the Russians, but that involves political allies, but what we are really after is control.

The cartel in Mexico and Arizona is another matter altogether. The control my cousins need to make our plan work is on hold until they finish school and come of age and marry. It is a requirement and expected. Since Deacon, Liam and I are older, we need to control things as much as we can. The last thing we need is an influx of drugs to swarm our cities with no control.

I enter the mostly deserted office building, except for the receptionist and weekend security on the first floor. I nod and take the elevator up to the floor that houses the boardroom.

As I walk toward the double doors, I hear my father's voice over my brothers and the other Kings.

I walk in and my father's eyes light up with pride. "You look refreshed this morning," he says.

My brothers both look at me with grins on their faces, knowing that I slept with Selena last night. It wasn't a secret that I took to my bedroom and never left until this morning. I scan the room and nod to the other five Kings, all with different last names to mask their true identities and that they are cartel kings.

Aiden, Mase, Colton, Leo, and Smiley are the younger Kings. Alex, also known as Smiley, is the older of the five and Mase's cousin. Leo is my cousin on our father's side. We are all part of the Mexican Cartel. Families that have united together and trust each other with their lives. Their fathers, like mine, married women in different social circles to support the facade for our futures. Our legacy and business.

. . .

"Damn, *ese*. You look like you put in an all-nighter but in a good way. Who's the chick?" my cousin Leo says, fist-bumping me.

"Why are you worried, *cabrón*? You get enough pussy in college and at the sex club you have going. Are you bored already?"

He gives me a smile. "You know how we do it in Hillside."

"You and Smiley do, but not these three married *chavalos*," Deacon chimes in. "How's Khalani, Lucy and Linda?"

"Waiting for this pussy to settle down already," Aiden says, tapping the table. "Come to think of it, *ese*. You three older *putos* need to get settled down and concentrate on what we are trying to do. Shit is getting hot and spending time fucking around will not get us anywhere."

"Except pussy," Smiley adds on a chuckle.

"Not me, I like my girl. I might take your advice, Aiden."

"If she is the one, *holmes*. Go for it."

I take a seat at the other end of the table and glance at my father. "What is this meeting about?"

"I will let you know shortly, but I want to hear who has my oldest looking so relaxed and refreshed this morning?"

"If you brought me here to piss me off, then it's working."

He leans back in the leather chair at the head of the table and puffs out his chest. My father is an older version of me that still maintains his physique, but where my dark hair is long on top, his is short on the sides with gray streaks.

"Fine, I'll get to the point. Since you are the CEO of the company, and you are aware of your duty to the King legacy, it has been brought to my attention that Elysium, in a year's time, will be appointed a new CEO from the founding family. I don't know who the guy is, but he will be knowledgeable and seasoned to take over. Since we need to have political ties, especially with the shit the Polish Mob has pulled with the shipments, there is only one other option. For you to get married, Relic."

My head snaps to attention at the word marriage coming from my father's mouth. Deacon and Liam frown at my father, knowing I'm not interested in marriage and like my life the way it is.

I fuck who I want and answer to no one. I get that the younger Kings were just talking about it, but my cousin is still single and does the same thing I do. Fuck different women. His tastes are a little deeper than mine, but we have similar interests in not settling down.

Smiley has the same mindset, but he runs East Hillside and likes the old-school way of doing things by playing the streets. He doesn't have to, but it's good that he does. It keeps us having control.

But right now, my father wants to control my dick and my life.

The image of a dark-haired woman with eyes the color of the clearest ocean pops into my mind. The one currently sleeping in my bed and the only one who has ever slept in my bed. I never fuck in my bedroom; I have five other rooms to choose from, plus a perfectly good pool and plenty of penthouses.

Selena is the only one that I have ever brought into my bedroom. Women get ideas when they stay the night, but with her, it's different. She doesn't nag or ask questions and hasn't led me to believe she has high expectations.

I left her there with instructions for Elanor to make her whatever she wanted for breakfast. But the message I received five minutes before I got here let me know she left and didn't ask for anything except if I left her a message.

I should have, but I don't want to lead her on, and right now, with my father telling me a marriage is needed to form an alliance, it's for the best that I didn't.

"Who do you expect me to marry to form this perfect alliance that you have in mind?"

He smiles, and it reminds me of *El Diablo*, Aiden's father, when he has a trick up his sleeve. "You already fuck his daughter, and she is already hanging on your cock wherever you go. I'm sure having her officially as your wife wouldn't make much of a difference."

I know who he is referring to and he is out of his mind.

"Sophia? No fucking way!"

Deacon gets up from his chair. "Dad. This is not right and you know it. That bitch is horrible and only good on her knees."

Mase stays silent, scratching his brow, while Colton gives Liam a look. Colton doesn't like these types of conversations. He has his new bride Linda, who he calls his goddess, to worry about with her new role with the Italian Mafia. He gives me a side-glance and nudges his chin toward Liam, silently telling him to speak up.

"No pun intended, Relic, but I have to say it. I don't agree either. That bitch is toxic, and Mia can't stand her," Liam says.

My father stands and leans over the table with his hands on the flat surface, giving me a murderous glare. "I don't give a fuck! Relic, you will marry Sophia Mitchell, and that's the end of it.

"The Mitchells already conduct business with us worth millions, and his daughter would be a perfect match. This will solidify our power and support from the government. The other Kings understand, and they are younger than you. You are the head of our conglomerate. You have a keen eye for business, and we are powerful. We have Elysium Holdings from Japan and the yakuza in our court.

"Elysium, one of the most important, with its history and Japanese influence with yakuza. Jiro has already taken control from his father and all we have to wait for is Elysium's announcement of their CEO."

My eyes harden, knowing I have to think about my duty to my family and not my dick. This is about my heritage and the future of my family and brothers. The Kings in this room have shed blood, sweat, and tears.

"When?" I blurt.

Liam and Deacon both raise their hands in annoyance.

"You've got to be kidding, Relic. You're not seriously going to consider marrying her?" Deacon speaks up.

Leo looks at me in horror, like I'm possessed. "Don't do it, *ese.*"

"Run, *carnal,*" Smiley adds.

"Enough!" my father growls at the other Kings.

"*Perdonanos, tio,*" Leo says apologetically. "We are sorry. We are just pulling his chain."

My father calms down, and he slowly takes his seat. He places his hands together. "It will be best to announce your engagement in three months." He looks to Leo. "Don't think you're off the hook either.

You better get all that fucking-around mess out of your head and think about the future, Leo. If not, it will be one of those girls in West Hillside." Leo snorts.

My eyes harden at what I must do. "Fine. If it's what I have to do, then so be it."

My father looks at me and nods, knowing I'm not happy but will do what's required for my company and for our family.

"I can't fucking believe this!" Deacon roars, pacing the board-room, not accepting. "Relic, you don't have to do this. It's not right. There must be some other way. A better option."

My father's expression turns to anger. "Deacon, stop. If there was some other way, then it would be done, but there isn't. Elysium is a powerful player with the Japanese, and I don't know who they have in mind to take over; it's all some big fucking secret. Yuri, Dimitri and the Russian Bratva are a wild card, and the Polish are scumbags, and we cannot afford risks. Relic can draft a solid prenup and marry Sophia, and that's final until I say otherwise."

The thought of marrying Sophia has my stomach churning in dread. I fuck her and she gives a good blow job, but that's it. I have never had any interest in her unless it's to keep my dick wet.

I can't stand her crazy jealous rants and her snobbish remarks, but she never cared if I was with other women. She said she understood we were not a couple.

Everything was fine, and she usually minded her own business until she saw Selena. Sophia was just convenient, and I always wore protection with every woman I took to bed until Selena.

A pair of blue eyes invade my mind yet again, and I hate myself because I don't want to let her go. One night with her is not enough, and I had planned to have more with her, but now my father's announcement has derailed my plans with Selena.

The softness of her skin and the wetness of her pussy wrapped around my dick have me hard under the table just thinking about last night. The sweet taste of her and her perfect body has me begging for more. I couldn't get enough of her last night, and I didn't want her to leave, but when my father calls for these meetings, it's usually important.

My duty to my family and my company comes first. My personal wants and needs don't matter. It's something I understood when my father handed me the company. As much as I want Selena, I have to let her go, even if it kills me. I want her more than I should, and I crave her like no other. For the first time in my life, I have to let go of what I want before I have the chance to keep it.

I glance at Aiden, Mase, and Colton, envying them right now. At least they got to marry who they love. I have to marry for convenience. All because of the political ties Sophia's father has with King Enterprises that will keep us in control. Elysium is a mystery. No one knows who is going to take over, and that can derail everything we have built if that person is not on board with us.

I wonder who the asshole is? Because of that *puto*, I have to tie myself like a dog on a leash to a woman I don't love.

Chapter Sixteen

The entire weekend, I couldn't get him out of my head. He occupied my thoughts, and my body craved him. The man lit my skin on fire, and when I fell asleep in his arms, I felt safe. The kind of safe a girl desires when she's alone in her bed, wishing those same arms were wrapped around her, whispering sweet nothings in her ear.

I knew it was stupid of me to want someone who made it clear it was just sex and it would just allow me to get hurt, but I couldn't help it. He showed me a side of him I don't think he shows many people and I liked it. I like the way he views things. It's simple and uncomplicated.

Lying in my bed, I place the pillow over my head and scream. When it comes to Relic, I'm so fucked. He told me he doesn't get involved in relationships of any kind and has no plans to marry, so why am I here daydreaming about more? I can't stop thinking about him and how he was with me alone in his room. But I know the answer.

He was amazing, the sex was amazing, and he held me the entire night. We talked about everything, what we liked and disliked, like we'd known each other forever.

When he laughed at something I said and smiled, it was breathtaking. That man has a face and body molded to perfection. It makes sense why he has women all over him. I just knew I couldn't be that vulnerable, but I've never felt like this before about anyone.

I'm getting dressed and ready for work, and my thoughts drift to my past when I would visit my grandfather in Japan every summer until I left for college. There was a boy that would come over.

His father knew my grandfather, and he would drop him off for the day's lesson. My grandfather wanted me to learn self-defense and Japanese culture. The katana sword was sacred and difficult to learn, but I did my best, and my father said it was necessary for me to learn and that one day I would understand.

Japanese families feel strongly about culture and loyalty. My father and mother instilled those same values back home. They made sure that I earned everything and had to excel. It was what pushed me to earn my scholarship to NYU.

My parents believed in me always, and I couldn't let them down. Loyalty and honor were big parts of my life, and so was my first crush. The Japanese boy that taught me everything he'd learned when I visited Japan.

I was surprised he knew English. It felt like he was learning from me the same way I was learning from him and what we didn't know, we learned together. We lost touch after I left for college, and I have never returned to Japan since then.

It's been five years, and I haven't heard from him. My grandfather would call me to see how I was doing and say that soon he would come and visit, reminding me that Japan would always be a part of me and to always honor my family and heritage.

Chapter Seventeen

SELENA

TWO MONTHS LATER

I haven't heard from Relic or seen him at work. He never called or reached out, and I realize how stupid it was to think I was any different from any other woman in his life. It was just one night of sex and a good time. He never promised me anything, and he made sure to keep his distance from me. His message was loud and clear, even if it hurt me deep inside. *A conquest.*

My probationary period at King Enterprises is almost up, and to be honest, I don't think I want to stay on permanently. Mia mentioned it was time for my evaluation and to expect a decision this week.

It's already Thursday evening, and I'm in my bedroom applying for other positions online with my mind made up to turn the position down and give my boss a two-week notice.

Mia will be sad, but I don't see how I can be myself there. My emails to Relic are robotic, he makes sure I don't need to explain my reports, and he tries to avoid seeing me. It's best that I leave and find a job elsewhere. Somewhere else where my work is not clouded by personal feelings. After sending my last application, I close my laptop, the door opens, and Mia enters my bedroom, sitting at the edge of my bed with a concerned expression etched on her face.

"Hey. Are you okay, Selena?"

Placing my laptop on the nightstand, I look up and give her a fake smile. "Yeah, everything is fine."

She crosses her arms over her black blouse. "You're a terrible liar. Tell me."

She gets comfortable, raising her knees, waiting for me to answer.

I sigh and tell her the truth. "I'm not going to take the position if they offer it. I'm actually going to put in my notice, and I've already started applying somewhere else. I appreciate everything you have done in getting me this position, and I know working at King Enterprises is a great opportunity, but it's not for me."

"Is it Relic? Did he say or do––"

"He didn't say or do anything," I interrupt her.

"Then why?"

Giving her a sad smile, I tell her the truth. "I don't fit in, and I made a mistake in mixing my personal feelings with my work. Sleeping with your boss and wanting more is never a good idea. He actively avoids me, and it will eventually hurt me professionally. I can't even explain my work to him because he makes sure I don't have to. It's for the best."

Her expression softens. "You fell for him, didn't you?"

Taking a deep breath, I admit it for the first time out loud. "Yes."

"Does he know?"

I scoff. "He is not interested in how I feel. I haven't seen or heard from him except for an automated email after every report I sent him for the last two months. It's obvious. He couldn't have spelled it out more clearly. One-night stand."

"What an asshole," she whispers.

"Leaving is the best solution I could come up with."

It would save me from having to see him or, worse, with someone else, making the knife in the wound dig deeper. I have to get over it. He was nice, amazing even, except after. After, he became what I feared, the man you want who doesn't feel the same way about you. I guess he will stay a memory. I just hope he does nothing to dirty it.

Chapter Eighteen

SELENA

In the morning, I finish writing my resignation letter in an email to Relic and HR, and I hover my finger over the send button on the mouse, looking at the screen. One of the applications I sent yesterday already requested a formal interview for tomorrow and I accepted. Anything to leave here as quickly as possible.

Closing my eyes, I click send on the email. One lesson I have learned is to never sleep with the boss. A message pops up from Relic, telling me to come immediately to his office. My stomach tightens in anticipation as I make my way to the elevator to the fortieth floor.

The elevator doors open, and I walk to the impeccably dressed secretary seated at her chrome desk. My heels echo on the marble floors as I approach the older woman, smiling as I walk closer.

"You must be Selena. He is expecting you."

I give her a nervous smile. "Yes."

She motions me to the double doors. "You can go inside."

"Thank you."

Opening the door, I walk inside, and the scent of him and his cologne hits me in full force, making the heat between my thighs rise like an inferno.

Get a grip, Selena. This man ghosted you.

His eyes find mine, and there is a hard edge to them. "Have a seat," he says curtly, motioning me to the chair in front of his desk.

Sitting with my back straight, I gaze at his beautiful face with his straight nose and chiseled jaw.

"You wanted to see me?" I say with indifference, like we're strangers.

"You're leaving?"

"Yes, I am."

"You were going to be offered the position if that's what you were worried about."

My mouth forms a thin line. "I'm sorry, but I have to decline, respectfully."

His nostrils flare, his expression hardens, and he seems upset. "Why? Your work here is flawless."

I lick my lips, and he tracks the movement of my tongue. I decide to tell him I was offered a better position, even if it's partially a lie. I haven't been offered the position yet, but I decide it's the best answer I can come up with.

"I'm grateful for the opportunity, but I was offered a better position somewhere else."

He leans back in his chair, and his eyes darken and it's like they are black instead of amber. His jaw is set, the tension crackling in the air.

"Come here," he demands while he presses a button.

He turns in his chair when I walk over to where his legs are wide open, and he pulls my hand closer. He gets up from his chair and places me flat against his desk in one swift movement. Before my mind catches up to what is happening, he slides his hand up my skirt and finds me soaked and ready for him.

"You want me, Selena? Say it," he commands.

I close my eyes, hating my treacherous body. "Yes," I hiss while he swirls his fingers over my clit from behind.

My skirt is lifted, and my thong is torn off. The sound of his belt buckle and zipper clinking before the warm tip of his cock is at my entrance.

"I've avoided you because I would be fucking you all day in my office. Since you have made your decision to leave, it won't matter if they hear you scream my name through my office door." Without warning, he slides his cock balls deep inside of me with one hard thrust, making me moan his name.

"Now they know I'm fucking your wet, hot pussy in my office," he whispers.

My eyes widen at the realization that I moaned his name really loud. He pounds into me from behind with his hips slapping against my ass, his belt banging against the glass desk with every thrust.

"Now they will all know who you're fucking. Do you know how beautiful you are? The men that work on your floor have been dying to take you out, whispering how fucking hot your ass looks in a skirt. It is why I showed up at my bar and took you." He leans over my back and his breath fans my hair. "Sam thought he had a chance. He just didn't know you were already claimed." He licks me right below my ear. "I lick what is mine, *preciosa*."

My breathing picks up as he pounds into me relentlessly. He grips my hips and goes harder. Oh my god. What the ever-loving fuck? My climax builds inside me like a firestorm, and I try to bite back the moan, but it's no use. His cock hits something deep inside me that no one has ever touched. The piercings on the tip of his cock rub my G-spot, making me come so hard that fireworks cloud my vision, and the loud moan I've been holding leaves my lips loud and clear for all to hear.

"Ahh fuck." He grunts deep in his throat as I ride the wave, spilling inside of me.

He pulls out slowly and hot cum drips down my inner thighs. I push up on his desk, and I feel a handkerchief slide between my thighs, wiping me clean.

He grabs me by the waist and turns me around so I can sit on his desk. He looks down at my thighs and nestles his cock again at my entrance. We both look down and watch as he fists his cock in his hand, using our arousal to slide his hand up and down before sliding inside me.

We both moan softly, and I hold on to his shoulders with my eyes closed. We kiss gently, tasting each other, and his hands undo the buttons of my blouse, revealing my breasts nestled in black lace.

"Beautiful," he whispers.

My hips move in circles, and he hisses. "I love when you're deep inside me. I want you, Relic. So much."

When the words leave my mouth, he stiffens slightly and pulls out, leaving me empty. He looks down at me and buttons my blouse in place. My expression doesn't hide the confusion on my face.

"I want you, Selena, but I don't deserve you."

"Why? Is it something I said?"

He gives me a sad smile. "It's nothing you said. I just can't be what you deserve. I'm sorry."

As soon as we started, it was over. He dresses so quickly that I'm still trying to put my skirt back in place when he's finished fastening his belt. He's trying to tell me we can't be anything more. The reality hits me like a slap in the face. He won't even look at me as he utters his next words.

"You don't have to finish the two weeks if you have to start at your other position. I will arrange a car for you."

If you want to know how it feels to be used and cast aside, this is it.

My anger getting the best of me, I snap, "That's unnecessary. I am not some whore you can just pay off to leave you alone. I don't want you to arrange anything. You said from the start you didn't get involved in any type of relationship, and I told you I understood. I just didn't think you were going to be so cold about it. This is the second time you've treated me like I'm nothing but a tramp after you fucked me. 'Fuck' is the term because the word 'sex' is too good for what we had and what you make it out to be in the end." I walk over to get a better look at his face because he won't look me in the eye. I want him to see the hurt he has inflicted, but his next words are something I never thought he would ever say to me. Ever.

"I want you to leave. Don't finish the day and don't come back to work here. We're done. We can't work together, and you obviously can't handle it."

I flinch like he slapped me and I swear I see something cross his face for a split second. Like it wasn't him saying these horrible things to hurt me, but that would be impossible.

It was him saying them to my face, like I'm some stalker that won't leave him alone.

My eyes lower in defeat, and the feeling in my heart is a stabbing pain I feel all the way to the pit of my stomach. "I'm sorry you feel that way," I croak, my throat constricting with a ball that suddenly wants to take control of my voice.

Looking around, I find my ripped panties on the floor by his desk, and I bend down to retrieve them.

His hand grips my arm, but not enough to hurt me. "I want you to get out," he grits out.

I stand quickly, my eyes filled with unshed tears, and I turn and practically run out of his office, wishing I had never met or laid eyes on him.

The next day, I'm getting ready for my interview, glad I don't have to return to King Enterprises. When Mia came home yesterday, she held me as I cried myself to sleep over how much I wanted a man who didn't want me and treated me like shit. I also cried because I knew it would never work and I let it happen. I let my emotions override my common sense and I completely screwed up my first job. I made a complete fool of myself.

Mia told me she saw Relic at work and told him in front of Deacon and Liam to stay away from me and never go near me again.

Everyone on his floor heard us, so apparently, the rumor mill is that I was fired after sleeping with the boss and got clingy. *Bastard.*

She told me Liam got upset at how he treated me and punched Relic in the face. I wasn't happy about that, but he deserved it. Liam stormed out and Deacon was ashamed of how Relic treated me. He basically threw me out of his building, asking me to collect my things and leave.

It's almost time for my interview, so I head out of the apartment building and wait for the Uber to arrive. I'm looking at my phone when a text comes through from an unknown number.

Unknown: I'm sorry for how I treated you. I don't expect you to forgive me, but I want to tell you I'm truly sorry for hurting you.

I type out a reply.

Selena: I understand. Bye, Relic.

I didn't know what to say to his apology, because my wounds are still bleeding. I need a fresh start, something different. I feel so hurt and lost right now. Me texting him, I understand is just me acknowledging that he doesn't want me in his life. He turned what we shared into something dirty. Something I don't want to think about.

The Uber arrives, taking me to the address they gave me, and we arrive at a tall building in the middle of Seattle, not far from the Kings' building. The building has familiar Japanese blossoms and I feel a sense of déjà vu. It reminds me of when I would visit Japan as a teen.

There is a Japanese sign on the wall behind the reception desk with a letter in bold. There are cherry blossoms drawn behind on the wall like they are growing. I am confused. The irony of me walking into this building with the symbol of the letter meaning katana and the cherry blossoms.

When I trained with the sword as a child, learning all the basics with my first childhood crush, I remember he vowed to protect me like a great samurai warrior. Memories of those moments replay in my mind as I stand looking at my surroundings.

I would giggle that he was being silly, but he would always tell me I had the most beautiful blue eyes. The receptionist watches me as I approach the clean desk and notice it is a man with Asian hair wearing a red tie and a suit.

"Hello, Miss Tenaka." I look at him curiously, wondering how he knows my name or why he is so sure I'm Miss Tenaka.

"How did you know my name?"

He smiles warmly. "They have been expecting you." He walks over, dismissing my question, and presses the button for the elevator. "Twenty-seventh floor." He bows after I enter the elevator.

Once the doors close, I press the button to the twenty-seventh floor and the elevator rises upward at a steady speed. The walls have a reflective material and I check myself to make sure my bun is in place and the best suit I could find in my closet looks okay. When the elevator reaches the floor, the doors open and there is an older Asian man with gray hair waiting near the French doors to the left.

"Miss Tenaka, right this way," he says in English but with a notably strong Asian accent.

Once inside, I notice the office is huge, with floor-to-ceiling windows and bamboo flooring. No one is sitting behind the desk or on the two chairs in the bare-naked room. There is only a huge rectangle box frame with a single light shining down on it that holds what looks like an original katana sword. When my eyes dart around the room, I notice to my right, a man is standing with his back to me, looking out the floor-to-ceiling windows at the city below. I didn't see or hear him enter. He wasn't standing there when I entered. *Weird.*

I walk closer, my heels echoing on the bamboo flooring as I take each step, and the older man turns around with a smile on his face. He is short and reminds me of my grandfather. With a heavy Japanese accent, he bows and greets me. "Welcome."

I bow right back, as is customary in Japanese culture. "Thank you."

We both straighten, and he motions for me to sit. "Please, sit. I remember your grandfather showing me pictures of his only grand-daughter when you were just a child."

I frown in confusion. "My grandfather? How do you know my grandfather?"

He grins. "Remember, when you were young, he told you one day everything would make sense, the training, the learning of your ances-tors, and that one day he would ask you to come back to Japan to receive your inheritance when the time was right."

I remember when I was fifteen, he said something like that to me, but I thought nothing of it.

"What does that have to do with why I'm here? I don't under-stand. I came for an interview. I applied for a job online."

He chuckles. "Selena Tenaka. This is your inheritance, known in Japan and the underworld as Elysium. Here in the states, the company is known as *E* in English but *I* for katana in Japanese. You were taught honor, loyalty, and to earn everything you work for, but now it's time for you to take your place as the CEO of Elysium. If you decide to take over what your family has built for generations, you will need to go back to Japan and learn everything there is to know before you can come back here and take your place. I will run things while you're gone at the instruction of your grandfather."

I swallow, taking in the magnitude of the stories told to me when I was a kid and piecing them together in my head. It was all true, everything that I was taught and the little tidbits of information given to me.

"How did you know where to find me?"

"That was easy. An old friend has been tracking you since you graduated from New York and moved to Seattle. When you were applying for jobs, we took the opportunity to be the first to bring you here before you left for somewhere else because we have been monitoring where you have been working and living. Your analysis skills are impressive, but we will fill you in on how we know about your work when the time is right."

"What friend has been tracking me without me knowing?" I cross my arms, getting annoyed. He looks toward the French doors behind me.

I hear the doors suddenly open, I turn my body to see who has come in and my eyes widen.

Jiro.

Chapter Twenty

SELENA

I watch an older Jiro walk toward us, the colorful tattoos on his neck and hands making him look dangerous as he walks in wearing a suit. He has gotten older and more attractive since I last saw him. He glances at me, but his eyes don't soften like they used to. Jiro looks at the older gentleman and bows, greeting him in Japanese, saying the older man's name, Daiymo.

"Jiro has taken his rightful place as the head of the yakuza and will oversee protecting you like his father has protected your grandfather. It was all arranged from before you two were born. The only difference is that you were born a woman and not a man."

I smile sarcastically. "Lucky me." Daiymo's eyes show amusement at my sarcasm.

I feel bad for showing disrespect to him in the way I answered, but really, yakuza? That means Jiro is the head of the Japanese Mafia. They kill people. It also means that I'm part of the Japanese Mafia.

My eyes move to Jiro and he looks at me with a dry expression with his head turned slightly to the side, studying me.

I wait a few seconds impatiently. His silence makes me lash out and I raise my left eyebrow. "Are you done?"

He opens the wrapper of a solid candy and pushes it in his mouth, making a sucking sound, sliding it to the side of his mouth so he can answer. "I was just admiring your choice of clothing. You look horrible. Your grandfather will not approve."

I roll my eyes. "If you haven't noticed, I was here looking for a job and clothes cost money."

He smirks and answers me like I'm a child. "You now have plenty of it. I will take care of it. Also, you don't go anywhere unless I take you. No more Uber or whatever you call that shit. It isn't safe for someone like you and who you are. No one is to know who you are until you come back. The friend you live with is not to know either. You will tell her in time. Just let her know you will be visiting your grandfather for a while."

I take a deep breath, annoyed. "You have my life all figured out, don't you? What if I had a husband or boyfriend?"

Daiymo takes his leave with a worried expression at my tone with Jiro as I stand.

Jiro walks closer in my personal space, and I take one step back. "Your life is mine to protect, and I guarantee you if you had a husband or a boyfriend, I would know. A man that you belonged to would never let you live with your best friend or alone. When was the last time you went out on a real date, Selena? Since you graduated and you dumped that asshole, you haven't been out with anyone except your best friend and her boyfriend."

I'm relieved that is all he knows of where I've been. He hasn't mentioned the bar or the restaurant Relic took me to. I take a step closer with a hard tone, and his cologne hits my senses, clean and intoxicating and very much belonging to Jiro.

"I never thought you would be a creep and stalk me for so long, but who I see or who I fuck is none of your business."

His face is an inch from mine. "It is now," he says softly as the whiff of his fruity candy mixes with his cologne.

My week keeps getting better and better. I shake my head in disbelief. "Creepy, but whatever," I mutter.

"Let's get you home and start getting the things you need the most. We leave Friday evening. If you need anything, call me, either a driver or I will take you anywhere you wish to go." He steps back, giving me my space, and we walk toward the elevators.

When we reach the lobby, the doors of the building open and there is a matte black Bugatti Chiron idling. *Impressive.* He walks forward, opening the passenger door so I can get in.

Once he slides in the driver's side, he drives off, roaring through the streets and taking me to the apartment.

"You've changed since I last saw you," I say, trying to relieve the tension.

I didn't think I would ever see him again, and not under these circumstances.

"You haven't. You're still beautiful." A hint of a Japanese accent he tries to hide seeps through when he says the word beautiful, and I find it's kind of cute. "If anything, you're even more beautiful than the last time I saw you."

"Thank you, I guess," I reply, my cheeks tingling with heat because he called me beautiful.

He pulls up at the entrance to the apartment and people gawk at the impressive car. When I open the door to go, he takes my hand and stops me to prevent me from leaving.

"Take out your phone."

I take it out as he demands and look at the message notification. It's a text, and I open it. It reads a foreign number with a message that says The Finest Boyfriend as a contact. I look up, and he smiles.

"Ha ha, very funny."

"Save it and call me if you need anything. There will always be someone watching you until I decide who will permanently be with you as your protection when I'm away on business.

"Okay."

I'm still wrapping my head around everything that is happening, so I'm frozen in place when he leans over and gives me a kiss on the cheek. "Missed you, Selena. I'm sorry I was being a jerk back there."

My heart is brimming with happiness that my childhood friend is back. It's not the way I thought it would pan out, but he is here. He must have done bad things. Things I haven't been exposed to yet.

Things I'm afraid of, but I also know I'm too curious now and want to find out.

"I guess you have seen and done things that are fucked up, huh?"

"Yes, and unfortunately, you will too. I'll try to not let you do or see more than you have to."

I swallow, not liking his last comment. I nod and slide out of the car, closing the door, knowing that a new chapter of my life will soon begin. I just hope I'm ready for it.

Mia makes it home later, and we sit talking on the couch. I told her that I went to the interview but later decided to take some time off and clear my head, and now I want to go visit my grandfather,

"Are you sure?"

I let out a breath of air, pursing my lips. "Yeah, for a little while. I miss him. He contacted me and asked if I would come. I haven't seen him in like five years, and I am a sucker for the old man. So, I agreed."

I don't like to lie to Mia, but it's not entirely a lie, just omitting other pertinent details. This will be good for me. I need space and the time to understand what taking over my grandfather's legacy entails.

"I get it, and with what happened with Relic, it would be good to get a change of scenery. But only if you go to the company gala with me on Friday. Please don't make me beg. I already see that look on your face," she says, jutting her bottom lip out like a child with her hands together like she is praying.

"He won't be there, right?" I ask, hopeful that I don't have to see him.

"Deacon said he wasn't coming and I want to at least spend some time with you before you leave."

I look down, feeling bad for holding back that I'm actually an heiress from Japan. Mia is my best friend and I hate keeping things from her since she has been there for me. I have stayed in her apartment, and she put in a good word for me and got me a job right after graduating. It isn't her fault I was stupid and fell for Relic. I thought I could keep sex and my emotions separated, but I couldn't. I tried, but I failed.

"Fine. I'll go, but I have to leave early to catch my flight."

"I can have someone take you."

"I've got it all sorted out. Don't worry," I say, hiding the nervous feeling that someone is probably downstairs watching me in this very apartment.

She smiles and gives me a tight hug. "I'm going to miss you, but don't stay over there too long and meet some hot guy and fall in love."

I snort. "I don't think so. I still have to get over Relic first," I say sadly.

"What a jerk. He could have just left you alone. He treated you awful and then told you to leave the building and not come back. What a colossal––asshole."

"He sent me a text apologizing. I guess I'm not worth a phone call or a visit. I'm sure I wouldn't have received either if it weren't for you guys making him feel guilty about it." Her expression softens with sadness at how I must feel. "I texted him that I understood and said goodbye. There is nothing more to say. It's clear he doesn't want me and definitely doesn't want me around."

Mia's expression is lost in thought as she says, "I don't know, but there is something that doesn't sit right with him wanting you to stay away. I mean, he fucks around, but he always lets them hang around. Do you know what I mean? Even if he moves on to the next flavor of the week or whatever. It's weird that he treated you like that," she says.

"Maybe it's because we are best friends, and he knows I will always be around. Probably doesn't want me to get any ideas about us having a relationship." I throw my hands up, tired of dwelling over Relic. "Whatever, fuck it. I have to get over him and I already cried the bastard out."

She comes up and gives me a tight hug. "I'm so sorry."

"Me too," I whisper as a single tear rolls down my cheek, failing to mask the fact that my heart is broken.

Chapter Twenty-Two

SELENA

I have all my things packed, ready for my trip to Japan. The driver Jiro assigned to me will take me to the gala. By the time I arrive, Mia and Deacon will be there. She assured me that my name was on the list at the hotel so I won't get tossed out when I arrive.

I sent Jiro a text that I would be attending a gala with Mia, and he said he would pick me up as soon as I texted him so we could take our flight to Japan.

There is a knock on the front door. I pinch my brows and close one eye to look through the peephole. It's a delivery guy with a big black box in both his hands.

I open the door and the young delivery guy greets me. He hands me the box once he confirms my name and says it's for me. I roll my eyes at the déjà vu while taking it into my room so I can open it. I pull the lid off and there is a delicate card inside lying in a bed of red tissue paper.

I still remember red is your favorite color.
Jiro

. . .

I smile and open the tissue paper to reveal a brown Louboutin shoe bag and the most beautiful red silk dress I have ever seen with a matching coat. I place the shoe bag to the side and hold up the dress and then the coat.

Gorgeous.

The cut of the dress is dangerously low but so sexy and chic, with a high slit almost to my hip bone.

The man has taste. The shoes are high and sexy, red suede with spikes. The coat is velvet to compliment the silk gown. Excited that I would be able to wear it tonight, I walk to my bathroom to get ready and dress.

Once I'm done showering, I dress and then apply makeup. I turn and smile at my reflection in the mirror, loving the way I feel in the new dress. Loving that it's from Jiro.

I look at the bedroom one last time before closing the door like it's the last page in a chapter and roll the luggage that I already packed the day before out the doors of the apartment.

When I make it out of the building, I notice the driver is waiting at the curb in a black Wraith. He lifts his head when he notices me and immediately moves to help me with my bag.

After the twenty-minute drive, we arrive at the hotel venue, and I am ushered to the entrance of the King Enterprise's fundraiser gala. The gentleman at the door finds my name and lets me in, indicating the table with my name tag.

When I look over, I spot Mia and Deacon already seated at a huge white round table with Liam, an older woman, and an older gentleman that looks just like Relic but an older version that is obviously his father.

When I make it to the table, Mia introduces me to Mr. and Mrs. King.

"Oh please, call me Victoria," Mrs. King says, welcoming me.

"Hello, Selena. You can call me Damon. Mia has told us so much about you."

I smile at how nice and welcoming they are, but Relic's father has a sharp edge to him that doesn't go unnoticed.

Liam is seated to my right and leans in close. "What's up, beautiful? You look amazing. I think I'll have to break a couple of guys' noses tonight if they keep staring at you," he whispers, making me blush.

"Selena, how has your move to Seattle been since graduating from New York?" Victoria asks, seated across from me.

I smile, looking at my best friend. "It's been great because of Mia."

"That's right, you two are living together at the apartment?" Victoria asks.

"Yes. It's like our old college days when Mia was attending NYU, and we shared a dorm."

"What do your parents do?" she asks, firing another question.

"My father's an accountant, and my mother is a teacher. They moved out west after they graduated, and then they had me. My father was supposed to move back to Japan, but my mother is an American at heart, so my father stayed and they raised me here in the states."

She eyes my hair, making the connection with my Japanese roots, and then her eyes meet mine, noticing that I'm mixed.

"You came out beautifully with blue eyes and beautiful long hair. It's very exotic," she finally says.

"Mother," Liam scolds.

"What, Liam? She's exceptionally beautiful, and her eyes are stunning," she says.

I blush at her compliment. "Thank you. That's kind of you to say."

That doesn't go so bad... until I see Damon and Victoria glance up behind me. I feel a presence that gives off this electric energy taking over the room. It's like all the air is being sucked out of the room like a vacuum, blurring the chandeliers and the whispers of conversation from the other tables around me. My stomach flips and I watch as Victoria's expression turns to admiration.

A man in a tailored black tuxedo moves into my line of vision as he greets his mother with a kiss on her forehead and hugs his father. Relic.

The person with him is the last person I expected to be with him. Sophia's eyes burn into me as she smirks after she greets his parents with familiarity.

I look at Mia, and her expression hardens as she watches her. My eyes move to Liam and Dean. Liam and Deacon both stiffen in their chairs as their eyes study my reaction with worried expressions.

My stomach drops as I continue watching them together. A knife stabbing me in the chest, twisting with jealousy and hurt. He looks striking in his tuxedo with his handsome face. The face that is the reason for my sleepless nights and puffy eyes when I awake in the morning.

My eyes follow him, but he doesn't look at me. When my gaze moves to his right, Sophia is staring at me with a knowing look on her face. My heart beats rapidly like a person having a panic attack, drumming in my ears.

I reach for my phone on the table and unlock it. My thumb moves over my messages, finding Jiro's number. My fingers fly across the keyboard.

Selena: Please be here to pick me up in fifteen. Don't be late.
Finest Boy Friend: Never.

"Have you all heard the great news?" Damon announces.

My head snaps up at his words. Sophia gives me an evil smile, reminding me of Cinderella's stepmother.

"Relic proposed to Sophia, and they will be getting married."

It feels like my soul just left my body. Victoria gives a dry smile and looks at Sophia, congratulating her while Sophia shows off a huge diamond engagement ring.

My eyes sting, filling up with tears, but I blink them back before they fill completely. My skin breaks out in a cold sweat. *Why her?* But I know why? I'm not good enough and I mean nothing to him. Now I know why he wanted to get rid of me. It was because of her, but what gets me is that he used me. That is the part that hurts.

"Liam, why don't you take Selena to dance?" Deacon says.

I respond quickly, so I don't give away what I'm feeling inside. Devastation. "Oh, that's okay. I'm about to leave."

Victoria looks surprised. "But you just got here."

"I just wanted to spend my last day with Mia, but my flight is leaving earlier than expected," I lie.

"Where are you going?" Deacon asks with a worried look.

I swallow down the huge lump in my throat as everyone waits for my answer. "I'm going to visit my grandfather for a while. I haven't seen him since I started college," I announce, not looking at any of their expressions because I keep checking my phone, anxiously waiting for Jiro to message me when he's outside.

"That's really nice," Sophia says with a sardonic smile and my eyes meet her face.

Liam gives her a murderous glare while Mia's hard stare is aimed at Relic. She feels the same way I do. He lied to me. It wasn't because he didn't do relationships. It was because he planned on marrying Sophia.

"I'm excited that the Mitchells and the Kings will be a unified alliance, and Relic has been dancing around Sophia for years," Damon says.

Deacon snorts while Sophia snakes her arm around Relic's possessively, her diamond engagement ring glittering in the light.

His gaze finally finds mine, and the hatred is clear in my eyes as they narrow, watching her flutter her fingers, making sure I notice the big rock he gave her over his chest.

My phone finally pings, breaking the hateful stare aimed at the man I fell for, the same man that just wounded me with all his lies.

"Please excuse me. I'm sorry, but I have to go. My ride is here." I glance at Mia. "Mia, I love you, and I'll call you as soon as I land."

"Okay, be safe," she says in a shaky voice.

I look over at the rest of the table. "Goodbye, Deacon and Liam. It was nice meeting you, Victoria and Damon."

"Bye, sweetheart," Victoria chimes in.

I look directly into Relic's eyes, blue meeting gold. "Relic and Sophia, congratulations. It's obvious that you two are perfect for each other."

His hand is fisted at the table. His gaze travels up my body as I stand in my red silk gown. I turn around and walk out. More like trotting in my heels, but who cares?

Once I reach the exit with my coat, the cool air blows over my heated face, and the tears I've been holding back stream down my face like a dam that's been opened. I sniff and try to dab my face with the edge of my coat as I spot Jiro's Bugatti.

"Selena!" A deep voice shouts my name right before I reach the car and I turn around. Relic is standing at the entrance, looking over people walking between us. "Selena! Give me a minute. I can explain."

I don't want to hear any more of his lies. He frowns when he tries to reach me and sees the car.

I turn around, dismissing him, hating the fact he saw me break down and cry. Quickly I slide inside the sports car and watch Jiro's face turn murderous as he sees the tears running down my face.

He floors the gas pedal, and the car flies like a bat out of hell down the street, the engine roaring loud inside the cabin of the car.

"Why is Relic King calling after you, and why are you crying?" he asks in a seething tone. His hands are gripping the steering wheel so tight it looks like he is going to rip it off.

I place my hands in my lap, trying to compose myself. "It's nothing," I say, then nervously wipe my face.

"Did he hurt you?" he asks, but I stay quiet.

He glances at me briefly while driving us to the airport. The tension rises as he pulls onto the private airstrip to a huge plane waiting for us to board.

He slides his fingers behind my neck, pulls my face toward his, wiping the tears off my cheeks with his fingers and says softly, "Let's go."

I have never been on a private plane before, and when I follow Jiro inside, I'm greeted with lush leather seating. Jiro quickly takes his seat. He motions for me to sit across from him so we are facing each other with a table in the middle with refreshments. I notice there is a stewardess standing patiently off to the side, waiting to see if we require anything.

Jiro puts his hand up to dismiss her and watches me with his dark eyes. I have never met anyone with eyes like his. Even when we were kids, he had these black-as-night eyes.

I can see that he lost that friendly demeanor he had always greeted me with. When I would come over in the summer to spend time with my grandfather, he would look at me like I was the sun. He was always smiling and happy that I was visiting and spending time with him.

"Tell me, what is your relationship with Relic King?"

"Why do you want to know?" I ask.

We are interrupted by the pilot indicating we are ready for takeoff and to buckle our seat belts and remain seated. I look at Jiro, and he is buckling his seat belt and turning to me to watch me do the same.

"My interest in your safety is my main concern, Selena. You are inheriting Elysium from your grandfather. I know it doesn't mean much now, but as soon as we are back with your grandfather, he will be the one to explain what your duties are and what will be required. I am just in charge of your safety and training."

I look at him and smile. "I still remember you always telling me you would protect me. You kept your word."

His expression turns to annoyance. "Stop evading my question by changing the subject. Why are you crying?"

I slip off the high heels and tell him everything except the details of when Relic and I were intimate.

"I'm sorry, and I apologize for how I went about asking. The Kings are dangerous, Selena, but we have an alliance with them, and they do not know of this arrangement. When he finds out that you're taking over Elysium, he is going to wish he never hurt you." He snorts and scratches his cheek and continues. "As for his marriage proposal to that snob... that is his family duty. Sophia Mitchell is a politician's daughter and Damon King's plan for the future. He thinks marrying Relic to Sophia is the smartest move. He just doesn't know who is taking over, and believe me, they think it's a man. In reality, Relic has no commitment to any woman. It is all for business."

I look up suddenly at his words, turning in my seat. "Do you have any commitments, Jiro? Do you just sleep with women and act like they don't exist when you're finished?"

He gazes at me intently. "No, I don't have any commitments, and I have my needs just like every man, but I'm very conscious of who I decide to take to bed. I am a powerful man in Japan, but it doesn't mean I don't have enemies."

I nod in understanding. "So then, you two are not very different."

"Yes, we are different. I care about your safety and how people treat you. He... obviously doesn't."

They are not words I want to hear, but there is truth behind them. It doesn't matter anyway. I will not be seeing him for a while. He will probably forget I even exist either way.

It is true what Jiro says about him, and it's best things between Relic and I end. Time heals all wounds, they say. I hope they are right.

Jiro looks up. "The seat belt light is off. I suggest you get some sleep. If you would like, there is a room with a bed through that door." He points at the door to his left. "I will sleep here, and you can have the room."

"How do you know Relic so well?" I blurt.

He stays silent with a look on his face like he's contemplating what to tell me. "Our fathers and your grandfather are old friends. Relic trained with me for the five years you were in college. We are friends, but when it comes to you, you're first. There is more about his alliances and upbringing I will tell you when the time is right."

"Thank you for being honest."

He nods and I get up from my seat.

When I open the door to the room, my bag is sitting on a bed with a white comforter and sheets. I smile inwardly because he already planned to give me the room.

I immediately get undressed and change into leggings and a cropped T-shirt. I set my Converse sneakers at the foot of the bed so I can put them on when we land, and I lie down on the most comfortable pillow and drift off to sleep.

My eyes flutter open when I feel a hand caressing my face. I can hear Jiro calling my name. "Selena. Wake up. We're here."

My eyes meet dark ones before I scan his face until I reach his throat with colorful tattoos sneaking out from his white T-shirt.

His expression turns soft and he whispers, *"Kirei." Beautiful.*

I don't move, not wanting to break this moment of getting a small glimpse of the old Jiro. We stay silent for another moment, and then it's over. He puts the mask back in place and gets up.

"We need to go. Your grandfather is waiting."

I quickly get up and fix my top, put my shoes on, grab my bag, and brush my teeth in the small metal sink.

I meet Jiro by the chairs we were sitting in when we boarded.

He studies what I'm wearing. "Put your coat on before you head out. You cannot be seen dressed like this, Selena. You know it's not tradition. I am supposed to take you right away to your grandfather so he can discuss things with you."

I stop and look at him like he has lost his mind. "Seriously, I have to be careful what I wear? I have never had an issue with my grandfather about what I wear."

"Please, Selena. Don't make this difficult. You look too... exposed."

I walk up to him and look up at his face, pissed off. "Get one thing straight, Jiro. I will wear what I want and will not be told what to wear, within reason. I will abide by certain traditional rules, but I was not raised like you. I was raised to have a say. I will wear the coat to not make a bad impression, but not because of any other reason."

He steps back as I turn to put on my long coat to cover the crop top and leggings. I turn around and grab my bag. "Ready," I say with a hard edge to my tone.

I follow him out to two Maybachs with men in black suits waiting with the door open to the first vehicle.

I slide in first, and Jiro follows behind me. The door closes, and we are off to my grandfather's home in Tokyo. It is dark outside, and you can see the lights everywhere from the buildings.

Jiro is talking on his cell phone in Japanese. He is telling whoever we have arrived and are on our way, but that's about it. He turns to me with his hard mask in place and repeats what I have already heard.

"I have notified your grandfather that we have arrived and are on our way. He says he is pleased and is waiting for your arrival. There is much work to be done."

"I am excited to see my grandfather," I say, giving him a grin.

I have butterflies in my stomach from what's in store for my future. My phone suddenly starts going off with a bunch of alerts from text messages once I turn airplane mode off on my phone.

I take my phone out of my bag and unlock it. I can only imagine they're from Mia. I didn't properly say goodbye or text her when we landed and she must have calculated the ten-and-a-half-hour flight it takes to arrive here from Seattle.

Mia: Where are you? You left, and I haven't heard from you yet. You must have landed by now. I need to make sure you are okay.

Mia: Are you okay? Deacon says Relic ran after you and you left in a Bugatti. Who the hell do you know that has a Bugatti? If it's a guy, I hope he is hot. Just sayin.

Mia: Okay, now I am worried, Selena. Is everything ok?

Jiro looks at me with my phone in hand. "Is it your friend Mia?" I nod. "You should call her when we arrive," he says with amusement. "Tell her your new boyfriend drove you to the airport." He lowers his voice and leans close. "Make sure you tell her he is the one that owns the Bugatti and is very hot."

My eyes narrow. "Yeah. Hilarious." I try to play it off, but my lips curve into a smile when he grins.

We arrive at my grandfather's estate, and it is still as breathtaking as before. It is as beautiful as ever, with teakwood double doors at the entrance and a cherry blossom tree in the center of a Japanese garden out front.

We exit the vehicle, Jiro barking orders ahead of me. Everyone bows to him as their leader. They look down as they address me with the utmost respect, giving me the same curtesy.

The doorman opens the door, and you can hear the water trickling from the giant Buddha fountain to the right against a wall, giving me a sense of peace and calmness.

We are guided to an area with red pillows on the floor around a dark table already set with tea.

My grandfather smiles, and I bow in traditional respect. He motions me to sit in the tearoom. The house is made in traditional timber and wood in a Taisho Roman style, with breathtaking views of the garden out the windows.

"Welcome, Selena. I hear from Jiro you have had a good trip from America."

"Yes, *Ojisan*," I answer to my grandfather in Japanese.

"Good. I want to be brief in discussing your role in taking over Elysium. First, you will become the CEO of Elysium, effective immediately. I will not publicize it for your safety. I will not lie to you and tell you that all of my business dealings are legitimate because they are not. Jiro is now the head of the yakuza, and we've had an agreement since you were a child with his father that Jiro would protect you when you were ready to take over."

"He could have told me before I left for college, and he didn't," I reply, letting him know I was disappointed in not hearing it from Jiro.

"Jiro was sworn not to tell you. So, please, do not be cross with him. Second, Jiro will train you to defend yourself at the highest level. There will be a time when you will have to end someone's life and you must be prepared to do so."

Could I really kill someone to defend myself? Am I that person? Does that mean that Jiro is dangerous and a murderer?

"Third. After you have had all your training, you will return to America. Jiro will travel back and forth, leaving someone for your protection when he is dealing with things here. I need you to analyze all business contracts regarding the imports and exports from the Russians, Polish, and the Kings from Japan to Elysium. I need you to make sure the contracts go smoothly. There are also political families with ties to the government. There is one King named Mason, whose father is in politics and is married to Luciana. She is *El Diablo's* daughter and a powerful ally, just like all the Kings' wives." He pauses and I try to not let my emotions give me away when he mentions the Kings. "Well, except one, when Relic King marries Sophia. Anyway, we all get a cut of the shipments so that the American government does not interfere. The details will be given on all the shipments by Jiro and the Kings. All the Kings are Mexican cartel and they are trying to legitimize their businesses."

I nod at my grandfather in understanding when he stops talking. It all makes sense. They are all Mafia Kings. Mia told me about Deacon and his mysterious disappearances, the bloody knuckles. Relic speaking Spanish and the way he carries himself when he deals with people. The house parties.

I glance at the tea and since I'm the youngest, I bow my head and serve him, then Jiro and myself. I place the pot on the center of the table and kneel on the pillow and wait until he drinks first as my elder.

When he places the saucer down with a clink, Jiro follows. I'm last and take a sip of the warm liquid, calming my emotions.

I tilt my head when my grandfather rises and begins to walk away.

"*Ojisan*, where will I be staying?"

He pauses, giving me his side profile and my insides quake. He knows. He saw it when he spoke about Relic and his marriage.

"You will stay here, and I will wrap things up with Elysium so that you can take over in America. I will live in the city. Jiro will provide you protection and train you here in the garden. It is peaceful and quiet. He will escort you everywhere, as I know you feel comfortable and trust him. He will protect you with his life. I also called your parents and let them know of your new position here under my direction. Since your grandmother passed before you were born, they are pleased you can keep me company," he says with a nod.

My grandfather is traditional, and when elders discuss delicate matters, it's different. Emotions are spoken with their body language or their eyes. Right now, he is disappointed. He knows his granddaughter. He sensed my sadness and heartbreak. I just hope he lets things take their course. It starts with rebuilding. My heart, my self-esteem, and my self-worth.

Chapter Twenty-Four

SELENA

I am shown to my room, which has a simplistic design of wood and limited furniture. There is a bed against the wall, it looks functional but not comfortable like back home, but maybe once I get in, it will be.

The room is private. It has a connecting en suite bathroom with a single white tub in the center with a wood table and a simple sink in the corner. The big window behind the tub has a beautiful view of the garden. You can see right through to the outside, but I don't think anyone can see inside if they were standing outside watching.

I turn on the hot water and pour body wash under the cascading water. The scent of Japanese blossoms fills the tub and I undress, letting my hair down from the messy bun I was sporting when I got off the plane.

Placing my phone down on the teak bench, I press play on my music app and "Hurricane" by Halsey plays as I get in the tub. After soaking for a few minutes, I lean forward to lather my legs.

The hairs on the back of my neck stand as a shadow moving by the door catches the corner of my eye. I call out, "Who's there?"

I close my eyes, cursing myself for not locking the door. My eyes pop open when the door slides open slowly.

Instinctively, I cover myself with my hands, my hair long enough to cover my nipples. I stand in the tub, ready to scream, waiting for whoever is going to walk through that door.

When the door slides open completely, I swallow when I see it is Jiro, frozen in place. He is wearing a simple white T-shirt and black dress pants. His eyes slowly rise, taking in every inch of my naked body until he reaches my eyes.

He tries to say something, opening and closing his mouth like a fish, but quickly composes himself, taking a deep breath. "I am so sorry, Selena. You need to close the screen behind you. I can see you through the window, and if one of my men looks through that window... I am afraid I will have to kill him." He says this calmly like it's nothing to end someone's life for looking at me naked through a window.

My eyes widen a fraction, still in shock that Jiro is talking to me calmly while I'm just standing here... naked.

He walks forward, trying not to look at my body, to close the massive shade on the window. I turn away from him, giving him my back, embarrassed at my stupidity.

Once the shade is fully closed, I think about how reckless it was to think someone couldn't see through the window. I was caught up in the peace of the beautiful garden.

He comes up close to me, my hands planted on my sex. His eyes caress my skin everywhere. He is close enough that I can hear the rate of his breathing pick up.

I try to avert my eyes, but my body is aware. Aware of him. I'm not scared, but I'm... confused.

"Look at me, Selena," he whispers.

My phone plays "Sober II" by Lorde as he breathes in deeply like he is fighting with himself. My eyes meet his, then they move down his white shirt to his black dress pants. The bulge in his pants shows a full-blown hard-on.

My eyes lift to his and they're as black as night, calling me to his darkness. "*Jirosan*," I whisper, getting lost in his black orbs.

I don't know what to say. I never would have thought he was attracted to me. When we were kids, I had a huge crush on him. I was always conflicted with emotion and confused because of my feelings for him. We have shared a bond and love since we were kids. In my mind, he was my samurai.

Relic makes me feel different things that I can't even name. Feelings that take my breath away. I had three boyfriends before sleeping with Relic, but never have I felt anything close to the type of feelings I feel for Jiro or Relic. The emotions in my heart are blurring, and I can't figure out where my heart belongs.

He continues to inch closer, and I don't stop him. I need to feel wanted. I want to feel needed.

He brushes his lips delicately over mine. I close my eyes and feel. When I was sixteen, I wished he would kiss me. I just hate that he finally does it when my heart is so fucked up, but I can't break the kiss. I don't want to.

I remind my heart that Relic didn't choose me. He chose to marry Sophia. My lips part for Jiro and he takes my lips with his delicately.

He cups my face while I place my hands over his hard chest, sliding them up and winding them around his neck, drawing him closer. My nipples pebble and the backs of his fingers slide down my chest and stomach to rest on my hips.

He slides his tongue gently, tasting my mouth. Kissing him back, I inhale his citrusy scent, getting lost in the moment. We are both panting when we finally break apart in need of air.

His forehead rests against mine and he says softly, "I hope that one day, you will look at me the way you looked at him when you left the hotel."

My heart breaks, cracking in two. He spins around and walks out, leaving me stunned in silence. I get out of the tub, throw a towel around my wet body, and run after him. He can't leave like this.

"Jiro, wait!" I call out. I step out of the bedroom, looking down the hall. "Jiro!" I call out again.

Nothing.

I don't move farther into the hallway, afraid someone else might hear me and see I'm wrapped in nothing but a towel with my hair dripping wet down my back. Fuck, that shouldn't have happened.

Turning around, I walk back into the bedroom and quickly get dressed. I grab my phone and text Mia back so she doesn't worry.

Selena: Sorry I haven't called. Everything is okay. I will be back as soon as I can.

Mia: I'm fine. Are you okay? I was so worried about you. You must be so hurt. Please forgive me. I didn't know he was going to show up. Deacon said he wasn't. Relic was pissed when he came back into the hotel after you left. I can't believe he proposed to Sophia. Deacon and Liam didn't look happy. Relic told me to call you and make sure you were ok.

Selena: I forgive you. Please don't mention me to Relic. He lied to me. I'm not interested in what that liar has to say. I'm done with him.

Mia: Okay.

Selena: I gotta go and will talk to you soon. It's late here in Tokyo with the time difference.

Mia: Okay, chica. *Talk to you soon and don't forget about me. Oh! Say hi to your grandfather for me.*

Selena: I will. xoxo

I hate not telling my best friend the whole truth, but I will in time. Mia met my grandfather once when we went to my parents' house for Thanksgiving when we were at college together. I never mentioned Jiro per se, just mentioned him in passing when I told her about my summers in Japan.

I lie awake for some time thinking of the kiss in the bathroom with Jiro, but I don't want to complicate things with my new role at my grandfather's company, the training, and everything that will take place.

It shouldn't have happened, and Jiro probably regrets it. *He walked away.*

Chapter Twenty-Five

JIRO

I can still smell her sweet scent on my lips. If she only knew what she did to me, she would run far away. Since having laid eyes on her at the company getting off the elevator, I couldn't get her off my mind. I swore I would always look out for her when we were kids and I have kept my feelings for her in check. I close my eyes as memories of when we were kids play in my mind like little snippets. Little reminders of how beautiful and soft she is.

"Will you always protect me, Jiro?"

"Always, Selena. I will always protect you from anyone."

She was always gorgeous as a kid and I had a crush on her. But I knew I could never act on it. I was born to lead and trained to become the head of the yakuza when my father stepped down.

I was sworn to protect Selena when she took over Elysium. She was trained in the katana's basics, but I will have to show her how to kill and defend herself... that is... if I cannot make it there first to protect her.

I care for Selena deeply, and her happiness means everything to me. I've had many women growing up, but no one comes close to making me feel like Selena does.

When she left for college, I tried to forget my feelings. I was older, and I had no business getting involved with a teenager at twenty years old. It was wrong.

I tried to move on and even thought I was in love once. Her name is Akemi, and she is beautiful in a traditional Japanese way. She knew all the traditions that women must show their significant other and tried to please me in any way she could, but I live a dangerous life, and I didn't want her to be a target. The worst thing about her is that she is a hostess at a club. A club that I own that makes her available to whoever gives her the right price. She was taught to please men, not one man.

Except she said what we had was different, but she would complain that I was indifferent to her affection. Maybe I was, or maybe I wasn't. So, I did what I felt was right to save her from heartbreak and ended it and took other women to my bed.

She cried when she saw me with another mistress on my arm at the club. Not all women that frequent the club are there to provide sexual favors. Women that are seen at the club are wives or mistresses and are never part of any criminal activity. They serve the yakuza and are not allowed to be in any of the ranks. I still run into Akemi from time to time, and I see that look she gives me. The same lovestruck look Selena had when she was running from Relic King.

I don't have personal issues with the Kings, but I now have an issue with a certain King. I will protect her from him and whoever hurts her. He doesn't care about her feelings if he's marrying Sophia. He was stupid to let her go. He thinks she is some girl that he slept with and isn't worthy of being in his world.

I watched him on the steps as he let her go, and I promised myself that I would always be there to pick up the pieces. Her pieces. I would never let anyone make her feel inferior, and there is no one that knows her like I do. Not even Relic King. He may be a cartel king in disguise, but I'm head of the yakuza. I have no problem making Selena my queen because, in my eyes, she will always be mine.

Training begins in the morning, and I must keep my inner turmoil at bay. My emotions cannot interfere or jeopardize business dealings.

Her training is what will protect her if she is ever in danger. The Russians, the Kings, and even the Polish will have a field day when they see that the biggest company in Japan, managing all the exports of drugs and weapons, is run by a woman. Especially a woman that looks like Selena.

The following day, I wake up feeling refreshed. I get dressed in leggings and a comfortable off-the-shoulder shirt and make my way to the kitchen to see a small assortment of tea and fruit.

I help myself and sit with my legs crossed at the table, enjoying the view of the beautiful garden and taking in the tranquility it gives. I hear someone coming up behind me and turn to find Jiro with a white V-neck T-shirt molded to his muscles, showing off the tattoos covering his arms. I notice that some traditional tattoos don't go past certain parts of the body, so no one can identify them as yakuza, but other tattoos are more modern. *Interesting.*

He stops next to me and says in Japanese, "You need to change, put on a kimono and customary geta."

I hate wearing the uncomfortable sandals worn by Japanese women.

"Why? Where are we going?"

"You will be getting your *irezumi*. It will cover the expanse of your back in traditional Japanese tattoos with Koi fish. The Koi fish you can have done wherever you like."

I nod in acceptance, having known that I would eventually receive a back tattoo when I was older but didn't know exactly the reason. Now I know why.

"I will wait in the living area until you finish." His tone is professional and curt.

I call out, "Jiro, about last night."

He holds up his hand. "Selena. That was a mistake and should never have happened."

I flinch at how he brushes it off like it means nothing. Regret is a bitch, like a dish served cold. "I couldn't agree more," I quip, walking back to my room.

"Selena, I didn't mean it like that."

I stop and turn around. "Don't worry, Jiro, I'll make sure it doesn't happen again."

I'm furious at myself when I feel the sting of his rejection. I'm sick and tired of men treating me like I'm a mistake.

We walk out to a waiting Maybach with a bodyguard that I must assume is part of the yakuza. He nods as I get in the car and Jiro closes my door.

Jiro sits in the front passenger seat and I look out the window, feeling lonely and mad all at the same time. The car drives forward, and I feel pressure in the back of my head from the tension that is like a band pulling until it's about to snap.

I reach to the back of my head, trying to seek relief by letting my hair down. I pinch my favorite hair clip together with my fingers to release my dark strands, sliding it off as my hair cascades down the side of my left shoulder, hitting the seat. Looking down at the hairpiece in my hand, I admire the diamonds.

I run the pad of my fingers over the natural stones, rubbing them as if they hold all my secrets and the answers to my questions, but all it does is remind me of Relic.

I feel like someone is watching me. My eyes lift and I find Jiro's gaze on me through the visor's mirror. He watches me and he knows I'm still upset. My eyes dart away, and I decide looking out the window is a better idea.

The car pulls up in front of a tattoo shop in Tokyo. Jiro jumps out before the driver to open my door, and I quickly put my hair back up, letting Jiro lead the way into the shop.

I am amazed that the shop does not differ from any other tattoo shop in America. It has the same setup, the counter in the middle, the colorful walls painted with tattoo murals.

Frames of tattooed art on the walls to the left and right, highlighting the available designs to choose from. We move into the area where the chairs are set up for customers to sit on, and I can smell the antiseptic.

Whatever tattoo design I have to get on my back, I want it to snake over to my arm, and I want the Koi fish going up one thigh. I remember reading that tattoos are a symbol and not just art on your back for women in Japan. As I consider this, I find myself drawn to finding something that represents peace for my inner soul to add to my skin.

A delicate Asian woman appears from the back room. She is young and pretty and has tattoos visible on every part of her arms. I watch as she greets Jiro and they both respectfully bow. She smiles coyly at Jiro, indicating they are quite familiar with each other.

"*Jirosan*, to what do I owe this pleasure? Are you here to finish a piece, or do you want something new?"

Jiro nods in my direction. "I am here to introduce you to Selena, and she needs an *irezumi* completed. She will take over as the CEO of Elysium and is under the yakuza's protection." The young lady turns to smile at me. "Selena, I want you to meet Hana."

"Nice to meet you, Hana," I greet her politely and bow.

"Nice to meet you, too. You are very beautiful, and the color of your eyes is unusual."

A nice way to point out that I don't look Asian. "I get that all the time, Hana. I don't seem to fit the mold."

She chuckles. "Jiro has his work cut out for him. And you do fit the mold."

She motions with her hand to follow her through the back door to a private room with a table for me to lie on. Jiro posts a bodyguard just outside the door, but he stays in the room. He looks serious with his yakuza mask in place, looking straight at Hana while she prepares the table, smiling at him.

"So, what would you like to have done?" she asks, but her eyes are on Jiro.

I look up and say, "I would like to have water around two Koi fish going up my thigh and a female with a katana sword on my back with a cherry blossom tree in the background. The cherry blossoms should go down my left arm. I also would like the clip that is in my hair to be drawn into her hair. The rest can be what is required by tradition."

Jiro catches sight of all the diamonds when I take the clip out of my hair and I hand it to her.

She looks at it and says, "It is exquisite. I have never seen a *kanzashi* clip with diamonds like this. It must have cost a fortune to have it handmade."

"My grandfather gave it to me when I was a little girl. Recently, someone surprised me by having it customized with all the diamonds as a gift," I say.

She smiles. "Well, whoever made that for you must think you are very special."

"Thank you, Hana. The hair clip means a lot to me, and I would love to have it drawn on my back. I trust your judgment in how the design will come together."

"Of course. Now, let's get started."

I immediately take off the kimono, standing clad in only my thong in front of Jiro, not caring that he is standing there when he has seen me naked. I can faintly hear his intake of breath as I lie on the table face down so she can get started on the pain I will have to endure.

She preps, drawing the tattoo outline on the stencil and then placing it over my back. I finally glance at Jiro and catch his gaze on my body like he is searing it to his memory. My hair slides to the side, it is so long that it almost touches the floor. I study him, watching as Hana cleans the area of my skin to place the outline and I can't make out what he is thinking as the sound of the machine takes over what my mind is trying to piece together.

. . .

Seven hours later, my back and arm feel raw, but I can honestly say it wasn't bad. She cleans me one last time before Jiro gets up from his seat to look.

"So, what do you think?" Hana asks.

He looks me in my eyes as he answers. "Beautiful, as always."

I look away and slowly get up, not caring if he sees my breasts, but he turns away out of respect.

Hana holds a mirror so I can see all the beautiful colors and the cherry blossoms. I see the hair clip, the detailed diamonds shining bright in the hair of the female warrior in her stance with the katana sword.

I smile at her. "Oh, Hana, it is absolutely beautiful! It's exactly what I wanted." I turn to her. "Thank you so much. You are so talented."

She smiles warmly and says, "You are very welcome. Come back and we will finish the Koi fish on your thigh and the rest on your arm."

"I will wait by the entrance so we can take you to eat," Jiro says, walking out of the room.

Once she places the plastic over the tattoo and gives me instructions so it can properly heal, I gently place the kimono back over my body.

"Okay." I move toward the door. "I'm starving."

"He has never looked at a woman the way he looks at you," Hana says, causing me to turn around and look at her.

"We are just childhood friends, and now in a partnership to fulfill our duties, nothing more."

"Selena, he can hide it from you, but I can see it. It's more than that. The man that gave you that customized hair clip wasn't Jiro, was it?"

I breathe in deep and hold it between my fingers before wrapping my hair up with a slight wince and admitting, "No, it wasn't."

"I think Jiro just came to the same conclusion as I did. Just be careful, Selena."

I look back at her one last time before I walk out the door and smile. "I will. Thank you. I will see you soon."

If she only knew that man doesn't want me. Neither does the one that was sworn to protect me. My heart wasn't included in that promise.

I walk out of the tattoo parlor and over to the bodyguard waiting for me to get inside the car. I wince when I slide into the seat slowly.

Once the door closes, we are off to a restaurant just five blocks down.

Chapter Twenty-Seven

SELENA

When we arrive, men are waiting at the entrance for Jiro to lead the way inside. I step out of the car, and a younger bodyguard catches my attention.

"Right this way," he says.

I nod and follow him inside the restaurant filled with people. Everyone stops and stares at Jiro and his men like a celebrity just walked in. The men look me over with interest, and suddenly, Jiro walks back and takes my hand like a sign of ownership.

All the men drop their stares and look away. I walk steadily in the sandals to the booth with soft cushions that I'm grateful to sit on. He motions for me to sit with a pillow on my back to relieve any rubbing on my skin.

He takes a seat right across from me and a hostess comes up to Jiro, giving him a demure smile. "Welcome, *Jirosan*. We see you again with another lovely lady," she says, her English not as polished.

I look at him with a smirk. How nice. He just took me to where he takes all his conquests, whores, or whatever he calls them. He gives her a hard stare like he wants to wring her neck. He orders for us both and dismisses her curtly.

I'm watching him intently and he barks. "What?"

"Everywhere we go, there are so many women you know. They seem jealous that you have brought me along. Let's be honest, it seems you have left a long-lasting impression with your cock," I say with a grin, realizing he isn't any different from Relic. They probably hang out or share.

The thought brings bile up my throat, but I wash it down with the glass of water that appears on the table and play it off like I don't care. I shouldn't. I don't have a claim on any of them.

His eyes widen at my statement. I shrug my shoulders slightly, laughing at his embarrassment. I couldn't help myself. Big bad yakuza boss fucks practically everything that walks in Tokyo.

"Is there anyone you haven't fucked?" I ask, giggling, but my insides are breathing fire.

"Selena, what I do or who I fuck is none of your business," he snaps.

"It is my business when you take me around and I am meeting all of them," I counter.

Guilt crosses his expression. "I-I am sorry, Selena. I did not intend to make you feel uncomfortable."

I look up at him, and he catches the sparkle of my hair clip. "So, he had that made for you?" he asks, throwing the ball in my court.

I'm taken aback by the change of subject. I instinctively touch it, and he watches the gesture.

I angle my head, looking at him. "He did. He took it while I was on an elevator with him. I thought he wasn't going to return it, but four days later, a package was delivered with the diamonds all over it."

Jiro's face hardens, and the muscle in his jaw tics. "I figured," he says dryly.

"It doesn't matter. Does it?"

A man in a black suit stops at our table. "Jiro, it's nice to see you. I had to stop and admire your friend. She has the most beautiful eyes and I wanted to introduce myself."

Jiro's expression turns to anger and he responds sarcastically, "Yes, she is very beautiful, and if I ever catch you near her, I will slit your fucking throat." The man stills as if he can see his life flash before his eyes. Jiro suddenly laughs and looks directly at the man. "That's a promise."

The man turns to me. "I sincerely apologize. I did not know."

I stay silent, not knowing what to say or what he means. The man turns to Jiro apologetically, but what he says next doesn't quite reach his eyes. "I apologize. It will never happen again, *Oyabun*." He bows to Jiro and quickly leaves.

Jiro keeps watching the man as he leaves and says, "If he ever comes near you, you tell me."

My eyebrows rise at his sudden change of mood. It stinks that Jiro is far from the boy I knew when we were kids. Instead, a monster and a killer have replaced him.

"You will have to learn to defend yourself, Selena. There are men that will look at your beauty and try to take advantage of you because of it. This is your first lesson."

I listen and then decide to use his own words against him. "Will you look at my beauty and take advantage of me, Jiro?"

His head snaps to the right to look at me. I'm testing him, and he knows it.

"I have seen you naked. Clean with a perfect shaved pussy. Have I laid you down and rammed my cock into your tight pussy and made you scream yet?"

Whoa. I never expected him to respond like that. I definitely wasn't prepared for the dirty thoughts going through my head, imagining him doing what he just suggested, but I'm a sucker for punishment and want to push.

"Do you?" I challenge.

"Do I what?"

I lower my voice above a whisper, so no one catches a hint of my next words. "Want to ram your cock in my tight pussy." He stares at me. I stare at him right back, waiting for an answer, challenging him to admit it.

The food comes, interrupting the tension between us and we begin to eat.

"No," he says quietly between bites.

Of course, he would say that. I was expecting it. I knew Hana was wrong. He just sees me like a friend he has a duty to protect.

"I expected as much. You have the responsibility to protect me when needed, and I have the responsibility of running Elysium. There is nothing more between us except friendship. This is good. It clears the air between us. Thank you."

"For what?"

"For being honest."

He nods in acceptance, but he doesn't meet my eyes.

My mind drifts to the night with Relic and the mind-blowing sex. I shift my legs under the table, suddenly getting wet, thinking of how his lips would taste me. The desire I would see in his eyes as he would fill me. The way he washed me in the shower and held me that one night.

"Selena?"

"Err——what?" I say, snapping back to reality.

"You were off somewhere. I was calling you."

"I'm sorry, *Jirosan*. I was just thinking... sorry about that." My gaze meets his, hoping he can't see the thirst in my eyes.

My pussy is wet, probably soaking through the thong I'm wearing. I need to stop thinking about Relic. He is a soon-to-be-married man, and I can't believe the shameless thoughts that fill my head when the subject of sex is spoken out loud.

Can Jiro tell?

No way. I am just overthinking.

He quickly settles the bill and tells me, "We have to get you back so you can bathe and apply the ointment so the tattoo heals fast. We have much training to complete after your last tattoo session with Hana."

"Okay," I say, slowly getting up and following him out to the awaiting car.

The pain in my back throbs a little, and he notices because he gently helps me into the awaiting Maybach.

He slides in next to me, and I take out my phone, wanting to listen to music on the drive back. Noticing a cable, I plug it in and open my music app to play Rhianna's "Kiss It Better." I can hear it through the speakers and close my eyes until the lyrics start.

When I open them, Jiro is gazing at me, listening to the music as I whisper the lyrics to the song on the drive back.

When we arrive, I slowly enter the house and head toward my room and the bathroom and undress. This time making sure the shade is drawn before releasing the confines of my hair. A knock sounds on the wooden door, and I wait until I'm in the tub to answer.

"Come in," I call out.

The door opens and Jiro walks in with liquid soap in his hand. He hands it to me and puts my phone by the sink. He says he will play some music from a small radio on a teak table in the corner. He selects "Love Is Madness" by Thirty Seconds to Mars, featuring Halsey.

"How do you know about this type of music?" I ask.

"I spend a lot of time in America, and I have interests there. Hence my car." He smiles.

"Yes, I love that car. It's so your style. Mia mentioned it in the text when we landed. I guess it left an impression."

"I know it's improper for me to see you undressed, but it's for your safety. I cannot have anyone else help you because of the nature of your role. Do you understand?"

"I understand."

He turns around to give me privacy. The soap he handed me to wash is lavender and smells wonderful, but there is a small bottle and I guess it is the soap to wash the tattoo.

Once I am finished, I grab the special soap for my back.

"Can you help me get the middle of my back, please? It is stinging."

He spins around, takes the soap from my hand and lathers it gently in his fingers before applying it to my back. He stops, rinses his hands, and takes off his shirt before he gets completely soaked.

He lathers his hands again and continues to wash my back, gently peeling off the rest of the plastic wrap toward my butt. The tattoo covers the expanse of my back down to where the plastic ends and he carefully rinses my skin like a doctor would a patient. Once I'm finished, he wraps a towel around me gently and steps into the bedroom, waiting for me to follow.

When I enter the bedroom, he has the ointment in his hand. "Please lie face down, Selena. I have to apply the ointment on your back."

I comply and lie facing down as he gently applies the ointment, caressing my back with his fingers. I turn my head to the side and smile.

"What are you smiling about?" he asks.

"Nothing, it's just that you give me Dragon Ball Z vibes."

He looks at me and chuckles. "Really?"

"Yes. The hair and your body. Except you have way more tattoos than he does."

"You know what that means?"

"What?"

"It means I'm better. Good night, Selena."

Chapter Twenty-Nine

SELENA

FOUR MONTHS LATER

I exit the bathroom and head into the bedroom with a fluffy white towel wrapped around my body after having dinner with my grandfather here in the house. I left Jiro and Grandpa in the tearoom to discuss my progress and business while they had their sake.

I roll my shoulders to release the tension that has built up in my sore muscles due to training. Jiro has trained me hard. Every day, the training intensifies, pushing me to my limit. Hardening my dissolve. Hardening my soul into a killer.

I see things differently since I have been here training day after day. Jiro doesn't train me like a woman but as an equal. When it is about Elysium or training, I'm not a childhood friend. I'm an ally. If anything, he treats me like I'm above him.

I'm facing the wall, lost in thought, when I hear my door open.

"Selena?" Jiro calls out to me.

"Yeah."

I hear his footsteps on the teakwood floor as he walks farther inside the room and closes the door. "Your grandfather has already left. I wanted to see if you needed me for anything."

Yeah, your friendship. Your love for me when we were kids. The softness of your smile or when you would make a joke and I would laugh. That is what I need, but I don't tell him that. I just stand motionless in my towel, staring at the wall, feeling alone. Utterly...alone.

I have reached out to Mia, but because of the time difference, it seems impossible to hear her voice or her laughter when she asks me if I have fallen in love with someone in Japan yet.

I send her texts and I know she will answer me when she is awake and vice versa. Taking over for my grandfather is my calling. I feel it inside my heart, but I also feel alone. I know they will judge me. I feel it in my bones. I don't look Asian enough, and I don't fit in American society because I feel that I'm missing something. A piece of myself is missing. It feels like I lost something along the way and I can't get to it. It feels like it's right there, but I can't grasp it with my fingers.

I guess I just want to feel because I know I'm getting colder on the inside, and soon, a monster that I have lying dormant will be released. I just hope I can control it. "Eyes Closed" by Halsey plays through Bluetooth speakers. Maybe Jiro won't think anything of it and he'll leave. He won't see the sadness filling me, threatening to finish breaking me.

I'm not enough for Relic and I'm not enough for Jiro. I'm just never...enough.

I always thought you shouldn't force yourself where you don't belong, but what if you want to belong? I want to belong to someone.

I feel Jiro's warm hand on my naked shoulder. "Selena," he says, whispering softly.

A lone tear slides down my face. Needles prick my throat and I swallow, pursing my lips to let a breath out slowly so I can answer. "Yeah," I croak.

He pushes my shoulder, turning me to face him and I blink back the tears that have pooled in my eyes. I hate to cry and fall apart in front of him.

In front of anyone, I don't want to be viewed as weak. Then I won't be enough to run Elysium.

I won't belong.

His thumb wipes away the tear that slides to my chin. He moves, hovering over me. I inhale slowly when he lowers his lips over mine. I close my eyes when his tongue slides in my mouth, kissing me softly.

I'm scared, but I kiss him back and realize I shouldn't feel guilty. I don't belong to any man, but I want to belong. And right now, I want to fall.

I open my eyes as Jiro trails his lips and tongue down my neck and over my breasts. He sucks on my nipple and palms the other. My breasts are full in his hands as he gives each the same attention.

I inhale sharply as he removes the towel, skimming his fingers down my stomach to the apex of my thighs, slipping an expert finger inside the folds of my pussy. I arch my neck, opening my legs, granting him the permission he seeks.

He slips another finger inside me, and I moan. His dark eyes are full of desire as he watches me. "Look at me, Selena." My eyes meet his. "You will never be a mistake, just my undoing."

I close my eyes when I lie back on the bed. He slips a third finger inside and I can hear the wetness of my juices as I fuck his hand. Making me feel. I don't want him to stop.

I moan mixed with a whisper, "Yes, please don't stop."

He removes his hand to settle his face between my thighs.

I open my legs wider as he replaces his fingers with his tongue, sucking on my clit like a storm. I get wetter as I cream in his mouth with my arousal.

He grunts, licking, sucking, and tasting me. I run my fingers through his straight black hair, loving his mouth and tongue on me.

His dark eyes lift, releasing his mouth from me to rasp, "This is what heaven feels like."

I snag the bottom of my lip with my teeth, watching him between my legs. "Don't stop... please," I whisper, loving the feel of his tongue as he fucks my pussy with his mouth.

I grind my hips, seeking more. He removes his fingers and grips my thighs, holding me steady. My fingers grip his hair as his tongue takes me over the edge on a moan. "Mmm... Jiro. Fuck."

I get up from the bed, his eyes following me as I pull his hand so he stands in front of the edge of my bed. He places the strands of my hair behind my ears, and I stand on my tippy-toes, cupping his face with my hands the same way he did the first time we kissed, and I lick my arousal glistening on his lips.

We both moan when he deepens the kiss while my hands lie flat on his hard chest, feeling every ridge of his muscled torso under the soft white cotton of his T-shirt.

I slide my hands down and he pulls back, breaking the kiss when he feels my fingers undoing the buckle of his belt, my gaze never leaving his. It's sexy.

He is sexy. His body is ripped and hard. Every edge is defined over taught skin. His eyes are expressive, deep with a promise. A promise I recognize from when I was becoming a woman and he was already a man. A promise that one day we would give in to each other, solidifying our connection.

I finish unbuttoning his pants, sliding them down with his boxers. My head tilts down to watch his cock spring free.

My eyes flick up to watch his lips lift in a knowing smirk. "Impressed?" he asks.

I look down and I admire the perfection as I palm his cock with my hands, rubbing my thumb over the tip. "Very," I say with a grin.

He hisses under his breath when I kneel and wrap my lips around his cock, taking the head inside my mouth with a firm suck. I lick his shaft up the length and back down to his balls while his fingers run through the long strands of my hair.

My blue eyes meet his dark ones with his cock in my mouth and he swallows like he's struggling and says in a husky voice, "I love watching your beautiful eyes with my cock in your mouth."

His hands hold my hair away from my face as he watches in awe as I take him in a rhythm. His eyes follow my mouth with his head tilting slightly, like he's savoring the moment forever.

I continue to suck, taking him deep in my throat, relaxing my muscles to accommodate him while tears leak from the corner of my eyes.

He wipes them from my face as he thrusts into my mouth, the tip hitting the back of my throat until he grunts one last time, whispering my name as his hot cum spills down my throat.

I drink his cum, milking his cock with my mouth, tasting him. Drinking him while licking my lips, making a popping sound when I'm finally done.

He rubs his thumb over my swollen lips. My head tilts and he strokes my cheek. "I want to be inside you, Selena, but I want it to be your choice. I want you to be sure."

I nod in understanding, thinking he is going to leave, but he helps me into the bed and slides in next to me under the white cotton sheets. My head rests on his chest and I fall asleep in his arms, giving him a piece of my heart.

I wake up to the sun streaming through the window and feel a necklace around my neck with a heavy square pendant resting on my chest. I look down, holding it in my hand. It is a gold necklace with a jade stone with diamonds encrusted around the flat stone. In the center of the stone, there is a gold letter written in Japanese kanji

Jiro must have put it on me while I was sleeping. I freshen up and head out of my room, walking barefoot through the house to the table where breakfast is waiting for me. I instinctively run my fingers over the pendant while unlocking my phone and see an unread text message.

Jiro: Good morning, beautiful, I hope you like your necklace. I had it made for you. The jade symbolizes strength and wealth. Where the diamond shatters, the jade brings the signal of death that will come upon those who wish death upon you. The yakuza is your protection. As the leader, I will always protect you. I will meet you at breakfast.

I smile, rereading the text. Jiro has been so honest and respectful these past months. I hear the front door open and close. My head lifts as he walks through the doorway.

"I got your message." I touch the necklace with my fingers while he bows. He is wearing another V-neck white T-shirt with loose pants. I notice that his ink runs colorfully up his neck, while on the other yakuza members, it stops. He is the youngest *oyabun*, or leader, to have ever taken control at twenty-seven years old.

At the time, it made little sense, but now I realize that my grandfather is older and needs me to take over earlier than expected. The realization that they have already planned my life has slowly taken a toll on my consciousness. But I am relieved that I belong to a legacy and have a future.

"Are you ready for today's lessons?"

I smile. "Yes, sir."

He laughs, making my stomach flutter. "I'm not doing a good job. You're showing your American roots already," he says, teasing me.

"I guess, but you're in charge."

He comes closer, reaching his hand out to stroke my cheek with his fingers. "That's not true. You're in charge now. You never have to want for anything. If you need to buy anything, just let me know. There is also a black card in your name on the dresser, in case you need anything."

"Thank you, kind sir. Are you my sugar daddy now?"

He snorts. "You don't need one of those. It's actually the opposite. They would probably think you're their sugar momma. Anyway, there is no limit, and you can buy just about anything. If there is anything else, tell me."

"Okay," I say, surprised I went from counting how much I have in my bank account to not having to worry about how much something costs.

SIX MONTHS LATER

We've trained every day for the last six months, and I've re-learned everything from katana, jiu-jitsu, tae kwon do, and weapons training. I'm exhausted when he goes into protector and teacher mode. He reports to my grandfather all my progress, and he says that I will have to look over the business side of things after training. My body has increased in strength in places I never thought were possible.

After that night, in my room, we talked about what had happened between us. He doesn't come to my room unless it is necessary. He's also decided to use one of the spare rooms in my grandfather's house. Unless he has business to take care of, he has dinner and breakfast with me almost every day. He is always respectful. I also notice he makes sure not to touch me in front of the yakuza members. His gaze doesn't linger on me, but when we are alone, I catch him watching me.

I should feel disappointed but I'm here for a purpose and that is for my family. And that always comes first. I understand Relic and why he chose to marry Sophia. I understand that there are certain sacrifices you have to make for your family. He just went about it the wrong way. I will never forget the way he treated me after.

Being with Jiro these past months helped me find myself. He taught me to control my emotions and seek inner peace because you don't know when someone wants to disrupt it and take it away. Emotions can run high and that is when you die.

I'm in my room looking at myself in the mirror when my phone vibrates from an incoming message.

Jiro: Be ready to leave at 8:00 p.m. We will have dinner with all the yakuza members to introduce you as CEO before we have the meeting with all the leaders.

It's time. I will be introduced as one of the leaders in the Mafia world. Am I nervous? Hell yes. Extremely so. But fuck it. I earned my place.

Selena: Okay.

I rub the necklace he gifted me instinctively while getting ready. I decide to wear garters under a kimono, opting for suede thigh-high boots and tucking a knife inside.

I pull my hair into a twist, securing it with beautiful red chopsticks I bought at a little store in Tokyo. I apply light makeup and opt for a nude lip with the red-and-gold kimono.

The kimono ties at the waist, but the slit allows a glimpse of my boot when I walk. When it is time to leave, I walk outside to the awaiting car. The young bodyguard I have associated with being one of Jiro's men stiffens and stares at me. I look at him like he has lost his damn mind as he puts his arm out, preventing me from entering the car.

"Forgive me, Selena. Does he know what you are wearing?" he asks in Japanese.

"Does it matter?"

"It's just that I want to make sure you're safe," he says nervously.

"Thank you, but I can handle myself just fine. *Jirosan* is there to protect me, not my virtue," I fire back.

He nods, and after I enter the car, he closes the door. He drives toward the hostess club Jiro instructed me to attend. When we arrive,

I'm greeted by more yakuza bodyguards. They guide me inside to a long table with members in black suits seated around it, with Jiro seated at the head of the table. He glances up at me as I walk forward and everyone seated at the table stops midconversation when they notice he isn't paying attention.

Jiro gets up from his chair and motions with his fingers for me to come. I walk up to him, and he looks at me up and down with a cold, hard demeanor. I should be shocked, but then again, when Jiro is in yakuza mode, he turns into this monster. An unfeeling asshole is what I call it. My eyes meet every member sitting at the table when he introduces me.

"I would like to introduce Selena, the new CEO of Elysium. She will be running things, analyzing every export and import to and from Japan. She is to be honored and respected, and if anyone disrespects her, it's like you disrespect me. She is very proficient in business analytics and will look over all of our contracts and be in charge from now on."

I nod at everyone's acknowledgment. None of the members look me in the eye, but I know it's a sign of respect. A pretty woman on the other side of Jiro suddenly moves. He smiles at her while she touches his bicep, and it hits me. He sleeps with her. I lower my gaze. My stomach clenches and I'm confused because I should feel honored that I have a place and a purpose. I shouldn't feel hurt or empty. I should be proud I accomplished something, but all I feel is lonely.

I glance at Jiro, hoping my mind is not making things up, but he doesn't acknowledge me. It feels like I don't exist to him. She whispers something in his ear, but I can't make out what she is saying. I don't know if I should feel hurt, but I sure as hell feel disappointed. I hear him say her name, Akemi.

Her expression when she looks at him is full of deep longing. He caresses her hand on his bicep and she lowers her gaze demurely. *Bastard.*

I feel like an outsider all over again. With my heart in my throat, I look around and feel like the ugly duckling in the story. The one that looks different from all the other ducks. The one that feels alone and unwanted. The one that always has to fight for attention. The one that always has to watch.

I find the courage within me to address every one of his men with my sharp tongue. "Well, gentlemen, since I am obviously no longer needed, may you all have a great evening."

They all nod, but the look on their faces is... shock. I whirl around and walk down the aisle without a backward glance.

I'm hungry, but the way I'm feeling right now, it's best if I eat alone. I miss Mia more than ever. I miss shopping at my favorite secondhand stores back home. Having a girls' night out where we can talk about nothing and anything.

I look up at one of Jiro's bodyguards standing at the door, knowing it's foolish to be alone, but I figure I have a driver that is also part of the yakuza. "Please send the car. I wish to eat somewhere else," I demand.

He nods and texts the driver. A minute later, the Maybach pulls up and I slide inside, not waiting for anyone to open the door.

I meet the driver's eyes through the rearview mirror. "Drive."

The car rolls forward and I quickly plug in my phone with the USB, opening my playlist and playing "Traitor" by Elley Duhe.

"Miss Tenaka? Where would you like to eat?" the driver asks.

"Do you know somewhere good to eat shrimp tempura?"

He nods, cracking a smile. I put my head back on the headrest of the luxury seat and feel my phone vibrate from an incoming text.

Jiro: Selena, where are you? Why did you leave like that?

Is he serious? He just treated me like I didn't matter once his little girlfriend was all over him.

Selena: Leave me alone. You just left me standing there like I was nothing and dismissed me. I don't want to talk to you right now. I want to be left alone, Jiro.

Jiro: Why? I didn't do anything.

Selena: Then you have nothing to worry about. I came like you wanted and you made the introduction. I left. It's not that hard to understand.

Jiro: You didn't even eat.

Selena: I don't want to eat with you. I want to be left alone. It's okay, Jiro. I'll get something to eat on my own.

I know I may be acting foolish but the way he ignored me hurts. We aren't together and he can sleep with whomever he wants, but it hurts seeing him with someone else. I shouldn't be upset, but I am. We fooled around, but it has been months since that night in my bedroom.

The man has his needs, and they don't involve me anymore apparently. I just thought he was different. I remove the necklace from around my neck and put it inside my purse, angry with myself. I just feel...alone.

The car finally stops in front of a busy market where they sell different types of Japanese food. People are walking in and out. There are different areas set up selling different types of foods.

"I will pick up your food, Miss Tenaka. I will also pick up something for you to drink. Please wait here."

"Thank you."

I relax in the car, waiting for the driver to come back with my food. "Lie to Me" by Tate McRae plays and I decide to let her album play all the way through. Tears roll down my cheeks. I'm confused and feel like I'm bleeding inside from a wound. And I hate it.

I wipe my eyes and suddenly see three black Bentleys pull up. Men step out and wait for the third car's passenger door to open. My eyes narrow on the figure and realize it's Jiro. *He found me.*

He walks toward the Maybach with a hard expression and opens the door, sliding in next to me. His eyes follow my hand on my thigh. My kimono is slightly open, exposing my boot and garter. I take a deep breath, holding the knife in my hand.

"You're going to stab me, Selena?" he asks.

I smile sarcastically. "You know, that is actually not a bad idea. What are you doing here? I thought I told you that I wanted to be alone. Preferably, away from you."

He smiles and laughs, the sound floating over my skin. "I wanted to eat with you."

"Ha, yeah right, could have fooled me. Looked like you had other plans."

The driver returns, handing me my food. Jiro tells him to drive around, and I sit in silence, enjoying my meal. He leans against the door facing me, watching me eat. After I finish my meal, I open a mint candy I had in my bag and push it past my lips. Jiro sucks in a breath as he watches me suck the candy with my tongue.

I stiffen when his hand touches my shoulder. He lowers his eyes, hurt by my reaction, but moves closer. He pulls my hair away from my neck and slides his fingers over my bare throat, noticing I'm not wearing the necklace. My eyes lift and he looks defeated. I'm sure he noticed I had it on when I walked into the restaurant. Jiro notices everything.

I glance in the rearview mirror and can see the driver's confused expression. He must be wondering what is transpiring in the back seat with his boss and the female heir of Elysium.

Jiro makes sure he keeps his distance from me in front of the others, but right now, I don't think he cares. Jiro slides his hand down my arm to the side where the opening to my robe is held closed. His fingers slide under, opening the silk to reveal my lace bra. He continues to glide downward with his fingers, opening it completely until I'm left in just my matching bra and panties, thigh-high boots and garters.

He stops and rakes his eyes over my body before slowly moving between my legs. He slides my body forward and grips the handle of the knife in my hand and places it to the side with ease. He throws his jacket on the floor before settling his face between my legs. And I let him. I can't resist. Because maybe... it's what I want.

I jolt as he suddenly slams his palm on the button to close the divider. He rolls up his sleeves and lowers himself again.

"Selena," he breathes. "Is this what you wanted?"

He moves my panties to one side, revealing my wet slit. He slides his tongue, licking my clit, and I moan from the pleasure.

"Yes."

He smiles. "I want you to know that you come before any other woman in my life. Until the day I die," he says before he begins the onslaught of pleasure, fucking me with his tongue.

God, it feels so good; he drives me crazy. I want him inside me, but I know he needs me to say the words. I'm ready and I come so hard, holding his face between my legs, not caring if the driver can hear me.

While I run my fingers through his hair, he looks at me and peppers kisses on my thighs, moving toward my breasts, taking one nipple and then the other, sucking gently over the lace of my bra. I feel goose bumps all over my flesh and the desire to please him just as much. I raise myself, unhooking my leg.

His eyes meet mine and I kneel between his legs, unbuckling his designer belt, reaching in and pulling his hard cock out. My eyes stay trained on him, and the buttons of his shirt fly everywhere as I rip it open.

I smile when he tilts his head and arches a brow. "It's my turn."

His chest is on display and I rub my hands over his smooth skin, feeling every hard muscle underneath his beautiful ink. He doesn't move, not even a flinch in his expression. He keeps a straight face, letting me do what I want. I push up on my knees and kiss a trail down to where his hard cock is anxiously waiting for me to milk it inside my mouth.

He softly grips my hair, caressing my back. Courage builds inside me, and I slam my hand on the button, opening the divider. It slowly lowers and I can feel the eyes of the driver behind me.

I take Jiro's cock in my mouth and moan at how the taste of him is sweet and salty in my mouth. His head tilts, watching me take him inside my mouth. I skim the head with my tongue until I reach the base of his cock and take him in my mouth completely.

I don't care what they think about why he left the hostess club. I'm not the old Selena who didn't belong. I'm reborn. I don't need to hide.

I suck him deep in my throat and I pull up slightly, teasing him, licking the underside of his shaft like he is my favorite dessert. His legs get rigid, letting me know he is about to come. When he grunts and my name escapes his lips, his hot cum shoots inside my mouth. My eyes find his and he knows I want more. I want him.

When I'm finished, I help him with his pants, biting my lip in concentration. His finger tilts my chin up to meet his eyes, and he rubs his thumb on my lip like he did that night, but this time it is so I can release it from between my teeth.

"Do you want to stay with me tonight?" he asks, but he sees it in my eyes and in my nod that I would say yes and go wherever he goes.

He covers me with my kimono, sliding the silk over my shoulders and tells the driver in a demanding voice, "Take us to the Ritz in Tokyo."

W e arrive at the hotel and enter the lobby, heading toward the hostess. Her eyes go wide when we walk up to her and she bows to Jiro, and I realize why she looks shocked.

I totally forgot about his shirt. He can't button the shirt back up because there are no buttons. I stifle a giggle as the hostess tries to look away from the view of his muscles and ink. When he addresses her in Japanese, she blushes, and I give her a hard stare.

"I want the penthouse on the top floor," he says.

"Yes, right this way," she says, leading the way to the reservations desk. She looks at the computer and enters the keys on the keyboard.

She hands Jiro a key after he pays, and he grabs my hand, walking toward the elevator that will take us to the top floor.

He leans against the elevator, not caring that he is half-dressed. I grin at him through the mirror of the elevator, and he smiles at me while we wait for the bell to signal we have reached our floor.

Once it does, we enter the tastefully decorated space with a living room, dining room, and two bedrooms. I walk to the master bedroom, which has a huge white bed and gray curtains on the windows, and into the bathroom, where there is an enormous bathtub.

He walks up behind me and turns on the water to the right temperature and undresses. I watch, mesmerized by his beautiful body as he removes his shirt and pants.

When we train, I try to keep my thoughts on each lesson and avoid ogling him when he moves with each weapon, showing me how to disarm an intruder or an enemy. When he stands close behind me, I try to hide the attraction I feel for him. An attraction that is more than just friends.

Out of nowhere, thoughts of Relic pop in my head and I compare the men. I put my hand over my eyes and close them, ashamed of where my thoughts went.

"What's wrong, Selena?"

I open my eyes and give him a smile. "Nothing."

"Then come and join me."

I undress slowly and he watches me with a lust-filled gaze as I step in the tub, sinking down in front of him, leaning my back against his chest. He kisses my neck and breathes me in.

"You smell so good, Selena. Your skin feels so soft and you're so beautiful. I'm dying to be inside you." He kisses my shoulder and I tilt my head to meet his lips. "I want to be sure you are ready. I don't want you to feel like it was a mistake." He kisses my back, lifting my hair and wrapping it around his hand. "Because that would kill me and whatever happens, I will always be here for you."

"I would never regret you and I would never think you are a mistake, but I understand why."

He doesn't want me to regret sleeping with him because of Relic. I don't know why he is worried about him when the man is marrying someone else. Maybe he thinks I haven't let go. What he doesn't understand is that I was left with no choice. It was obvious that Relic had no interest in me. He doesn't love me. I was just another conquest. Another body to warm his bed for the night. He found the right woman to marry and serve his family's purpose. I have had enough time to think. I have let enough time pass to understand that, in his eyes, I don't belong in his life.

I wasn't enough.

After our bath, my eyes grow heavy when I slide in the king-size bed with Jiro. He holds me and before I drift off to sleep, he whispers in my ear, "When you're ready."

I wake up in the middle of the night thirsty and look over and smile when I see Jiro sleeping peacefully. When I get up, I quietly walk around the room and find my robe and throw it on to go to the kitchen.

Once there, I grab a bottle of water and make my way to the freezer for ice. I open the refrigerator door and roll my eyes, annoyed.

"Great, no ice," I mutter.

I walk back to the bedroom and grab my knife and quietly let myself out of the suite, leaving the door propped open with the doorstop so I don't get locked out in the process.

I pad down the green-carpeted hallway with the ice bucket in one hand and, with the other, keep my robe closed with my knife concealed.

A nagging feeling grows stronger, but I keep walking until I reach the ice machine. I place the bucket under the ice dispenser, and a large hand comes up from behind me, covering my mouth.

Shit.

All the air in my lungs rushes out, causing my eyes to blur when someone pins me to the wall with great force.

"There, there, don't scream, and I will make this quick."

My eyes try to focus, but I recognize his voice as he pushes my face up against the wall, holding me in a fierce grip.

I'm having trouble breathing, but I concentrate on calming myself down. I'm relieved he hasn't noticed the knife. I recognize the man. He is the same one that went up to the table the first time I went with Jiro to the hostess club. Jiro warned him that if he touched me, he would kill him. I guess he doesn't care or has a death wish.

"I've wanted to fuck that little tight cunt since I first laid eyes on you. You're a whore who gives it to the yakuza. I have had their left-over pussy before but couldn't wait until he tires of you. Soon enough, he won't even notice you left, but I have recently found out that you mean more. You're an important little bitch that would be in my best interest to kill. My business associates would be pleased with how easily I could get rid of you," he says with a heavy accent. "You thought he could protect you," he seethes.

Jiro has trained me for this exact thing. When my fingers get a good grip on my knife, two other men walk into the tight space and begin touching my ass.

They speak in rapid Japanese, arguing about who will be first and taking turns raping me before they kill me. Bile rises in my throat at the thought, but I swallow it down, replacing it with rage and adrenaline.

He turns me around, and right when he tries to open my robe to grope me, I slide the knife into his stomach.

His eyes widen, almost bulging out of his face, stunned, not believing I have stabbed him. I use the few seconds I have to flick the knife again, open the wound and gut him. I watch as he stumbles back, holding his stomach and spilling his intestines on the floor. The other two guys that entered with him are watching in disbelief. I'm relieved, but it is short-lived when they lunge to grab me while the guy falls to the floor, trying to speak, but all I hear are gurgling noises.

Spurts of blood spray as he continues to try to speak. The distraction leaves a window for me to stab the shorter one in the throat. The third one on my left uses his advantage and grabs me by the hair.

Ignoring the throbbing pain, I push off the wall with my feet in the small space, using my weight to throw him off balance, knocking us both against the ice machine. I'm relieved when his face slams into the metal machine, but it's not enough for him to release his hold on me. His hand snakes around my throat, squeezing out all the air until my eyes burn like they are going to fall out of my face. I have seconds left before I pass out and realize I still have my knife. In one swift motion, I slice the sick bastard in the groin. He howls in pain.

I grit my teeth. "You wanted to rape and kill me, you sick bastard," I spit, holding the knife by his dirty pathetic cock.

Suddenly an enraged Jiro appears, looking at the massacre I have created with the three men. His eyes blaze in a fury. He looks at me and where I have my hand holding the knife, catching every word I just said.

I dig the knife in deep and swipe down, cutting his cock right off. The man falls to his knees, screaming in agony. He watches in horror as the blood paints the floor, my kimono, my arms, and my hands.

My hands are shaking when I slice the man's throat so he will shut up. "Stupid motherfucker, you fucked with the wrong bitch. I'm not a yakuza whore." I say shakily, spitting on his dead corpse.

Jiro takes the knife from me and goes to the man that attacked me first and slices his throat from ear to ear. "I told you I would slice your throat if you ever touched her, you piece of shit."

He looks at me and sees that I am still shaking from the rage.

"Jiro!" I whisper-yell pleadingly. "What have I done?"

"What you were trained to do. What I prepared you for in case this happened and I couldn't make it in time."

I close my eyes and say in a hoarse voice, "*Jirosan*, get me out of here, please. I want to leave, please," I repeat.

He grabs my hand and we run quietly back to the room. "Selena, get your stuff and let's go."

He grabs his cell and makes a call, speaking in rapid Japanese. I make out that we are to get a car somewhere.

"Let's go. A cleanup crew is on the way, and I don't want them to see us still here. Someone knew we were here and targeted you. They were waiting for you to come out alone."

We reach the private elevator, and he enters the key that allows us access to the parking garage. I look down at my body and I'm covered in blood, the smell of copper and death clinging to my skin like perfume. I want it off me. My mind replays what just happened over and over.

I just slaughtered three men like they were nothing, and I couldn't stop. I can hear myself breathing rapidly, like I just ran a marathon. My arms feel heavy and my throat feels like sandpaper from where the asshole squeezed my neck. It hurts every time I swallow.

The elevator dings and I run barefoot in the direction Jiro is leading me. "Hurry, Selena! My car will be waiting for us three blocks from here."

"I need to throw the boots and garters away, Jiro. My hands have ruined them with all the blood."

He finds a trash can in a back alley and throws them in there to be lit on fire by one of his men. He opens his phone, reads a text, then continues to run until we reach a black Phantom parked behind a building.

He opens it, and I slide in carefully, aware of my bloody hands on the clean interior. He revs the engine, and we take off in an unknown direction. I sit still in the car in an awkward position, like I have a stick up my ass.

"Are you hurt, Selena?"

"No, why?"

"Why are you sitting like that? Are you sure?"

"I don't want to mess up your beautiful car," I reply because it's the only thing that makes sense in my head right now.

He looks at me briefly with an irritated expression. "What? The car? Fuck the car. I will buy another one and burn this one. I'll take care of what happened back there."

I close my eyes, shaking my head. I'm a fucking murderer and a monster. Training is one thing, but acting out what you learn and using it as a weapon is another thing entirely. I know deep down I will never be the same. Ever. The feeling of dirty blood and the smell of death are painted all over me like a canvas.

We pull up to a tall building with black windows, and he parks in a parking space in the garage.

"Where are we?" I ask.

"We are at my place. A place no one knows exists. Well, except for you."

Chapter Thirty-Three

SELENA

He gets out and opens the door to help me out of the car. I have my arms locked in place against my body, feeling numb inside. I follow him as the elevator opens, and we are taken to the top floor.

The elevator opens to a hallway with a solid wood door. Jiro places his thumb over the pad and the sound of an electronic lock buzzes and turns green, unlocking the door that opens to the biggest open-spaced loft I have ever seen in Tokyo.

It takes up the entire floor with beautiful wood floors and an impressive view of the city.. I stand in the middle of the loft, frozen, not wanting to touch anything. I'm barefoot and must look like a crazy bum from the street after a zombie apocalypse. He turns on the shower to my right.

The loft is an open concept that allows you to see the shower with only a frosted glass door keeping the teakwood floors from getting wet. His bed is closer to the floor-to-ceiling windows, and I watch as the steam from the shower permeates the air like smoke. He comes up to me and guides me by the hand to the shower. Removing my hands from my waist, he slides the kimono off my body.

I'm standing naked, covered in dried blood, realizing that I'm cold, or maybe it's because I'm shivering from shock. Silent tears run down my cheeks.

"Come, Selena," he whispers. "I'll make it go away. Trust me."

He walks inside with me and washes the blood from my skin, but I can't stop crying.

"Make the feeling go away, Jiro. Please," I plead. My eyes close while I lower my head in defeat.

"I will, baby. Trust me. I will."

His body wash smells just like his cologne. Fresh and clean with a bit of citrus. He washes my hair and face gently as I lean into him. When he is satisfied that I'm clean, he washes himself and I just stare at the frosted glass, replaying what happened. What I did. What I had to do. It was self-defense. I needed to kill them.

He dries me with a fluffy white towel and brushes my long, wet hair. He peppers light kisses near my ear and whispers that everything is going to be okay, his breath like a caress on my heated skin. I wait, lost in my thoughts, as he moves around the room.

We walk toward the bed, and he lays me on the mattress, pulling the covers over us both, the soft sheets on my naked skin like a cloud. He turns to the nightstand on his right. I can hear porcelain clinking together. I turn my head and he motions for me to sit up, placing the small cup of hot tea to my lips. I take small sips and lie back down, letting the warmth of the tea soothe my sore throat.

He kisses my cheeks where my tears slide and then kisses me deeply. I kiss him back, sliding my tongue in his mouth, tasting him, rubbing my hands over his chest up to his neck.

"Jiro?"

"Yeah?"

"I want you inside me," I say into his mouth.

He pulls back slightly, looking into my eyes. When he sees what he needs, he pulls down the comforter, exposing my breasts. He sucks them lightly and I writhe under him, needing more of a connection.

All I want is him inside me, taking away all the terrible memories and replacing them with his. He reaches over to his nightstand, tears the wrapper open with his teeth and slides on a condom before settling between my legs.

I can feel the tip of his cock at my entrance. He rubs the pad of his thumb over my clit and my hips lift off the bed, seeking more. He holds himself upright with his left hand, and his eyes lock on mine. I'm lost when he slides his thick cock in slowly, inch by inch. I arch my back when he is finally balls deep inside me, stretching me. Filling me.

He takes a deep breath and holds me to him by sliding his hand over my back like a puzzle piece that was missing and finally fits.

"I knew you would be perfect. Everything about you is perfect," he rasps against the skin of my neck. "So. Fucking. Perfect."

Both my hands cup the sides of his smooth cheeks, and I whisper against his lips, "You will always be my hero. In this life and the next. Near or far. Together or not. You will always have a place in my heart."

His body moves, grinding inside of me, and I hold on as he makes love to me. I hear the noises of how wet I am. How wet he makes me.

My head tilts back, my hair sliding behind me. "Harder, Jiro. Please," I plead as my climax builds.

He answers by pounding into me. Each thrust is harder than the last. He suddenly stops and pulls out, turning me around in one swift movement.

I whimper when I feel the loss of not having him inside me.

He places me on all fours, caressing the skin of my ass. "I love the feel of your ass, Selena," he whispers, ramming his cock inside me.

I mewl, "Yes."

His balls slap against my clit as he pounds me from behind. All you can hear are the sounds of skin slapping skin as he grabs my hair gently and tilts my head back so he can place kisses on my sore throat. It doesn't hurt when I feel this good.

"I love being inside you. I love watching you. I love making you mine."

As my orgasm climbs, I moan. A huge wave of pleasure crashes inside me, my voice echoing against the walls as I call his name. My scream of love for him escapes from my lips.

"Don't stop," I say breathlessly.

He answers by continuing to fuck me until I finish coming like the sea returning to the deepest part of the ocean.

He stills as his hot cum spills inside the condom, filling it so much that it drips down my leg. I stay on the bed on all fours, turning my head to watch him as he climbs off the bed to get a washcloth to wipe up our mess.

When he is done, I lie down, pulling the covers over our sated bodies. He kisses my hair and holds me until we both fall asleep.

Chapter Thirty-Four

SELENA

I slowly wake up to Jiro kissing me on my neck before sliding his tongue down my body to the sore lips between my legs. He looks up when he realizes I'm awake and pushes my legs wider.

My body responds to him when his tongue swirls on my clit over and over. My fingers run through his hair, feeling the soreness in other parts of my body from my attack last night. The only soreness that is welcome is between my legs, almost forgotten now with the pleasure the man between my thighs is giving me.

Jiro's wicked tongue drives me over the edge. He raises his body and is at my entrance, sliding his sheathed cock inside me.

I close my eyes as my swollen walls accommodate him and he takes it slow.

His movements are soft as he slowly grinds in and out. My fingers snake over his muscular ass, pushing him deep. I want to feel him deep inside of me. The pressure of an intense orgasm builds, coming to the surface.

"Come for me, Selena," he demands on a groan, gripping my hips.

I gasp when it's too much. "God, yes. I'm coming!"

"Selena," he breathes, feeling my pussy convulse around his cock, squeezing him, pushing him over the edge. "Fuck."

I can feel his heat inside the condom matching mine as he grunts while he caresses my nipples with his fingers.

Once he pulls out of me, I get out of bed and head to the shower. He follows me inside, turning it to hot but not burning hot. I stand in the spray washing myself. My eyes flick up when he stands in front of me with a grin on his handsome face.

I avert my gaze and he says, "It will pass."

"What will pass?" I ask, my brows pinching.

What does he mean?

"The feeling of taking someone's life who deserves it. It gets easier. I know it's not what you wanted to hear, but they were going to hurt you."

I take in a deep breath and sigh. "I know that part. It wasn't why I did it. It was the way I did it. It makes me feel like a monster. I didn't think I was capable of taking three of them out like that."

He leans forward. "That means you have a good teacher," he says, his accent sneaking out.

I notice it has diminished, but I can still hear it when he gets emotional or when he is having a serious talk with me about my safety. He goes all yakuza mode on me. But I like it. It makes me feel safe. He makes me feel safe.

"I get it," he continues. "My first time was when I was twenty years old. Someone attacked my father, and I had no choice but to kill him with my bare hands. My father knew then I was ready to take his place and honor the yakuza. It is all I have ever known."

"I understand."

We finish our shower and dry off, and he gives me his shirt and a pair of shorts to wear. I bring them to my nose and inhale his scent.

My eyes lift and I blush when he catches me and smiles. "I like that look on you."

"Very funny," I say sarcastically when I finish sliding my head through the shirt. "I must look like a freak."

"You can never look like a freak, Selena. In my eyes, you will always be beautiful."

My heart flutters from my love for him. I don't want to get hurt. It took me almost a year to recover from Relic.

"Jiro, about us…"

"I don't want to talk about that right now. Just let it be."

I loved him as my childhood friend, but now I love him as a man. What do you do when you have just slept with one of your best friends? The only thing I am certain of is my love for him will never change. It doesn't matter what happens. I will protect him and have his back the same way he has mine. We have this unspeakable bond between friends and an unspoken truth between lovers.

It's solid.

It's real.

It's us.

He slides his pants over his hips and says, "I am going to have your stuff brought here. We have an office building in Tokyo, but since they attacked you, I must finish what's left of them. I need you to look over the five shipments that we have had this month. Someone is stealing from us, and I don't know who it is, Russian Bratva or the Polish. I know it's not the Kings." My head snaps at the mention of the Kings. "You will have to go back to America, Selena."

Already? I don't want to go.

"I don't want to go back right now." Not when I have fallen in love with him.

"You have to, Selena. It's not safe. Especially when you discover who is stealing from us. The shipments have been short for the past three months. We need to know because they're Elysium's underground contracts involving Japan. The Kings will have your back, but here in Tokyo, I can't be around to watch you all the time while I deal with other business. Last night, you were attacked because someone gave our location away. They were watching us, or I have a rat."

"Will you come with me?"

He gives me a torn expression, and I know he is going to tell me he can't. "I can't, Selena. I have business here."

The sting of tears pools behind my eyes, but I blink them back. I'm not ready to go back, but I understand he is trying to protect me. I have to be strong. This is who I am now. I have to accept this as my present and my future. There is no room for emotion. Emotions cause you to make mistakes. Mistakes that can cost you your life.

I glance at him with a mask in place, and he realizes that I've accepted the reality of who I am now. The CEO of Elysium, like they wanted. The killer they wanted. But I will never be the Selena they remember.

"When do I leave?"

"As soon as possible, Selena. I'm sorry."

Chapter Thirty-Five

SELENA

I look at myself in the floor-length mirror as I wait for him to come back. He left my clutch on the teak table by the entrance. I open the purse and pull out the necklace Jiro gifted me, holding the jade in the palm of my hand. The stones glitter in the light.

I glance at the bed where we made love. Where I have to leave our love behind. The memory of us will stay in this room because where I have to go, he won't be there. He will come to me to make sure I'm safe. That I'm not in harm's way. *"Let it be."* His words.

It means it happened, and that is all that there is to say. I step forward and place the necklace on his nightstand.

"I love you," I whisper. "Goodbye, my hero."

Once Jiro returns with my things, I quickly dress and pack my stuff. He hands me the files I need to look over. "These are the files with the weights that indicate the shortages. It will give you time to sort things out in Seattle. You need an apartment and a car. There is enough money in your account to cover everything. You have all the money in the world to buy whatever you want."

"The Kings don't know I am taking over Elysium or who I am?"

My stomach clenches when I mention the Kings. Not because of

Relic but because of Mia and them seeing me again under different circumstances. Dangerous ones.

"Not yet. I will introduce you to the leaders and you will have the answers for them by then. I will be there in a week."

The elevator doors open inside the loft that leads to the garage. When the elevator doors open, I pause. There is a fleet of cars to choose from in a garage. It is like a dealership full of luxury cars. I don't remember seeing all these cars last night, but I was in shock and covered in the blood of my enemies. I'm still tripped up because the driver is on the opposite side compared to the US when I scan the row of cars.

"They're all yours?"

He clears his throat and grins. "They are."

"Nice, we're taking the Bentley."

"I love it when you are bossy," he teases.

"Get used to it."

We slide in the car after he grabs the key from a lockbox hidden inside the concrete wall and drives the twenty minutes to the airport.

Once we board the plane, I sit in my seat with the files in my hand to begin my search to find out who is stealing from us while the plane takes off. I make it my mission to find out who it is. I will find out everything by the time the plane lands in Seattle. It will help me take my mind off leaving Jiro.

After ten and half hours, right before the pilot lights up the sign signaling that we are landing, I find it. It is the Russian Bratva one month and the Polish the month after. They alternate, probably to take the heat off each other, but what makes little sense is the Russian shipments are the only ones hidden.

If they keep this up, we will not meet the cartel's requirements and will fall short. Which means we are shorting the Kings. *Fuck.*

Out of five shipments, it's fifty million in three months alone. There is probably more, but I only have the files for three months. I would need to review more. I pick up my cell phone, hoping I get a signal. Once the bars light up on my screen, I text Jiro.

Selena: I found it!

Jiro: I knew you would find it! They have been at it for eight months. I miss you, Selena. I am sorry you had to leave so abruptly.

Selena: I will see you when we meet with the others. Bye, Z.

I smile inwardly, calling him Z. He gets annoyed that I call him Z, but I think he secretly likes it. He said he was going to shave his head in a buzz cut to get back at me, but I think he would look hot either way.

I text Mia. God, I miss her. I want to catch up and go shopping for a night out. I need it.

Selena: Hey girl. I am back. I just landed.

Mia: Omg. Yes! Do you need a ride? I miss you so much. Let's go shopping and go out after. It can be somewhere the Kings don't own. Deacon will probably find me later, but so what.

Selena: I don't need a ride. I will meet you at your apartment.

Mia: I'm home. Omg, Selena. I want to scream right now. Let me call Deacon and let him know.

Selena: Okay. I will be there shortly.

Once I exit the plane, I get in the waiting Wraith and give the driver Mia's address. After the thirty-minute drive, the car arrives at Mia's apartment. I tell the driver to wait there to take us shopping.

I walk into Mia's almost empty apartment. "Mia," I call out.

"In here," she says, walking out of her room with her handbag slung over her arm.

I smile. "Ready?"

She runs up and gives me the biggest and tightest hug. "I missed you so much," she says with tears in her eyes. "You are my best friend, and I cannot be without you for so long. It's been almost a year!"

"Me too, Mia. But I have to tell you something, and I don't want you to find out through Deacon."

She gives me a worried expression and says softly, "Okay."

I tell her everything except that I slaughtered three men and her eyes go wide.

"All this time, and you're like a millionaire, maybe a billionaire."

I nod. "Yes, it's why I had to leave."

I tell her about Jiro and that he owns the black Bugatti that drove me to the airport from the gala.

"I couldn't tell you over the phone. Please, Mia, don't tell Deacon yet. They will find out that I run the Japanese operations and they know Jiro and who he is."

She stays quiet and raises her brows, taking a deep breath.

I get worried and grimace when she says nothing. "Are you mad?" I ask.

"What? No way! My best friend is a badass bitch. I can't wait until they find out." She smiles. "You know, from time to time, Relic asks if I reached out to you."

I should feel happy he asked about me, but I can't. I won't. I don't care. Not when I'm in love with Jiro. My face must have turned sour because she scrunches her nose.

"Okay. Maybe you are not happy about that." She angles her head. "He didn't get married," she says, and my insides flutter at the fact he isn't married.

Wait. That would mean Jiro knows. And he didn't tell me.

"Didn't he have to marry Sophia so he could keep his imports and exports flowing because of her father?"

She snorts. "Who, Relic? No way. Since you left, he has been on a downward spiral, making her life miserable with different women. He practically fucks them in front of her. It's like he wants to punish her. She has this illusion that she belongs to Relic King. The title and the power are all she cares about. She wants him in any way she can get him. She even parades around with a necklace that says Kings on it, like a stamp of ownership. She knew it was a marriage of convenience."

I'm still surprised he allows her to be under the Kings' protection in the city. I place my hand on my neck, remembering the necklace Jiro gave me and feeling the emptiness, but I don't regret taking it off. I don't regret giving it back.

"Anyway, let's go," she says, waving her hand and dismissing the topic of conversation. "We have to go shopping."

I laugh, and she smiles back. "Oh, also... I'm moving in with Deacon," she announces proudly.

"That is great, Mia! I am so happy for you. When is your last day here?"

"This weekend."

"I have to find a place now that I'm back. It shouldn't be hard since I have money."

"I will help you out if you need me to."

I snake my arm through hers as we walk out of the apartment. "It's okay. Get settled in with Deacon. I'll be fine."

She locks up and I lean against the elevator on the way down. "Alright, I don't want to hear you complain... and before you say anything... I want to say this now. Everything is on me and there is a driver waiting for us downstairs."

"No fucking way!" she blurts. "You have a driver like the Kings?"

"Gotta treat my best friend to a shopping spree and go out like we just turned twenty-one," I say with a laugh.

We head out to Jiro's Wraith, and I'm excited that I'm hanging with my best friend again, trying to be normal even though inside, I am nothing but a monster. That is the only thing I don't want. For her to fear me.

Mia isn't a Mafia princess or a killer. She is a small-town girl that graduated college and met the man she hopes to marry one day. A man that is a Mafia king, but I'm sure he doesn't tell her everything. She is carefree and full of love.

I give the address to the driver and we head to the area where there is nothing but designer stores.

"Miss Tenaka. *Oyabun* instructed me to take you anywhere you wish to go. If there is anything you need, he says to just text him, and I will make arrangements."

Mia's eyes go wide, giving me a knowing look.

"That won't be necessary. Driving me around is enough. I appreciate the message."

"Whatever you wish."

When we arrive at the boutique and get out, Mia grabs my arm and says softly, "So, tell me about this Jiro and don't lie. Be honest. I saw the look on your face when the driver mentioned his name."

"What look?" I ask, playing dumb.

"The pissed-off look of a woman who wants to hate the guy she is crazy about when things are left unsaid. Tell me about Jiro. What happened?"

I can't tell her everything that happened, so I keep to the safe parts. The sexy parts.

"We're childhood friends. Our fathers had everything planned for us when we were kids and we remained friends for a long time. He's the one that was mentioned at Thanksgiving when we went to my parents. We both secretly had a crush on one another and when I was in Japan, we slept together."

She giggles and places my hair behind my ear. "It was good, wasn't it, bitch?"

My cheeks heat like they are on fire and I sigh. "What do you do when you sleep with your childhood friend? Because I sure as hell don't know. But yeah, it was amazing. It's like having sex with a man that you know will protect you against anything or anyone."

"So, what's the problem?"

"He doesn't have time for someone like me. We are just friends. He has business and duties in Japan, and I'm in charge of running things from here. It wouldn't work. I'm already a target over there."

"Okay. Enough about the whole family duty shit. I have enough with Deacon and the Kings. I want to know about Jiro, the man."

"Okay, fine. It's like fucking Goku from *Dragon Ball Z* but with ink all over his arms and chest.

"Fuck me. Selena, that's hot."

"I know. Imagine being around a man like that for almost a year, getting all wet when he just looks at you, and you're confused because he's one of your best friends from when you were kids."

We walk into the boutique, and the lady recognizes Mia instantly. She tells the girl in the back to get the latest collection of designer clothes, snapping her fingers. We spend three hours in the store, and I think we buy everything.

I pull out my black card and the girl's eyes light up. "Oh, I thought we were putting everything on the Kings' account," she says.

I smile, handing her my card. "Oh, that won't be necessary. I will cover it." She swipes it, and it goes through with no problem. A girl can get used to this.

The driver pulls up and puts everything inside the Wraith. We make a stop to buy makeup and everything we need for a girls' night out.

"Selena. Let's go to this new dance club that recently opened. They play the latest music, and I have been dying to go.

"Okay, but I need to see if I can buy a car first. I can't pull up in the Jiro's Wraith, not until the Kings find out. They might recognize the driver," I say nervously.

"All right, baller. What bad bitch car are you going to buy?"

I smile at her. "A red Urus, of course. It's one in the afternoon. They are still open for business."

I tell the driver to take us to the exotic dealership and open my purse to make sure I have my ID while talking to Mia. "I will be staying in a hotel for the weekend until I can find a place. We can get ready there and head out tonight."

She nods with excitement, clapping her hands and doing a little dance. "I'll text Deacon so he doesn't freak out."

"How are you guys?"

"We are doing great. Taking things slow."

"Remember, if he fucks up, I will kick his ass," I tell her playfully. If she only knew, I mean every word.

We arrive at the dealership and slide out of the car. We don't look like we are here to buy an expensive car like a Urus—me wearing leggings, a bomber jacket, and wedge sneakers. Mia is also wearing leggings, sneakers, and a sweater.

A young salesman, looking at us like we are lost, greets us. "Can I help you, ladies? Are you waiting for someone?"

"No, I am here because I want to buy that red Urus right over there, and I want my tag to say my name on the back." He turns to the car and then back to us. "That car is two hundred eighty-nine thousand dollars."

I shrug. "No problem. Can I pay the amount with my black card?"

He smiles and says, "You can pay part of it, but I am afraid I would need a wire transfer for the rest."

"That can be arranged," I quip.

Mia glares at the young salesman. I ignore him and text the driver to tell him I need a wire to buy the car from my account. Five minutes later, my phone vibrates from an incoming text.

Jiro: Give me the amount and information. I will send confirmation to the dealer and give them my number so I can speak with them.

Selena: Okay. Thank you.

I walk up to the young salesman. "Can you call this number? They will wire you the exact amount with fees, but they want to speak to you first."

"Absolutely. You have amazing eyes, by the way."

I roll my eyes at his attempt to flatter me because he realizes I'm not broke. I give him my identification so he can hurry with the paperwork. "Can you hurry? We have somewhere we need to be."

"Yes, Miss Tenaka," he answers, looking at my license.

I admire the car with Mia, and she says, "Now this is a bad bitch car."

I feel like a kid buying a new toy. "I've always wanted one," I tell her. She gives me a happy smile and I snicker. "Now I don't have to Uber."

We both laugh at our inside joke and the salesman comes back with a smile on his face. "I'll get her washed and ready for you. You said you wanted the tag to say your first name?"

"Yes, please."

"Your boyfriend said to add some other finishing touches."

"I don't have a boyfriend," I say.

"I don't know about you, but you're something more if a man just dropped three hundred grand on a car for a woman that is not his girlfriend."

I try to hide my shock as he walks away. He didn't. I can't believe Jiro.

I glance at Mia, and her mouth is hanging open. When she recovers, she says, "I definitely have to meet Jiro."

"We're just friends."

"I don't think he sees you as just friends, sweetheart. Relic has some serious competition. This is going to be good."

My head snaps up at the mention of Relic's name. "What do you mean?"

She sighs. "Deacon kept asking me about you because Relic didn't know where you went the night of the gala. He told his parents off and insisted that he wouldn't marry Sophia. That's why he treats Sophia so badly. Not physically, but she gets angry because she is so hung up on the notion of her and Relic that she just takes it, I guess, and she hates the mention of your name. I can't put my finger on it, but she's a mess." She blows out a puff of air, making her hair fly forward. "I really hate that bitch."

I smile but my heart drums. My mind goes back to the fact that he wouldn't marry her, but then the hurt I felt after finding out he proposed to her takes over. The nights I spent crying myself to sleep.

"Don't pay attention to her. She is just a spoiled little rich girl that looks down on others who are less fortunate. She needs a good punch in the mouth a couple of times," I say, breaking a smile. If she only knew, I would love to be the one to do it.

After two hours, the salesman returns with keys and papers in hand. "Everything is all set. The plate is available because we have a tag agency next door. Just sign on all the highlighted areas, and the title will be in your name. Insurance is all paid for the year and I will send the paperwork to Elysium," he says.

"Yes, that would be perfect," I say.

The car is parked out front. The shiny red paint gleams under the dealership lights. I smile inwardly, loving the new perks of being a Mafia boss.

We leave in the new Urus with the driver following us to the hotel I have booked for the weekend. I smile and turn to look at Mia as she presses all the buttons and feels the leather.

"This is badass, Selena." I smile, turning the music up with the windows down.

We pull up to the hotel and the valet runs in our direction. The driver exits the Wraith and opens my door. Once I'm out, he does the same for Mia. We walk to the reception desk and pick up my room key, sending all our purchases to the suite.

Mia looks at her phone. "Deacon says he will meet us at the dance club a little later so we can have fun for a couple of hours on our own. I told him we would not overdo it by drinking ourselves stupid and that we just want to dance and have fun. It's been a while," she says.

We take the elevator to the suite and as the elevator doors open, I say, "No problem. Let's get ready. I am going to wear the red silk minidress with the open back, and the red-bottom shoes. Matches the car."

"Yes!" She beams. "I love it. I am going to change into the Balmain minidress with ankle booties."

Once we shower, I walk out dressed, and Mia gasps. "Selena, that is beautiful. Your back and all the ink and your thighs. It's... exotic."

I turn around at her reaction and smile. "I got it when I first arrived. One of Jiro's friends did it."

"Is that the hair clip Relic took and customized for you? The one on the warrior? It's the same one, isn't it?"

"Yes," I tell her. "He meant a lot to me at the time, but I don't regret it. I think I'm over it, though, and I will never forget how he made me feel like I wasn't worth fighting for. I felt like I couldn't breathe at the gala when I found out the real reason and his lies. The way he asked me to leave that day in his office. When Jiro came for me, it was like I could breathe and find myself."

"I am so sorry, Selena."

"Time hasn't changed how he made me feel at the gala. Whatever we shared was nothing more than what he has had with any other woman."

"He is just an asshole that will eat his words soon enough."

I brush my hair, needing to let the past go. "Doesn't matter. That was all in the past."

"He doesn't deserve you, Selena. You deserve someone who will tell you they love you and cannot live without you."

"Wishful thinking," I say.

We leave the hotel and arrive at the dance club. We step out when I leave the Urus with the valet. We walk up to the entrance, and I tell the guy at the door that I want to buy a VIP table. He looks Mia and me up and down, checking our IDs with his flashlight.

"Right this way, ladies."

I hand him my card, but he shakes his head. "It's on the Kings' account." Deacon must have called when Mia told him where we were headed earlier.

We enter the dark club with lighted tables toward the VIP section. The music is loud. The bass thumping in the huge space. The DJ plays "Regardless" by Raye and Rudimental, and we order shots of tequila, dancing to the music.

The club is filled with bodies. We have the attention of other men drinking at VIP tables, and they salute us from afar. Ignoring them, Mia and I smile at each other, having the best time.

We dance for hours, pacing the number of drinks we consume. Suddenly, the crowd parts with sparklers and bottles held high, and we see Deacon, Liam, and Relic being escorted through the crowd toward our table.

The women stare at the tall and menacing gods passing through. They look like tattooed models walking through the club. My stomach clenches when Relic comes closer, worry clawing my gut.

He doesn't know.

Liam reaches me first and gives me the tightest brotherly hug ever. He picks me up, and I have to hold my short dress to keep it from riding up. "There's my girl!" he says, loud enough for everyone to hear. I look down at him with laughter in my eyes. He kisses me on the cheek. "Hello, beautiful. I have missed you."

"I missed you too, sexy."

"I love it when you talk dirty to me, baby," he jokes, setting me down.

Deacon comes up and gives me a hug. "How are you? Everything good here?"

"Yes, I'm great. Everything is great, except they won't let me pay."

"Relic made sure you girls wouldn't have to pay," Deacons says.

My eyes meet his golden ones and then I watch as his eyes rake my body up and down as he walks forward. His gaze is intense. I take a step back, but he takes one closer.

Deacon moves to take a seat on the black couch next to Mia. Liam takes the other couch while the waitress sets the bottles of liquor on the table. We're the only two left standing. He lifts his hand to touch my cheek and I flinch, turning my head away.

His hand falls before his fingers brush my cheek. "Beautiful as always," he breathes. *No, How are you? How's it been?* Nothing.

I avert my gaze, not acknowledging his compliment, and take a seat next to Liam. He is safer and more fun to be around. Relic is too intense for me right now. I'm sure it surprised him I didn't melt in front of him. That happens when someone breaks your heart and you let go and fall in love with someone else.

He sits across from me, studying me. Mia must notice the tension in the air. "Don't Call Me Up" by Mabel plays, and she gets up, holding out her hand to me. I take it and she pulls me up to walk over by the railing, where we sing and sway our hips to the music. The guy at the VIP table across from us salutes and nods his head to me again. He is feeling brave, but so am I, and I salute right back.

Relic doesn't miss the gesture, and I notice his hands clenching into fists as he turns around to glower at the guy. The guy gets nervous and looks away.

What a bully.

Liam and Deacon are smirking at the scene playing out in front of them. I glance over at Relic, the expression on my face giving him the message loud and clear. *I'm over you.*

Turning back around, I can feel his eyes burning the skin on my back. I feel like I'm on fire. Someone cages me in from behind and I'm on high alert, but then I glance at the tattoos covering the tops of his hands. Hands belonging to the man I couldn't get out of my thoughts for months.

He leans forward so I won't escape, his breath fanning my skin. My long hair is swept to the side of my shoulder, and he brazenly slides his finger down my spine to my tailbone, his fingers scanning the tattoos on my back. Goose bumps rise all over my skin at his touch.

I should push him away. I should turn around and tell him to go fuck himself. But then I remember he doesn't know where I came from or why I came back. He doesn't know that I know who he is. Who they all are and how we will be involved in the future.

He chuckles close to my ear and says, "Resist me all you want, but we both know that you are wet right now. I bet if I slide my finger in that tight cunt, you will come on my hand."

He is so full of himself. Just the word cunt has me as dry as the desert, turning me off. Better yet, there is nothing he has done so far that turns me on. Because I'm not that woman. The one he can dismiss after making her feel everything. The one he threw away. I glare at him with hot anger, gritting my teeth. I'm surprised I haven't chipped a molar.

"Funny how you expect me to fawn all over you. But that is what you expect of me, isn't it? For me to see you walk in a room and get wet because you figure I'm stupid and can't help myself. But to be honest, I wouldn't stoop so low." I get in his face, tapping my finger on my chin. "Aren't you supposed to be married?"

He pulls away with a look like I have slapped him. I'm not a toy that he can play with whenever he wants. I'm done being toyed with. I turn around to dance with Mia, dismissing Relic King.

Mia glances at Relic, shrugging her shoulders. He watches me dancing with a confused expression. I guess he has never been turned down.

Liam throws gasoline on the fire and shouts, "Bro, you fucked up with her big time!"

My turn to watch Relic giving Liam a shut-the-fuck-up glare. But Liam keeps laughing.

"No, dude, really, she can't stand you," Liam says.

A woman gets through the bouncers and whispers in Relic's ear, but to my surprise, he dismisses her. I watch the exchange with a look that says, *exactly*.

Masking the way my stomach clenched when she was close to his body, I saunter up to him and place my hands on his chest. I motion with my finger, and he leans closer to my lips. "I'm surprised you didn't shove your fingers inside her cunt to see if she was wet," I whisper in his ear.

His head whips up, and he gives me a smile. "I miss yours."

I scrunch my nose at him and reply, "With what I just saw, I doubt it."

Mia mouths *It's time to go*, and Deacon gets up. "I will take Mia home," he says, caressing the side of her hip. I am okay with driving. I haven't had another drink since we arrived.

"You don't need an Uber?" Relic says. Mia and I look at each other and laugh hysterically.

"What's so funny?" The guys ask at the same time.

Mia calms down first, shaking her head, trying to catch her breath. "I don't think Selena will ever have to Uber again. We went car shopping today, and she picked one out. It's in valet," she says with excitement in her tone.

I hand Liam my ticket so he can give it to the valet as we walk toward the entrance. They all wait for my car to arrive so they can make sure I leave safely. The driver Jiro sent to make sure I was safe is waiting for me by the exit, keeping himself hidden.

The Urus pulls up, and the valet driver gets out, holding the door open so I can get in my car. I turn and give Mia one last hug. Relic's standing next to his brothers, probably in shock.

Relic walks up to the valet and takes the door from him as I get inside the car and tips the valet for me. Once I'm seated, he grips my chin gently, turning my face to look at him, and before I can object, he ducks his head and presses his lips against my cheek in a soft kiss.

I wasn't ready for tingles to break out all over my skin or for the memories of us to come back.

"The joke's on me, isn't it, Selena?"

His words should be satisfying, but they are not. Not when I wanted him so much. Not when we stayed up and talked for hours, getting to know each other on a deeper level. Then he tainted everything with his lies and he broke me.

"You were never a joke to me, but you made me feel like one. Look, things have changed, Relic. I have moved on and so have you. Just let it go."

"I can't," he says quietly.

"Trust me, you have to," I tell him, closing the door and leaving him standing there to watch the taillights of my car.

After the fifteen-minute drive through the city, I get to the hotel room and change into comfortable pajamas to sit and look over the contracts from the files Jiro gave me. I don't want to think about Relic and I don't want to think about the way my body responded to a simple kiss on my cheek. I feel like I'm betraying my love for Jiro, even if we left things unsaid.

Selena: I need the other files from the previous three months. I want to know when it began.

Jiro: You're back from a night out already?

Selena: How did you know I was out?

Then I remember the driver. His driver.

Jiro: I have eyes everywhere, but I instructed the driver to keep tabs on you.

I cannot get mad when he is just trying to keep me safe. He is making sure I don't run into trouble.

Selena: Okay. Well, I guess you know my plans before I share them with you.

Jiro: I will send them in the morning. Are you alone?

My heart races. Would he be jealous if I weren't?

Selena: You know I am. So why are you asking?

Jiro: You're right. I would know if you weren't. You left something on my nightstand that led me to believe you wouldn't be alone tonight.

Selena:. The part of protecting me doesn't mean I can't love anyone or give myself to anyone.

Jiro: Who do you love, Selena?

Selena: I have always loved you since we were kids. That will never change. I love you, Jiro. You will always be my hero.

Jiro: We have a meeting set in three days with the Kings. We will let them know what you found and then set up the meeting with the

Russian Bratva and the Polish fucks. It's time the Kings know who you really are. I will be there in the morning.

He dismissed my last message, and I cannot lie and say it doesn't sting. He has shown me I mean more to him than any other, but he has never said that he loves me. Maybe he does, but not in the way I want him to, or maybe being the head of the yakuza doesn't allow room for love.

I grip my phone like it holds the fate of my future and respond the only way I know how.

Selena: Okay. See you soon.

I hit send and then another text pops up from Mia.

Mia: I will see you in the morning so we can have breakfast.

Selena: Jiro is coming.

Mia: Oh my god, yes! I can meet the man that has my best friend over a King.

Selena: Eye roll. If a King finds his queen, he will be unstoppable. That is why he must always protect her from anyone.

Mia: I love how that sounds. See you.

SELENA

I wake up and head to the gym to get in a workout before Jiro and Mia arrive. I will probably order room service so no one sees us together before it's time. Jiro is most likely going to get mad I told Mia, but she will keep my secret from Deacon and the Kings for a bit.

I finish my workout and re-rack the weights in the medium-sized workout room. A guy walking over to a machine on my right gives me an appreciative smile and a little wave. I give him a friendly wave back, so I don't seem rude.

After my fifty-minute workout, he watches me walk out and grins. He's cute in a boyish way, fit and tall, but nothing like Jiro or Relic. Probably has a regular job and is trying to find a girl to have a family with one day. Not a bad boy or Mafia boss that fucks women with no commitments. I take the elevator up to my suite, leaning hard against the wood paneling of the elevator car, feeling the pressure of my emotions.

Walking out of the shower in my hotel room, I hear a knock at the door and look through the peephole to see that it's Mia and I open the door.

"Hey, you look refreshed," she says, walking inside.

"I worked out this morning, and I was flirting with a guy, waving at him like I'm back in middle school."

She laughs. "You are so crazy. Where should we go eat?"

"I thought we could eat here in the hotel to be discreet."

"Okay."

The hotel room lock beeps, and my head whips toward the door. I sag in relief as Jiro lets himself in with a key. Of course, he could get a key to my room.

Mia stares at him, quirking a brow. "Damn, she wasn't kidding. Boy, you are fine with that Goku vibe," she says, and the cocky asshole smiles with perfect white teeth and a small dimple on his left cheek, making my heart skip a beat.

She continues to drool over him like he is a fine steak and I shake my head. "Mia, stop it. It will go to his head," I scold playfully.

He takes in my short sweater dress that molds to my curves and my designer wedge sneakers I bought yesterday.

Mia watches him intently when he walks up to me and rubs his thumb on my bottom lip I didn't realize I was snagging between my teeth.

He pulls me close, and I breathe in his cologne as his arms circle around me, holding me close. My hands slide around his waist, and I place my cheek against his hard chest. He slips his hands down to my ass and pulls me closer, so I can feel how much he misses me.

"If you two don't stop it, I'm going back home to fuck my man. Jeez, the sexual tension in here," she says, fanning herself.

I quickly step away from him, breaking the spell he has over me, bringing me back to reality and the reason he is here.

"Mia, this is Jiro. *Jirosan*, this is Mia, my best friend since college. She's Deacon King's girlfriend."

He smiles and nods his head. "Pleasure to meet you," he says with a bow out of respect that she's special to me.

She shakes her head, her short platinum hair swaying with the effort. "You're in trouble, girl."

"What do you mean, trouble?" His brows pinch together.

"Nothing," I assure him. "She talks in riddles sometimes." When I see he still has a worried expression still crossing his features, I confess. "Don't worry, she knows who you are, Jiro. She is sworn to secrecy not to tell the Kings until the meeting."

He gives me a relieved smile. I was right. He was worried they already knew before the meeting.

I collect the files and put them away, and Jiro teases Mia while she leans on the dresser. "For the record, I was her friend first." Oh no, he didn't just pull the best friend card.

Mia raises her hand. "Hold up. You are her lover, not her best friend." She points her thumb to her chest. "I'm her best friend. You lost the best friend card the day you made love to her. The way you look at her, it wasn't just sex."

I turn white like a sheet at her brazen behavior. "Mia!" She looks at me with a mischievous glint in her eye. "What? I'm just trying to clear the air. He did. I can see it. That means anyone else can see it."

I glance at Jiro, but his mouth is set in a line. He nudges his head to the door. "Let's go."

"I thought we should order in."

"It's not necessary," he says.

We make our way to the hotel restaurant and take our seats. I see the guy from the gym, and he waves. I giggle and wave back. Jiro watches the interaction and gives him a murderous scowl.

"What?" I ask.

"Who the fuck is that?" he growls.

"A guy I met at the gym. Why?"

Jiro rubs his hand over his face. "Do you want him to die?"

"What?" I ask like he has lost his mind.

Mia whispers, "Shit."

His jaw muscle twitches, and he takes off his black hoodie. Everyone stops and stares at his unique ink. It screams Japanese yakuza.

He rubs his hair, and his muscles move under his white T-shirt. He turns and stares at the guy with a sneer, and the guy quickly gets up and leaves.

"You didn't have to do that, Jiro," I scold him, rolling my eyes.

Jiro gives me a satisfied smirk and says, "He's a pussy and ran off the second shit got thick."

Mia raises her eyebrows, pursing her lips. "Wow, you are intense."

After Jiro calms down, we place our order and discuss the plan for the day now that he is sure that it's safe to speak in front of Mia.

He takes a bite of his toast and says, "I have what you asked for. I also suggest we go and get you a place. You cannot be in a hotel because I can't have security here and not draw attention. Especially after the second meeting with the others."

"Okay. I will go with Mia, and we can look at places that are move-in ready."

"Good, I'm coming along. I need to know where you will stay anyway. I need to make sure it's safe."

"Fine," I say. He does need to know, and it will be good for him to come along. I want to feel him out. Every time the conversation about us comes up, he tenses and avoids talking about it. Jiro calls someone and they send him a list. We finish eating and head off in my car to look at places.

He decides to drive, so he hands me his phone. I see his screen saver and my heart races. I'm confused but surprised at the same time. It's a picture of me lying on the table with my tattoo finished and... I'm practically naked. I'm wondering when he took the picture without me noticing. I glance at him and he gives me a knowing smile. Little fucker, he knows how to get under my skin.

"What's the password to unlock the phone?" I ask.

"It's your birthday."

I smile inwardly, but I know his business comes first, and it will always come first. I look up the addresses, and we head to the first one. It's in an expensive part of the city by Lenora Street. We walk up, and I immediately fall in love with the building. It's secure and modern, with clean lines. The receptionist shows us the two-bedroom apartment, and I fall in love with the space.

"I'll take it," I tell her and the lady smiles. "When can I move in?" I ask.

"The apartment is ready, so whenever we receive the funds, the same day," she says.

"I can have the money wired into an account in fifteen minutes," Jiro says behind me before I can answer.

"Okay, perfect," she says.

Jiro makes a couple of calls, and when he ends the last one, I blurt, "Please, let me pay for the apartment."

He shakes his head with a look of horror playing across his features. "Not happening. I'm supposed to take care of you, remember? And I'm paying the entire year."

Mia smiles and walks over to the white granite kitchen counter, smoothing her hand over the surface. "The apartment is gorgeous, and it has everything you need."

I know she's changing the subject, so I will drop the payment issue. I will not be a pain in the ass and make this difficult. I sign the papers and grab the keys from the receptionist before we leave the building. I need some furniture but no big deal. I can order it online and they can deliver it.

We drop Mia off at the hotel so she can pick up her car. I collect my things and check out of my room. Jiro follows me back to the apartment in his Chiron Noire and we sit on the living floor with the files he brought over and I give him a rundown of everything. I've been trying to analyze and piece everything together.

"They have been stealing here, too." I point at a line item in the second file. "The amount ordered doesn't match here, and there are inconsistencies with the shipment's weight versus the rate." He nods in understanding, and we continue going over the files.

After three hours, I yawn and lean back against the wall with my knees drawn together. "I am exhausted, and I need some sleep," I tell him.

He helps me up and grabs my keys. "Let's go."

"Where?"

"To my place. You have no furniture. You can sleep at my house. I'm driving you to the meeting anyway. Get some clothes and come with me." My eyes meet his gaze, and I don't argue. I'm so tired, I can't think straight.

We make it to his place, and this apartment differs completely from the one he has in Japan. It has all-white chrome with a simplistic design. It is cold and sterile. This apartment reminds me of when he is cold and distant. I hate it. But I wash up and fall asleep in his arms.

SELENA

The next morning, I wake up to an empty bed. My phone vibrates on the nightstand with an incoming text.

Jiro: I left you breakfast. I will pick you up in an hour for our meeting with the Kings. All they know is that the new CEO of Elysium will be presented to them.

Selena: Okay.

I eat the simple breakfast of fruit and tea and make the bed. I dress in a knee-length silk kimono with red-bottom shoes and decide to wear my hair up with traditional chopsticks. I apply makeup and red lipstick and wait for Jiro. We didn't have sex last night and he made it a point not to. I guess it's because so much is at stake and today is the day that my secret is out.

It is the day that Relic and the Kings find out who I really am and what my place is in their world. This isn't about love. This is about my place. My legacy.

I hear the door open to his apartment and he stops, raking his eyes over me from the tips of my shoes, taking me in slowly until he meets my eyes.

"Ready?" he asks.

"Yeah."

He holds my hand as we walk to his car. He helps me inside and then we head to the Kings' building. I plug my phone in and play "Bad at Love" by Halsey to avoid conversation. I'm nervous. My hands are clammy, and I feel a wave of nausea. How will they react? How will Relic react? I shouldn't care what he thinks, but maybe I do.

When we arrive, I have butterflies in my stomach and I take a deep breath, trying to hide that I'm nervous. Jiro escorts me up the familiar elevator to the Kings' boardroom and I let out a slow breath.

The elevator dings and he tells me to wait outside the door of the boardroom, staying silent and compliant. I can't believe they will all find out that I'm the CEO of Elysium. My stomach drops when I realize that both Relic and Jiro will be in the same room.

The door suddenly opens, and I walk in to looks of confusion on all their faces. Deacon, Liam and five other men with similar tattoos are seated on the right. I have no idea who they are, but they all have the same crowns on their necks. They have tattoos on their arms and look younger than Relic, but not by much.

"What the fuck?" Relic says in shocked disbelief.

"No fucking way!" Liam bellows.

I glance over to see Deacon's reaction, but his eyes are closed, his hands in his hair.

"This is going to be good, *ese,*" one guy next to him says with a smirk. "Real good."

I narrow my eyes at them and put two and two together. They are Mexican cartel and related to the Kings. I read the files and analyzed the names. I can't put a face to each man seated, but I know they are all family or related in some way. Maybe even close friends like Jiro and me.

Jiro pulls out my chair, and I take a seat.

"It's true. I'm to take over Elysium. My grandfather is a *Tenaka* but is known by *Ito* to some. My grandfather and Jiro's father are old friends, business partners and allies. I found out a week before I left for Japan when Jiro came for me. Our families planned this and I'm sorry that I kept it from you all until now."

I turn to Deacon, and I know what he must be thinking. That I didn't tell Mia. "Mia already knows. I told her when I arrived and made her promise not to tell you three until today."

"Now the car and everything makes sense," Liam blurts.

I smile, and he winks, looking happy compared to Relic's angry expression. My eyes flick to Jiro, but he makes no move to leave my side.

"She has analyzed the shipments and manifests. She has found that the Bratva and Polish Mafia are stealing from the shipments, alternating every month. They're in it together and it's why we're short with the Kings in Hillside," Jiro explains as they all listen intently.

"Motherfuckers," Deacon blurts.

"The plan is to have a meeting and discuss it with them before we go to war. Less blood to spill," I add.

Relic laughs. "Really? Who the fuck said you can decide on what is best?"

Jiro tenses next to me and slams his hand on the table, getting his attention. "Get one thing straight, Relic. Don't you ever talk to her like that," he seethes.

Relic leans back in his chair. "We go way back, Jiro. We even trained together. We're boys, more like brothers. How is she going to show up looking like that and demand anything representing Elysium?"

"She can hold her own," Jiro snaps back. "She also has me."

Relic's eyes darken, and the gold that is usually there is nonexistent. Deacon and Liam watch the exchange with keen interest, along with the other five Kings.

Jiro removes something from inside his hoodie and I realize it's the Jade necklace with the symbol of the yakuza. My eyes widen as he delicately places it around my neck.

"You forgot this on my nightstand back home. Never take it off. The yakuza will always protect you," he says softly.

Liam places his hand over his mouth as if he is wiping something off his face. My eyes scan the others and Deacon is looking up at the ceiling while the others smirk.

Relic's eyes are slightly narrowed, and his hands are gripping the table so tight you can see the white on his scarred knuckles.

It's in that moment that I realize Jiro purposely wanted it to be known we slept together for whatever reason. He wanted Relic to know.

"All I ask is that when I'm taking care of business in Japan, you keep an eye out for Selena," he says.

"I'll keep her warm for you, Jiro," Relic says in a challenge and then glances at me. "Right, *preciosa*?"

"Damn, *ese*."

My eyes look at the guy that just spoke. He is good-looking with a bad-boy vibe. "My name is Leo, by the way." He gives me a wink. "These *vatos* next to me..." He points to each one and gives me their names. "This is Aiden, Mase, Colton, and Smiley. I'm Relic's cousin. Our fathers are brothers. If my cousin gives you shit, you tell me."

"And what the fuck are you gonna do about it, *pinchy cabrón*?"

"Make sure she is taken care of, *carnal*. You obviously have a problem with her leading and I know why," he says, giving me a knowing smile. He lowers his voice like Relic isn't listening. "He acts like a bully when he likes a girl."

I grin at him. I like him. He loves to pull Relic's chain and he must be dangerous because he isn't afraid of Relic. The men in this room are all killers, and I'm one of them.

Chapter Thirty-Nine

SELENA

"I know this is like a pissing contest, but I'm not here for that. Yes, I've known Jiro since I was five. He knows me. The old and now the new me. Jiro will always protect me." I look into Relic's eyes. "He knows about us, Relic."

"I knew it!" Smiley says, then holds his hands up. "Sorry."

Jiro remains silent as I continue. "I will honor my grandfather's wish. I was raised American, but I am part Japanese. Those are my roots. It's with me, inside me. Jiro showed me where I truly belong. I will not fail you all, and I'm sorry if this is hard to take in. Excuse me," I get up and walk out the door.

I'm furious at Relic and disappointed that he thinks I'm not good enough. He practically laughed in my face.

When I'm about to get in the elevator, Deacon steps out of the room. "Hey, come back."

He motions for me and Jiro to come back inside the boardroom, and I walk back inside with my arms folded across my chest. "What?"

Liam speaks first. "We're sorry we treated you like shit. It's hard to swallow, but we can trust you. Your plan is solid and a smart one. Keep your enemies closer and all that."

Leo points at Deacon. "Correction. You three treated her like shit." He points to the others. "We just met her."

"Keep at it, *ese*," Deacon says. "I'm going to go tell one of the girls you mess with that you want to make it official."

I almost burst out laughing at the look of pure horror that crosses Leo's face.

"Pfft. That is low, *ese*. I thought we were family, *carnal*."

Liam smiles and gets up to give me a brotherly hug. "I will protect you if he doesn't," he whispers. I smile and kiss him on the cheek.

Relic sits like a statue and says nothing, giving Jiro a murderous glare like he wants to strangle him, but Jiro leans on the wall watching Liam hug me. His face remains expressionless.

I pull back and turn to the rest. "I want all of us to air out any doubts we have about each other. You guys are all brothers and I think it best we get all the questions you have out now. So, ask away."

"I have a question about the elephant in the room. Are you and Jiro together?" Smiley asks, first looking at Relic and then at Jiro.

"No, we're not," Jiro answers. I stiffen at his quick remark and feel like he just slapped me. *Asshole*. Relic looks at me with curiosity, and I can see his hands on the table loosen their grip when Jiro continues. "She needs to be protected here. She is a target in Japan. There are people who want to get to me through her. They have realized she means more to me than some hostess in one of my yakuza clubs. Some know she is to take over Elysium and the protection I can offer is only so much when I am dealing with other business. I don't even trust my men with her. She was meant to run Elysium here anyway, and it's best if she has family she can trust. I can send one member to watch her. His name is Yan. But if they come for her with the Bratva, she will need more than Yan at her disposal."

They all nod in understanding. I don't know if I should feel angry or happy at what he just said to the Kings.

Relic speaks up finally. "She will have to follow my direction at all times, and she is not to be out alone. She shouldn't go anywhere alone until we settle this issue with the Bratva and the Polish. I don't think they will be too happy when they find out the new CEO of Elysium just fucked up their little operation. Especially when they see she's a woman." I hate the way he talks about me like I'm not right here.

Jiro turns to me. "Please listen to him, Selena. Don't go against them and rebel. Nothing can happen to you."

"Okay, but I am doing it for my grandfather and no one else," I snap. "I also have a duty to my family, and I will see it through."

I can see from the corner of my eyes that Relic is bothered by my last remark.

"Mia is aware of everything then?" Deacon asks.

"Yes, I told her everything, and she met Jiro when we looked for apartments yesterday. I found an apartment and just need furniture before I move in."

"So, where did you sleep last night?" Relic asks.

"She was with me," Jiro replies.

Colton claps his hands together. "This shit just got good, *ese*. It's like watching a telenovela. I can't wait until Linda, Khalani, and Lucy hear about this."

"Shut up, Colton. I want to see how this goes down," Mase chimes in.

Liam smirks, leaning back in the chair. His finger points between Jiro and me. "So, you two are not together, but you sleep with each other?"

I roll my eyes. He would say that shit. He loves to stir the pot and enjoys riling his brothers up.

"No," I snap. "Let's get this straight. I'm not with anyone, and frankly, my sex life is not your concern. If I want to fuck someone, I will. And it's not your business to interfere. I don't interfere in your fuckfests you have going on at your club." I glance at Relic, but he looks away. "Except you, Deacon. If it's not Mia and she is not okay with it, I will kick your ass."

Leo raises his hand like this is a classroom. "So that means you are free to have sex?" he asks with a smile.

Relic pins him with a stare and points at him. "Go anywhere near her with your dick and I'll chop it off and your little sexcapades will be over."

Leo tilts his head back and laughs. "Not if she agrees. Good luck, *primo*. You have finally met your match. Now I know why you didn't marry that snobby little bitch Sophia."

"Enough!" Relic bellows.

The Hillside Kings all get up and Aiden says, "We are heading out. If you need us to kill, you know where to find us." He turns to look at me. "You're perfect. Don't let this *pinchy vato* tell you otherwise. He just has his head up his ass."

"Thank you," I say.

He is the quieter one but honest. I appreciate his honesty. It means a lot to me right now. I avert my gaze and find a spot on the desk to avoid looking over at Jiro. I'm hurt by the way he dismissed me when asked about us, but deep down, I knew it when he wouldn't acknowledge that what we shared meant more. And now I know why he held back and didn't make love to me last night. He put me back in the friend zone. He hurt me by not telling me his feelings, but that is the way Jiro is. He hides his feelings. He only gives you beautiful pieces when the emotion is too much and words need to be said.

The Hillside Kings leave the room and I glance back at Relic before I leave too. "Don't you have a wedding to plan? You can still marry her, you know."

It is a jab because I don't want Jiro and him to have bad blood because of me. But it is also a reminder that he is supposed to be married. His eyes go cold and dark and Liam laughs along with Deacon.

"What is so funny?" I ask. What did I miss?

Liam speaks first, "He doesn't want to marry Sophia and as much as she is dying to marry Relic, he is planning to let her down really soon."

I frown in concentration. "Doesn't that complicate things with political interferences in the States with the shipments from Japan and Mexico?" I ask. "If you don't marry her, I mean."

He shakes his head. "Her father was caught fucking some young girl in one of our back rooms and it's all over the internet. He will likely get divorced and not be reelected," Deacon says.

For some reason, I think this had to be a setup from the Kings. I think the Kings are ruthless when they want to be.

"She is only around until her father loses his political position and then she will be kicked to the curb," Deacon continues. "She can probably keep fucking Relic if he wants or suck his cock."

I look at Relic and his eyes are like gold flames, probably looking for a reaction on my face, but I give him none. I will die before I show him or any man that another woman they take to bed bothers me. If a man truly wants you, he will die before he lets you go, and you will never have to wonder if you're enough. I have fallen in love with two powerful men like an idiot. I'm not good enough to keep either.

"Are we done?" I ask. "When is the meeting with the Bratva and Polish?"

"Day after tomorrow," Jiro says.

"Good, gives me time to get a bed at least." Jiro looks down with his hands in his pockets.

I turn to Liam, remembering I don't have my car. "Liam, can you take me home, please?"

"Of course, I would be honored," he says with laughter in his eyes.

"I have been dying to get in that GT-R."

"I love it when you talk dirty, Selena."

As I follow Liam, Jiro stops me by holding his hand on my elbow. I look over. "What?"

"I will send your stuff over to your apartment."

"No need. Save yourself the trouble. I can buy new things. Consider it a gift from me to your whores back in Japan."

Jiro stares into my cold eyes like I have kicked him in the balls. Good, he sees it. The hurt. The emptiness.

I hear Relic whisper to Jiro as Liam and I wait for the elevator. "Let it go, brother. She will come around."

When the elevator door opens, I hear Jiro respond. "No, brother. I hurt her. When she comes around, it will not be the Selena we thought we knew."

I get in the GT-R with Liam and look around so I can play music to keep my head from exploding. I am in a dark place. My emotions are everywhere.

Liam gives me the cord to plug in my phone and doesn't make any comments about what happened. I think he senses that I'm hurt and I'm trying to play it off.

He takes off, roaring down the street. He eats the road toward my apartment while I play Halsey. This car fits his personality. I have always thought of him as a loving brother who rescues me from the awkwardness around Relic. He would make any woman proud to have him by her side.

He gets me somehow, not getting into small talk, knowing I have this dark cloud raining down on me. I notice he knows the way to my apartment. I am sure Jiro gave the Kings all the information about where I live and where I will be working.

When I was back at the apartment, I called my parents and told them I had made it back to Seattle. They think I am just running the company for my grandfather, not knowing that it includes dealing with Mafia bosses and killing whoever crosses me or is a threat to Elysium. If my father knows, I know he is not telling my mother.

We arrive at my apartment. I jump out of his car after giving him a friendly kiss on the cheek, and he waits until I'm inside the building.

Once I am in my apartment, I almost jump out of my skin when I see an Asian man I recognize as a member of the yakuza. My hand is on my knife, ready to take him out.

He puts his hands up. "I apologize, Selena. My name is Yan. Jiro told me you knew they would send me here as your protection while he is away. I didn't mean to startle you."

I sigh in relief and regain my composure, watching him lower his hands. "Yes, he mentioned it, but not that you would be a creep in my apartment."

"I didn't mean to scare you."

"It's okay. You're just doing your job. I get it." I let a breath out between my lips. I nudge my head to the second bedroom. "You can have the spare room."

"Oh, no need. I am in the apartment across from this one. I was assessing your apartment and waiting for you. He told me you would be arriving, so I waited."

I study him and decide he's decent enough. Not too imposing, with soft Asian features, he has the traditional yakuza look down. He won't blend into a crowd, but if Jiro sent him, it's because this guy can fight. He is fit and looks agile.

"Okay. I just need to get furniture for this place. You don't have to drive me or anything, just tag along like we are the best of friends."

He smiles. "Whatever you wish, Miss Tenaka."

"I can order things from a furniture store online, but the bed I need to see in person for same-day delivery," I tell him, motioning for him to tag along.

We head out to the furniture store, and I pick the biggest, softest bed they have and pay extra to have it delivered the same day. I head to different stores and pick textiles for the apartment, and the last place we make it to is the grocery store. Yan looks exhausted from my shopping spree.

He stands quietly and waits until the delivery guys leave the apartment after setting up my bed. "I have something Jiro had made specifically for you. It's sitting on the counter," he says in Japanese. I walk over to the counter, curious to know what's in the big black box.

Yan opens the box, and it's a katana sword, along with smaller knives in a holster. "He says you can train in the Kings' gym. He had it made for you, but be careful. It can slice a man in half."

I turn the sword and admire the craftsmanship. It's beautiful. I turn to face Yan. "Please tell him thank you. It's beautiful."

"If I may be so bold, you could call him. I'm sure he will be pleased to hear it from you."

"I don't wish to speak to Jiro unless it's about a business matter. You can tell him thank you for the weapon that will most likely take the lives of those who wish death upon me."

Yan was most likely not expecting my reaction or the fact that I was not interested in calling Jiro. He walks toward the front door and bows before he leaves. When the front door closes, I place the sword back on its holder and I break. Trails of uncontrollable tears I have been holding all day flow down my face.

I tried to stay busy with settling into the apartment to forget about the pain of loving and not being loved in return. It feels like I'm cursed. Broken. Men that leave me their gifts of torment. I have tried to love and then love again, unrequited. Unrequited love seems to be the only love that will ever last.

SELENA

On the day of the meeting with the Bratva and Polish Mob bosses, I'm nervous but also dying to see the faces of those pieces of shit when they realize I have found them out.

I hate thieves, and that they are in it together is the worst part. I decide to wear over-the-knee boots so I can strap the knives with the attached holster to conceal them. The stockings underneath the boots will allow the knives to slide out smoothly. I wear a loose kimono-style top tied tight around my waist, covering my butt.

I'm not going to the meeting like I am presenting a PowerPoint. It's possible things could get messy, and to be honest, I'm itching to get this over with and eliminate the threat.

Jiro was right. Once you take the first life, it gets easier when you know it is coming. I think my time has come to accept it. I text Yan that I'm ready, and he comes to my apartment door, holding it open so we can go to a discreet warehouse in the city.

We head to my car and hop in. He enters the directions that the Kings sent him in the GPS, and we drive in that direction.

After a while, we arrive at the warehouse based on the GPS. It looks old and abandoned, but looks can be deceiving. This must be where the Kings do their dirty business. We get out of the car, and Yan leads the way inside the warehouse that smells like gunpowder and death.

I see another door that leads to a meeting table. All three Kings are seated at the table, along with two other men. One is a big Russian man with an angry scar running down his cheek. His eyes tell me he's a cold-blooded killer. The other man, with brown eyes and puffy cheeks, must be the Polish Mob boss. He gives me the creeps.

I wonder how they are in business to steal together. The Polish Mob and the Russian Bratva are rivals, so something doesn't smell right. These guys don't look like bosses. They look like guys that were sent by the bosses. They are too smart to be alone in a room with the yakuza and the Kings.

I figure the Kings want to send a message either way. I see Jiro standing to the right by the door as I enter. Relic's eyes turn gold like honey when I walk through the door, watching me carefully. The Polish guy leers and runs his tongue along his lips and it is the exact reaction I was expecting from the disgusting creep. He gives a vibe that he rapes young women for fun.

"So, this is the one who is going to run Elysium from Japan?" the Russian says in a heavy accent. "She looks good enough to ride my cock with those pretty blue eyes."

Jiro gives him a murderous glare.

Relic narrows his eyes. "That won't be necessary. She has information on you both that you might find interesting to hear," he says in an icy tone.

The Russian fixes his gaze in my direction, dying to know what I could have that would be interesting. I sit down with my hands under the table, making sure my knife is within reach.

Deacon waves his hand and says, "Selena, this is Nikolai. He was sent by Dimitri, the head of the Bratva. And this is Joseph Wisnewski. He is the third in command for the Polish Mob and runs Chicago."

I study them, not saying a word until it is required, but I smile, masking the monster that will soon come to the surface. I pull out the manifest that shows all the discrepancies from the last six months and slide it across the table. Copies, of course.

The Russian takes the file and opens it as I speak. "Gentlemen, you have forty-eight hours to return the money you have been stealing from the last shipments. We all know you have been alternating and taking cuts to avoid being caught." They both look at the files, then at each other before their gazes land back on mine.

"So, what do you think I am going to do?" Nikolai asks. "Just give you the money because you come here with this paper and a face that I want to put my cock in after I fuck that cunt you must have under that little kimono?"

The word cunt gets my blood boiling; it's a word I detest, especially coming from this sick Russian fuck that needs to be put out of his misery. I'm not the only one that feels that way. The Kings look like they want to throttle the Russian.

Joseph laughs. "I will take my turn after you're done, Nikolai. I would love to hear her scream."

Relic and Liam keep straight faces, but their eyes are like dark skies. Deacon's expression is like a storm of thunderous clouds rolling in, like he wants to just kill them and get it over with. I know Jiro is biding his time by keeping silent.

But I have to take control, or this will get messier than I thought. They will never see it coming if I act now. I smile at the Russian. He obviously thinks with his cock and not his head.

Since he is the bigger of the two, I take my chances with him first. I shift and let my top open slightly, revealing my bra, and the Russian's eyes fill with lust. You can almost hear his disgusting thoughts.

The Russian smiles. "You want to ride my cock, don't you, my little Mulan? It's funny because you don't look Asian. But I like to mix my food too."

This asshole. I rise from my seat and saunter behind him, smiling. Over his shoulder, I see his cock is hard in his black slacks. I smile coyly in front of the other men and rub my hand over his shoulder. His head is facing forward and he is staring in the others' direction.

The expression on the Kings' and Jiro's faces look uncomfortable watching the show. Joseph is salivating and rubbing his cock, sitting next to him, making bile hit the back of my throat.

"You want me to ride that Russian cock in front of everyone, don't you?" I purr. "Take it out."

The Russian rubs himself. I sneak one last look at Relic and Jiro, their eyes blinking in disbelief, not believing that I am going to sit on the disgusting Russian's cock. I smile, discreetly keeping my other hand near the knife in my boot.

They all watch the Russian as he unbuckles his pants to take out his nasty dick, and that's my cue. I grab the knife and swipe it along his throat from ear to ear. Blood, the color of crimson, pours down his neck while he chokes on his own blood.

The men are up with guns drawn, but I am not done with the Russian because all I see is red. I grab his hair and pull his head back, opening the wound while he tries to cover his neck with both hands. Taking my knife, I stab his eyes over and over, blood squirting everywhere like a broken faucet.

"I hate that word. The word cunt disgusts me. It's a word for whores," I snarl at the already dead Russian. I glance over at Joseph and see the guys all have their guns aimed at his head. Joseph decides it's best to lower the gun he has trained on me.

"Tell your boss and that dirty fuck Dimitri that they have forty-eight hours to return the money to Elysium, or I will maim every last one of the fucks he sends my way before I cut out their insides."

Joseph repeatedly nods with pure fear and understanding. He knows I'm not fucking around. "We will have your money, but I am not sure about retaliation."

"You tell them if they come for her, there will be hell to pay and not only from the yakuza and the Kings," Relic barks. "You will have pissed off the entire cartel because we will let all cartels know the Polish Mob and the Russian Bratva have been sticking their dirty hands in the cookie jar. Remember that, you stupid fuck. You're lucky I don't cut your fucking balls off right here and now."

Jiro gets the rat off the chair and pushes him outside. I can hear the blows of his fist connecting with his face. The Kings lower their weapons and watch me with a worried expression, as if trying to wrap their minds around seeing me slit a man's throat with a sardonic smile on my face.

"Please don't tell Mia what you just saw. I couldn't bear it if she was afraid of me," I plead.

"Don't worry, Selena," Deacon says in a soft tone. "She loves you like a sister and you will always be her family. She will always see you as the Selena she holds dear to her heart."

I look down at my bloody hands. "Is there a bathroom so I can clean up?"

"I'll clean up the mess with the Russian," Liam says, walking out to get what he needs.

Relic walks over to me and says softly, "I will take you somewhere so you can clean up. Yan will stay here and assist Jiro. I will have someone pick up your car. You will ride with me."

I am in no position to argue, and I follow him to a matte-black Maclaren. He opens the door, and for a split second, I hesitate, not wanting to ruin the beautiful interior. I look away and take off my top. From the corner of my eye, I see him removing his dress shirt, revealing his hard muscles underneath a white tank top.

My stomach flutters when he hands me the shirt so I can put it on over my bra. The smell of him that I had yearned for on so many nights hits me. I breathe in his male scent mixed with his exotic cologne while he waits for me to get in the car.

He closes the door, and I keep my hands crossed in front of my stomach, not wanting to ruin the interior, and stare straight ahead. I feel his gaze on me, and luckily the shirt is more like a minidress. I peek in his direction because he is not putting the car in motion. He just stares at my thighs and it feels like he is starting a fire on my skin.

"What?"

"I like you wearing my shirt."

"Yeah, I'm sure you tell all the ladies the same thing."

"Funny, thinking about it, you're the first."

"Well, I am wearing it because I don't want to ruin your precious car. Not because of anything else."

He gives me a grin. "I really don't care about the car. I didn't think you wanted that asshole's blood on you longer than it had to be. I also didn't want you to spoil your new car. I am sure you paid good money for it."

"I wouldn't know. Jiro paid for it."

His hands tighten on the steering wheel, and he presses the gas. We remain silent the rest of the way. After a few minutes, I realize we are not heading toward my apartment but to his house. I don't want to be at his house. It brings memories of our night together.

"I am having a party later tonight. Mia will be there. Let's get you cleaned up and go shopping for some clothes to clear your mind."

I don't want to argue. I just want the blood off my body, and I really miss being normal right now. If Mia is coming, I want to be there. I want to hang out with her.

The sun is setting when he pulls through the huge gates of his house and parks. I get out of the car and we enter the modern house. He guides me by the elbow to his bedroom and closes the door.

He goes to his bathroom and turns on the shower. I stand at the threshold, and he turns around. "I figured this would be more appropriate to get clean. The other bathrooms in the house have tubs and I don't want to scare my housekeeper away," he says.

The memory of the morning when I made the walk of shame hits me in the gut. "Makes sense."

I walk farther into the bathroom and remove my clothes in front of him because I don't care if he sees me. Instead of leaving, he just stands there, arms crossed over the tank top that hugs his beautiful chest.

I can still remember how it felt underneath my fingers and I'm confused about where my thoughts run to. I move to stand under the spray of hot water, getting used to the temperature before removing the stench of metal and death from my skin. I free my hair from the confines of the hair sticks, place them on the shelf, and rinse my hair with his shampoo, remembering the smell of it when he was eating me out the last time I was in his room.

Through the steam clouding the shower, I can see him removing his clothes. I should ask him what he is doing, but I don't.

My eyes fixate on his cock when it springs free from the confines of his boxers. I rub soap all over my body, remove all the blood and rinse my hair one last time with my back turned. I can hear the small steps he takes when he walks in the shower.

My skin feels hot, and if I step back, I know I will run into his chest. He washes himself, and I turn around to see the soap running down the grooves of every dip and curve of the muscles on his body.

I rest my back against the cool marble tiles, needing relief from the heat in my body, needing to quench the numbness inside. He angles his head to the side as his eyes follow my hand down my belly to the folds of my pussy. His cock goes rock hard as I put my fingers inside and rub myself.

A moan escapes my lips as I finger myself faster, rubbing my clit in circles. Relic moves closer, taking a deep breath, looking down at the pleasure I'm giving myself. This isn't for him. This is for me.

He grabs my breast and pinches my nipple and my pussy leaks on my fingers. When he tries to touch my pussy, I slap his hand away, denying him. His eyes go dark when I deny him. I don't think Relic King has ever had a woman deny him anything.

"You are driving me crazy, Selena."

I respond by trailing my right hand down his wet body until I grab his cock. It grows harder in my hand. I stroke his cock while he watches my fingers inside my pussy. He raises my chin with a single finger so he can ravage my mouth and I let him taste me.

This isn't about him.

This isn't about Jiro.

This isn't about love.

This is about control.

He fucks my mouth with his tongue as I fist his cock, stroking him to an orgasm. We come at the same time, and his grunts mix with my moans in the shower. When I am done fisting his cock, I slide my fingers inside my mouth to taste him and I cannot lie. He tastes delicious.

If I want to be honest with myself, everything about Relic King is delicious.

I just can't let him know that.

Chapter Forty-Three

SELENA

After the shower, he hands me a black T-shirt, sweats and a pair of slides that are huge on my frame. I can't complain and I have found that I secretly love to wear his clothes.

He gets dressed in a white V-neck and sweats, wearing a pair of slides too. He is probably doing it so I don't look weird shopping in a designer store with men's clothes on. We walk through the house, and I see the same gray-haired housekeeper named Elanor, and she gives me a warm smile.

"I knew you would be back. I had a feeling about you."

"Oh no, it's not... like that," I say, shaking my head.

"I may be old, but I'm not deaf and he never has had a woman sleep in his room before. *Eres especial.*"

I raise my brows, surprised to hear that revelation. Relic King makes his girls sleep in a guest bedroom and never in his bed. So, I am the only one to have ever slept in his bed. Not even Sophia? That is interesting. I wonder what else Relic is hiding underneath his cool facade.

"That's enough," he says, looking at her pointedly.

She brushes him off with a wave of dismissal. "*Andele,* go along you two. I have a lot to do before I leave with the party and all."

"It was nice seeing you again."

I don't even feel embarrassed she heard us. Relic leads me to the garage, and I scan the impressive collection of vehicles. All are black, except one that is red. Odd. He doesn't look like a red car kind of guy.

He walks to a lockbox and opens it to reveal all the keys to the cars. He selects one and turns to me. "This one is for you. It was the surprise I had for you that day in my office. The day that..." he trails off.

The day he threw me out and said we were only a fuck. Yeah, I remember. I look down at the key in his hand, confused. "You bought me a car. And you had it this entire time?"

His eyes meet mine. "Yes."

I can't believe he bought me a car and has kept it in his garage. "I don't know what to say. I shouldn't accept it. I already have a car. I really appreciate--"

"Please, I will not get rid of it. I bought it for you because I couldn't stand you not having a car."

I walk toward the red convertible. Is he serious? Normal people would buy someone a used car or a Toyota, but a Rolls Royce Dawn? It is beautiful and classy. Any girl would die if a man like Relic King bought them such an extravagant gift. The only problem is that the old Selena would have swooned. The new Selena isn't so easily swayed.

I walk around it, secretly admiring its beauty. The car is badass. It has black leather seats with the logo in red stitching and black rims. There is a license plate in the front, and it reads *From a King*. I continue to walk around the car and stop when I see the back plate reads *SHES HIS*.

I look up and his eyes are dancing with laughter. My mouth curves into a smile. "So, you expect me to drive this thing, letting the entire city know?"

"That was kind of the idea."

"I'll accept it, but let's get one thing straight. I'm not yours."

"Fair enough. I have time."

"Time for what?

"To change your mind."

I snort. "You're out of your mind."

With a devilish grin that tugs at my heart, he opens the car door so I can get in the driver's seat. I slide onto the soft leather, and he walks around to get in on the passenger side. He shows me all the car's features and laughs when I jump at the sound of the garage door opening.

He points to the buttons. "This one is to the front gate of my house in case you need to come here. If there is anything you need or if you're in danger, you can come to my house, Selena."

"Okay. Thank you, Relic," I whisper.

His eyes caress my face, and he lowers his voice. "I love it when you say my name like that."

I give him a playful smirk. "Yeah, don't get used to it, playboy."

I back out of the garage and the wind blows through my hair, drying the wet strands as I drive with the top down. I feel free and exhilarated, like nothing matters. From time to time, I can feel Relic's gaze caressing my face, but I won't give in to him. I learned that lesson hard and fast. If you let your guard down, he will break you. I have the sharp edges of the pieces from when he did it to me.

Chapter Forty-Four

SELENA

We arrive at a designer boutique that sells swimwear and head inside. Relic sits down on a couch toward the back and watches me shop. I have two bathing suits in my hand, but I can't seem to choose which one I want. It's not like I don't have the money to buy both, but I remember when I was dead broke and had to watch how much I would spend.

His parties are basically where women go skinny dipping, so I select the turquoise suit—which is a thong and the tiniest matching bikini top—and a see-through minidress cover-up with cutouts. I feel naughty tonight and want to feel comfortable in my skin.

I return the white minidress with an open back to the rack and place the fifteen-hundred-dollar sandals back, selecting the pointed, clear wedge sandals. As I pick out three other outfits for everyday loungewear, I glance at the blonde behind the counter. She hasn't once asked me if I need help.

Maybe it's because of how I'm dressed, but I notice she keeps staring at Relic on the sofa. I'm picking out lingerie on the other side of the store when she feels brave enough to walk up to him.

"Can I help you?" I hear her say.

"Yeah, you can. You see that woman shopping over there?"

"Yes," she says coyly.

"I want to buy everything she has touched in the store in her size, and if you don't have it in her size, order it. You better get to it because you have about twenty minutes."

I turn around to see the blonde open and close her mouth.

He gets up and glares at her. "Hurry and stop staring at me. My girl has been in this store the whole time and you haven't even asked if she needs help."

I walk over and he places a hand on my lower back, guiding me to the register. "What are you doing?" I whisper.

I watch the girl zipping around, boxing and packaging everything I touched in the store. She is red and sweaty, looking everywhere but at me. "I'm sorry about that, um... the total is one hundred fifteen thousand dollars and twenty-two cents."

I attempt to pass her my black card and Relic snatches it out of my hand. "Taking you shopping, *preciosa*." The girl stands there slack-jawed when he slides the card over to me and opens his wallet. He pulls out his own and hands it to her. "I think she gets the point now to stop staring at me," he says with a wink.

Cocky bastard. But I like it. It's why I fell for him.

"Fine, but don't get accustomed to it. I can pay, you know."

He chuckles. "Not with me, *mi reina*." He addresses the blonde. "Help us put the bags in her car, would you?"

She stammers, "Y-y-yes, Mr. King."

We exit the store, and he opens the trunk. The salesclerk brings the packages and places them inside.

When I slam the trunk closed, I turn toward her, handing her a one-hundred-dollar bill. "Never judge a book by its cover. It might turn out to be a good book," I tell her.

She looks away, embarrassed, and hustles back to the store.

We get in the car and Relic drives us to a small restaurant on the outskirts of the city. Even though it is a small venue, there are many people dining. He parks and we walk inside and up to the hostess. I'm not dressed for the occasion, but she doesn't seem to care.

"Good afternoon, Mr. King. Your table is ready, right this way."

They must think I am the flavor of the month, but it doesn't bother me. *Liar, you know it bothers you.* My thoughts get the best of me sometimes, confusing the shit out of me.

The table is in a far corner of the restaurant. Twinkling lights and sheer white curtains on the windows give it an airy, romantic feeling and I'm in love with it. It's like a different world from earlier this morning. Like traveling through a different time, and this morning was just a bad nightmare.

We sit, and the waitress comes to the table. She's an older lady with kind eyes.

"*Como estás*, Mr. King. May I get you the usual.?"

"*Si.*"

She turns to me. "What would you like, sweetheart?"

I give her a warm smile. "Water would be great, and a steak salad, please."

"Coming right up. And by the way, you have the most beautiful eyes."

I blush. "Thank you, very kind of you to say."

Relic stares at me and when she leaves, he says, "You have a beautiful smile, Selena." He leans forward, placing his forearms on the table. "Especially when that smile is for me."

"Then don't piss me off, and maybe I'll reward you with one from time to time," I tease.

His eyes light on fire, but the moment is broken by the interruption of our food and drinks.

He changes the subject, and I don't know if I'm happy about it or sad. "So Yan will meet you at the party and you can go home afterward."

"Okay." I am relieved he has my back so I can fulfill my newfound role and make my grandfather proud. I most likely have a target on my head after what I did to the Russian, but I don't give a care at this point. I realize the protection from Jiro and the Kings serves one purpose, to follow the tradition from my founding fathers and keep the money and shipments flowing and alliances protected. The criminal empire will never cease to exist. It will be passed down or taken over in a never-ending cycle. It's the same with countries. Power is passed down, or it's taken over, but it will never stop.

"What are you thinking about?"

"Nothing, just things I need to get for the apartment," I lie.

"Hmm." He can tell I am not being honest, but he lets it go.

"Thank you for taking me shopping and helping me forget about earlier."

He gives me a knowing grin and says, "I have to take my girl out."

"Who said I was your girl?" I challenge.

He raises his eyebrow and rubs his hand over his stubble.

"I like it."

He frowns in confusion. "What?"

"Your stubble. I like it."

His eyes glitter at the compliment. "I will leave it then."

SELENA

We leave the restaurant and head back to the house so we can get ready for the party Relic has planned for tonight. I pick one of the many guest rooms in his house to get ready because I refuse to be in his room while I get dressed. It makes me feel like we are together, and we most definitely aren't. It confuses my role and I need control over my emotions.

Mia shows up with a knock on the door, and I let her in.

"Whatcha doing, bitch? Heard you went shopping with King himself. I bet he bought you everything in that store."

"I tried to pay and he wouldn't let me." I sigh.

"Well, what did you buy and what are you going to wear?"

I smile mischievously when I pull out the turquoise thong bikini, see-through minidress, and clear wedges.

Her eyes light up. "They're beautiful!"

"Thank you. Let's get ready."

When we are both dressed, I look at her, all sexy in her shimmery silver thong and matching top. "Deacon is going to fuck you in the pool with that on. You know that, right?"

She smiles. "Funny, I would let him."

I laugh. "Would be kind of hot."

"So, what do you think Relic is going to do when he sees you in that thong walking around his house?"

The light goes out of my eyes for a second. "Watch me walk around in it. I have been burned by that match before, not interested."

"Damn, it's that bad, huh? Is it because of Jiro?"

"Jiro and I are just childhood friends. He has made that clear to the others. We had sex, that's it."

"Ouch! It's weird though. He doesn't look at you like that. It's the same look Relic has when you walk into a room. Like you are the only thing that matters. Like they can't breathe if they don't get your attention."

"Nope, it's just their obligation toward me because of Elysium. When I was Selena, the business analyst taking Ubers and saving for a car, I was a poor nobody and just a good time to Relic. And to Jiro, a childhood friend he didn't have time to call."

"It makes sense you would feel that way."

"Did you know he bought me a car before I left?"

Her eyes go wide. "Really? He never mentioned anything."

"He gave it to me today."

Her eyes light up. "See, now that's where Relic King is a confusing man. What did he buy you?"

"A red Rolls Royce Dawn convertible."

"He knows your favorite color is red. It means he is just as interested in you as Jiro."

I take out a few items from my bag. "I guess."

After applying some perfume and lip gloss, I let my hair down, not confining it tonight. We leave the room and head to the party. I can hear the music from the patio playing "Ap" by Pop Smoke and the smell of marijuana is in the air.

People are arriving in droves, dancing and drinking. Like the last time, there are girls in the pool with almost nothing on. Everyone is looking at us curiously as we walk toward the jacuzzi the Kings love to hang out in. I see Relic and Liam with girls in the jacuzzi. Deacon is waiting for Mia to join him, sitting on the edge with just his legs inside. I don't follow Mia and take a detour to a table with liquor bottles and empty cups. I pour myself a Malibu drink with pineapple while I watch Mia smile at something Deacon said.

Liam waves at me from the jacuzzi, and I wave back and give him a smile. He motions for me to come over, but I lift my cup and show him I'm drinking. Anything to avoid going over there. He puts his hands up in an exasperated gesture that grabs Relic's attention.

When Relic spots me, I spin around to avoid his gaze. I spot Yan and motion for him to come over to me. He is wearing a white T-shirt, showing his yakuza tattoos, and swim trunks.

When he is in earshot, I tease him and say, "Please don't bow in front of these people. They will eat that shit up."

He smiles. "Yeah, yeah. I get it. America is a little different from Japan, but it's fun and crazy as hell." Yan leans close and says, "Are you trying to give people a heart attack, Selena?"

I look at him in confusion. "No. Why?"

"If you don't mind me saying so, the men cannot stop staring at you. If Jiro were here, I don't know what would happen, but none of it would be good."

"He is not here, so it really doesn't matter." His expression tells me he didn't like my answer, but I don't care.

Mia joins us and pours a shot, offering me one. We drink one together. "Why don't you want to go over there and hang out with the Kings?" she asks.

"It's a little too crowded for me, Mia. You know the girls will look at me as a threat to their claim to His Highness. I'm trying to have a good time."

She laughs with Yan at my comment. "How about we tell the guy that is in charge of the music over there to play a crazy bad bitch song, and we can dance? Yan will stay and watch our backs."

I nod and we make our way up to the DJ and tell him to play Doja Cat. He does, and we dance, swaying our hips seductively. Two guys enjoying the show come up behind me, and I watch Yan run his hands through his hair, not sure about the whole thing.

Relic storms out of the jacuzzi, all wet and dripping like a god thundering his way over to us. "Yo, Mia. Deacon wants you!" he says in a hard tone.

"O-okay," she stammers when she sees his murderous expression.

Relic gets in my face. "You think your little show is funny? Shaking your ass in a thong in front of everyone, just begging to get fucked." He leans close and his teeth are clenched. Get out of my house!" He yells in my face.

It feels like he hit me and I take a step back. I can't believe he is throwing me out of his house in front of everyone. I look him in the eye as I walk back up to him, arching my neck because he is still tall, even in my wedge heels.

"Gladly. I will never set foot in your house again. I can promise you that. And just so we are clear, don't come near me. I'd prefer to die than have you save me," I say sarcastically, walking away with a stone-cold glare, the rage inside of me dying to surface.

"Relic, what the fuck!" Liam shouts.

Mia runs to catch up with me. "Selena, wait!"

I keep walking, fueled by my own anger, and go straight to the guest room. I gather my things.

Yan enters quietly with an apologetic expression, and I hand him all my stuff.

"Did you come in my car?" I ask.

"Yes, Jiro told me to pick you up in your car."

"Good, thank you. Can you drive me somewhere to get something to drink and eat? I'm not in the right state to drive, Yan."

"Yes, of course."

I throw on leggings and a loose crop top, and some Vans. Mia barges in the guest bedroom with tears in her eyes and I stop in front of her. "Look at me," I tell her. Her eyes meet mine. "You stay here with Deacon. I will be fine. I'm not alone. Okay?"

She looks sad and I know she feels bad for me. "Selena, I am sorry. He is such an ass sometimes. I don't know why he did that in front of everyone."

"Don't worry about it, Mia. Please do me a favor." I pull out the key to the Rolls. "Give this to Relic. Tell him I will send him the money he spent today and that I want nothing from him, ever."

She nods, taking the key from my hand. "Okay, will you call me later so I can make sure you're okay?"

I smile and give her a hug. "Of course. Go be with Deacon. He loves you."

"He wasn't even mad. Relic was just being a jerk."

"Exactly. He is not stupid and acts like a deranged asshole."

I walk through the hallway and slam right into Liam. "Selena, I have been looking for you. Are you okay? My brother is an asshole." He looks into my eyes. "You don't have to go."

I look into his worried expression. "It's okay, Liam. I'll be fine. I just want to get out of here. I don't want to see your brother. If he is there, I won't be. And if I am there, I'll leave."

Chapter Forty-Six

SELENA

Yan drove me to an old diner. I don't know how he found it, but he did. He's so nice and respectful. I am grateful for the neutral company.

He looks at me with a concerned expression as we sit at the table. "I know it's none of my business, but are you okay? You did the right thing to leave. I think you're very brave and a special person and he doesn't deserve you. He doesn't realize his jealousy made him act carelessly. I also noticed that he has lost you."

I lift my eyes from sipping the hot coffee. "I don't think he ever had me, not the real me anyway. I was just vulnerable because I didn't know who I was or where I belonged. I will always love and respect *Jirosan* for that. He showed me who I was and where I belonged. He gave me balance."

"From the outside looking in, you have two men that will do anything for you. I know their actions don't make sense, but it's because you make them feel alive and they will protect what they care about the most. And that is you, Selena."

I scoff. "Yeah? So, what the heck was that back there? You don't throw the person you care the most about out of your house, in the middle of a party with your family and friends, like they're trash."

He sighs. "Yeah, that was not good, was it?"

"I will never forget it. The look on everyone's face. The girls that were fawning all over him, enjoying the moment."

I continue to eat and my phone dings.

Mia: I know you told me that you would call me when you made it home safe. I gave him the keys and the message. He was silent and didn't say a word after you left. He doesn't want to talk to anyone. He just keeps drinking. I have never seen him drink like this before and I am worried. Liam and Deacon are staying with him to make sure he doesn't do anything stupid. He punched the guys in the face that were dancing behind you. Selena, he's out of control.

Selena: He's a big boy and can handle himself. He has plenty of people who care about him. I need to stay away from him. It's for the best.

Yan is staring at me intently.

"It's Mia. Here, look." I show him the text message thread.

He reads the text message and shakes his head. "See, I told you." Suddenly, his smile falters when two large men walk into the diner.

They look Polish, and the hair on the back of my neck stands, sensing danger. Yan glances at me and I pull out cash to leave on the table. We both get up, heading to the back exit.

We reach the Urus and hop in, and the men hurry out of the diner. I pull away and look through the rearview mirror. Fuck, they're following us in a black Ford Raptor. They must have been watching me, waiting until I was without the Kings.

I press on the gas while Yan is loading the two guns from the glove compartment. He hands me my knives and I keep them in my lap to have better access. He hands me a pistol and leans out the window, firing his gun.

The gunshots echo in the cabin and I look through the mirror, watching as the Raptor swerves and speeds up, gaining on me. They must have a modified engine because it shockingly keeps up with the Urus. I duck but keep my eyes on the road when I hear the bullets ding the car when they return fire. A bullet breaks my back window, shards of glass flying everywhere. I duck my head farther and take a sharp turn, trying to lose them while Yan gets on his phone and texts someone.

"I am texting the Kings and Jiro on a group chat, sending them our location."

"Okay, can you see them behind us?"

I floor the car, but this side of the road is dark. I honestly don't know where the fuck I'm going, but I keep driving. Just when I think I've lost them, the truck comes and sideswipes the Urus.

The car swerves and I let go of the gas and apply the brake the best I can. The Urus goes down a ravine, slamming into the bank, causing the airbags to deploy. I look over at Yan to see if he's okay.

"Are you all right, Selena?"

"Yeah, you?"

"Yeah."

We are both breathing heavily from all the adrenaline. I can hear voices and they're definitely Polish. Fucking bastards, they're getting closer.

I scan the car to see if there is a way out. The only way we can escape is through the rear passenger door. I would have to squeeze through the back and open the door slowly to clear an exit. I motion with my hand to Yan toward the rear passenger door. All I feel is numb, but my fight or flight kicks in and the only thing I can think of is to fight back.

I go out first with my knives in hand. The gun must have slid somewhere on the floor, but Yan has his pistol and we both make it out just when both men unload their guns on the car. The sound of bullets causes my ears to ring. They sent them to kill me, not to capture me. There is only one way out of this. It's either they kill us both, or I cut their heads off and send them back in a crate.

We make it past them and hide behind a tree as quietly as possible. One of them knows English but has a heavy accent as he singsongs, "Selena! Come out, and I promise I will fuck you before I kill you. We would love to make you scream."

Fucking bastards know my name. I'm going to fucking slaughter these sick fucks. I see one and nod to Yan and make a motion that I will go first, and he can shoot the second, but we have to move at the same time. "One... two... three... go." I run behind the one that called my name and stab him in the kidneys with one knife and the other in the neck. He goes down on his knees, and I slice his neck from ear to ear. I hear a gunshot, and I know Yan took the other one out.

I can hear the man trying to gasp for air, choking, slowly dying. I turn and look at him holding his neck, trying to keep the blood from seeping out, but to no avail.

"You thought you could find me and kill me? Guess what, motherfucker? The joke's on you. The only thing you're going to fuck is the animal that comes to feed on your beheaded corpse." I grab the sharpest knife and cut his head clean off to finish the job.

Yan comes over, and his eyes go wide in shock at what I have done. I look at him with a blank expression, noticing the other man is dead from a gunshot wound to the head. I take my already bloody knife and cut his head off too. Yan looks worried at how calm and collected I am while putting the heads next to each other, their dead eyes looking upward.

"Who's coming?" I ask.

He checks his phone. "The Kings will be here in five minutes."

I sit down on a fallen tree next to the heads. "Are you hurt, Yan?"

"I should ask you that, but I'm fine."

"I need to send these heads back in a crate to those Polish assholes."

"It can be arranged. Jiro is also on his way."

I shield my eyes from the blinding headlights of the destroyed Urus. I know I am covered in blood for the second time today. Well, the second day in a row. It's one a.m. I hear the voices of the Kings and get up.

I see Deacon first and he looks at me, panting. "Are you okay, Selena? Where are they?" I stay silent, pointing to the bodies and he furrows his brows.

Liam comes running and stops. "Holy shit! Their heads are cut off!" He looks at Yan and he points in my direction.

Liam walks over to me. "Selena," he whispers. He touches my cheek, and I turn my face away, not wanting to show him how I feel.

I was angry, and I channeled it all into causing death and destruction. I'm a killer. I get up and go to the car to see what items I left that I can salvage and I need to find the gun. Yan quickly comes to help me. I hear Relic's voice.

I can tell he has been drinking, but he is not incoherent. "Where is she?" he asks.

"She's over there, brother," Liam says. "I don't think it's the right time--"

"No, this is my fault," he interrupts Liam. "I'm to blame for not protecting her and kicking her out."

Yan helps me and finds the gone and any items that can be salvaged. I look at him and he nods silently, telling me that everything is out.

I walk over quietly and grab the decapitated heads by their hair and walk up to Relic. He's standing in front of a tree with everyone else. I stop and hold the heads up, then release my hold and drop the heads at his feet with a thud.

"Here, redeem yourself and send these back in a crate. Let them know I will decapitate every single one of them that comes to hunt me down."

He looks down at my disheveled clothes, covered in blood. He reaches out to touch me, and I flinch, moving out of the way. "Don't touch me."

Liam moves toward Relic, placing a hand on his shoulder. "Come, *carnal*, leave her alone. She's had a rough night." Relic looks away in defeat. Liam glances at me and says, "Look, I will stay with you and Yan. We will take turns keeping watch until Relic and Deacon handle retaliation or whatever our next move is."

I give him a nod. I don't want to argue. All I want is a shower.

Chapter Forty-Seven

We head back to my apartment building in Liam's car. Wearing a hoodie Liam gave me, I follow the guys up the stairs and make it inside the apartment. After I enter my bedroom, I take off the clothes, careful not to dirty anything, and place everything in a bag to burn later.

The Kings said that they would burn the car and take care of the rest. I walk over to the bathroom and step in the shower, but instead of standing under the spray, I sit on the floor, letting the hot water slide down my body. I have cuts that are stinging, but I just don't have the energy to tend to them. I pull my knees under my chin and sit staring at the cream-tiled floor, wishing the emptiness away.

When the water runs cold, I turn it off and sit back in the same position, falling asleep on the tile floor, not caring if blood is still on my skin. I give myself to the sleep that wants to swallow me into its dark abyss.

When I hear a knock on my door, I don't move to get up. It must be morning because sunlight is streaming from underneath the door. It felt like I only closed my eyes for a split second.

"Selena!" Jiro and Liam call my name.

They knock harder, but I make no move to get up. I don't have the energy to deal with Jiro right now. I just lie here feeling the chill of the cold, still feeling empty. I hear the lock give way and Jiro bursts through the door with Liam right behind him. Jiro lowers himself to the floor and turns on the hot water. I push up on the palm of my hands, squinting my eyes from the spray of the water wetting my skin.

"Damn, Jiro, I didn't know she was in here like this. She wanted to be left alone," Liam says in a concerned voice as he turns around out of respect that I'm naked.

He glances up at Liam with a hard edge to his voice. "I am going to fuck up Relic for this. I trusted him with her. I trusted him not to treat her like she was one of his whores. Because of his stupidity, they could have killed her."

"I know, Jiro. I don't know what is wrong with him lately."

"I need to bathe her and put her to bed," he says, pushing my hair softly away from my face.

"All right. Relic will be here shortly," Liam says as he leaves.

"Selena. Come on, I've got you. I'm here," Jiro says in a soft voice as he helps me up. He takes off his now-wet shirt and runs his hands over my arms to get me warm.

I tilt my head and meet his dark eyes and he smiles. "There you are," he says. "I'm going to wash you, okay? I will tend to your scrapes, but you have a deep one on your arm."

I glance at my arm and he's right. I'm not sure if I need stitches because there is dried blood everywhere. He washes my body and hair, and when he is finally done, he wraps me in a towel. After he cleans my wounds with antiseptic and dresses them, he carries me to the bed and slides in, holding me against his chest. He caresses my cheek with his fingers until I fall asleep in his arms.

There is a knock on my bedroom door, and I turn, feeling Jiro stir. Jiro blinks a few times and wipes his hands over his face, getting up with a yawn to open the door. All I hear is a fist slam into a face in a brutal punch. I bolt up, gripping the sheet to cover my naked body.

Relic storms in and punches Jiro in the face and the next thing I know, they're wrestling on the floor.

"You motherfucker," Jiro spits. "I trusted you to watch her and take care of her, and because of you, they could have killed her. You're always treating her like shit."

"Both of you, stop it!" But they don't listen to me. They have each other in a headlock, trying to choke each other out.

"You came here for what? To fuck her and let me see you in bed with her? We had an agreement."

Agreement? What agreement?

"Yeah, asshole. From now on, I am going to fuck her, and there is nothing you can do about it. From what I can tell, you kicked her out of your damn house in front of everyone. You might as well have handed her to those Polish fucks."

Liam pushes through the door. "What the fuck? Relic, let Jiro go."

Jiro doesn't let up. He wants to kick Relic's ass.

Liam tries to reason with him. "Jiro, let up, man. We're no good if we kill each other."

Jiro finally releases his hold and gets up. Relic pushes himself up and wipes his face with his shirt, ruining it with blood from his split eyebrow.

He turns to me with a hard glare. "Did you fuck him?"

"If I did or didn't, that's none of your business. You wanted me out, so I am out."

"Look at me," he demands. My eyes glare at his because he has some nerve. "Was his cock inside your pussy?"

When he asks the last part, I notice his eyes are dark and full of lust. I am naked and he can see it. He calms down as I pin him with a stare, but he must see I'm confused. He realizes nothing happened and that he's overreacting, but I saw it in his eyes. He wasn't mad about me sleeping with Jiro. He was mad because he wasn't a part of it.

"I know I fucked up. Jiro has to retaliate, but you will stay with me until this is over. Yan will always be with you wherever you go if I am not with you. Yan can stay at the house too."

I glance at Jiro, and he leans against the wall. "Swallow that pride of yours and stay with him," he says. "For your safety. I know you can handle yourself, but if they send more, you can't cut off all their heads." He smiles at me. "Is that your signature, *Onna-bugeisha*?"

I smile because it means female warrior. I'm honored because there are two types, one that fights in battle and the other defends her home. "Maybe."

Relic slides my hair behind my ear and places a tender kiss on my temple. "Get your stuff, you have thirty minutes."

Chapter Forty-Eight

RELIC

I walk out of her room, knowing I fucked up with her badly. Knowing she was with him in the bed caused my feelings for her to bubble to the surface. I panicked and acted out, not thinking clearly.

I put her life in danger. She could have been killed because they were after her. They waited for her to be at her most vulnerable and almost took her from me. The look in her eyes when she beheaded those men was the same look she gave the Russian. It is a look that will have grown men running in fear. When she strikes, she strikes hard, with no fear. I can feel the light leaving her eyes. The light I used to see before she left for Japan. And it kills me I can't reach her.

I need to keep her safe, and the best way I know how to do that is with her by my side. I know Jiro has had a strong connection with her since they were kids. It guts me I'm not close to her like he is, and he was there for her. He held her when she was in her darkest moment, and it should have been me.

I feel like a total asshole when it comes to her. A rage inside me erupts when I see other men looking at her, ogling her, fucking her with their eyes. I want to rip them apart.

I am not used to feeling this way about any woman, but it's different with her. I can't get mad at Jiro when he is always there to pick up the pieces. He has made her strong. I need to know how he really feels about her. How we'll move forward from here. Because I know he will never let her go, and I'll do anything for her.

"Jiro, I need to ask you something and be honest with me," I say when I see him in the kitchen washing his hands.

"What is it?" he asks.

"Are you in love with Selena?" He closes his eyes briefly as I say her name. I can see he is madly in love with her.

"You're the third person in my life I have said this to, her grandfather, my father, and now you. She doesn't know and has never known because I have never told her. But I have shown her. I have been in love with Selena since I was five years old. I thought it was infatuation, a crush. When she left with me for Japan, we trained, we slept together. She told me about her relationship with you and how it meant nothing to you. Just sex."

He dries his hands and rests back on the counter. "So, I didn't feel I was getting between you two. I waited for her to decide. We were at the hostess club so I could introduce her to the yakuza members. They were impressed, but they were worried about my feelings for her. They could see it in the way I looked at her. This girl, Akemi, we used to see each other a lot, and I thought I was over Selena and in love with her, but when my father told me it was time to bring Selena to Japan, all the feelings I thought were just infatuation for a girl when I was a kid all came back. It was then I realized I was still in love with Selena, and honestly, I will always love her until the day I die. It will always be her."

"Why do I feel there is a 'but' coming?"

"I have many enemies, Relic. People that will hurt her to get to me. As much as I love her, I am a danger to her. I would die for her. It is what I've vowed to do my entire life. To protect her. It is why I need you to look after her."

"How do you want me to protect her when she can't stand me right now?"

"She's still in love with you. She just doesn't want to admit it, but I see the way she looks at you. As much as it kills me inside to know

I'm not the only one she loves, I will take that risk knowing she is alive and protected. Even if it is with you. Her safety is what really matters. Trust me, I didn't want to send her back here, but it must be done. She is really no different from you and me. She has a legacy to protect and honor."

Liam walks through the front door and smirks at Jiro. "Dude, tell me he didn't catch you fucking Selena."

"No, asshole, he wasn't. He was just helping her sleep."

"So I can trust you to watch her this time?" Jiro asks.

"I'll try not to piss her off."

"I'm leaving Yan to help out while you are doing... whatever the fuck you do when she can't be around."

"I agreed to watch her, but in my house. I won't be an asshole, most of the time," I tease.

"Please, Relic, don't fuck it up. I love you like a brother that I never had, but for Selena, I will go to war."

"All right, I get it, you lovesick weirdo."

Liam chuckles. "I knew it, fucker! You are in love with her. You try to hide it with your hard demeanor and shit, but I see it when you look at her and I saw it this morning. Dude, you've got it really bad."

Jiro snorts. "Shut the fuck up, Liam. She doesn't know it yet. She will in time. I have to go back and infiltrate the Polish fucks that did this, and then I have a meeting with the Russians. I will be back in a week or so unless something happens. She goes to work for half a day in the Elysium building, and then you'll take her back to King Enterprises so you can keep an eye on her in the meantime."

Liam and I nod in agreement.

"I will brief the others." I pull my phone and send an alert. He goes back into the bedroom and tells Selena the plan. The only problem I will have is keeping my hands off Selena because Jiro or no Jiro, I can't get enough of her.

Fifteen minutes later, she comes out of her room dressed in leggings and a little shirt showing her stomach, and my dick gets hard watching her.

She has the most exotic look about her and those eyes. I remember the way her pussy gripped my cock when I was inside her while she was moaning my name.

I shake the thought from my head and get a grip on myself. After I help with her stuff, the first thing we are going to do is replace her car. She won't accept the one I bought her, so I'll get her the one she lost. I know she loved that car, and it is entirely my fault that they attacked her.

She hugs Jiro goodbye and I want to tear her from his embrace, but I can't forget they have a connection. I won't interfere with what they have. I'm just a jealous asshole because I can't hug her right now. I turn and look the other way.

I have no right to give her shit about how she will also be mine... I will just have to show her.

Chapter Forty-Nine

SELENA

I say goodbye to Jiro, hoping he's careful. I know he is going to get revenge for the attack on me. He told me his plan. As much as I don't want to right now, I have to stay with Relic. It's for the best, but at least Yan is with me and can watch my back. I owe him my life. He had my back when no one was there, and I trust him implicitly.

I saw Relic's expression when he walked in, so I know he feels guilty and maybe that is why he went at it with Jiro.

Jiro will come back with more information on the Russians. It wasn't the Russians who attacked me but the sick Polish creeps. Even if our relationship is not on the best of terms, I will be safe with Relic because one thing I can count on, they don't fuck with the Kings.

Liam will drop Yan off at Relic's while I leave with Relic to God knows where he is planning to take me. We are in his Maclaren, and "Wants and Needs" by Drake is playing on his car speakers. I look at him out of the corner of my eye. He looks hot in a cream hoodie, slightly fitted matching pants, and sneakers. I was in shock when he asked me if Jiro fucked me. What was that all about? Relic isn't the type to get jealous.

We pull up to a warehouse, and the sign on the front says *Exotics*. *He* must have some Kings business to deal with here.

The door opens, and a Mexican man with a lot of ink comes out. "What's up, King?"

"Nothing much, *Loco*. You got what I am looking for? Is it ready yet?"

"Of course, *ese*. You know I got it."

"Good. Let me see if she likes it. I'll wire the *feria* in about fifteen."

"I know you're good for it, *carnal*. That's your *hyna*?"

Relic smiles and doesn't answer.

"Never mind, *ese*. My bad, none of my business. I will be inside. Let me open the garage door so the light is better and you can bring her in."

What the hell is he talking about if she likes it?

He opens my door, and I look up at him. "What are we doing here?"

"I have a debt to pay." He smiles and holds out his hand.

I sigh and take it. "Alright, but don't get any stupid ideas. I'm just here for the ride. I need to get settled at your place, preferably in my own room. The one farthest away from yours would be nice."

He laughs, and it's the sexiest laugh. "Why? Are you afraid you'll get lost and end up in my bed?"

I stand up. "You would think that, wouldn't you? What's wrong, miss me? That bitch Sophia and your whores don't make you come hard?"

His eyes narrow, and mine don't flinch at the challenge. "Are you offering to make me come hard, Selena?"

I sigh. "Let's get this over with, Relic."

He keeps my hand in his, and I follow him inside the warehouse. There are about thirty exotic cars gleaming under the lights. Ferraris, Aston Martins, you name it, this place has one. They even have a Bugatti.

He guides me through another door to a private bay where there is a black Urus with red leather interior, like the one they had to burn last night. But this one has the emblem of Elysium on the front plate.

I'm shocked at how he could find one so fast and customize it.

He opens the door to the driver's side, and I look up at him. "Do you like it?" he asks, caressing my cheek with the backs of his fingers.

"Of course, who wouldn't? It's beautiful." I slide onto the driver's seat, rubbing my fingers on the steering wheel, admiring all the black and red stitching.

"I had it modified the same way as the red one Jiro bought you. The only difference is that I added some modifications to the engine and had it tuned to be faster."

I angle my head to look at him. He already analyzed how I got run off the road by those assholes. "Thank you. How much?"

"I took care of it. It was my fault you were in danger. The least I can do is replace your car. With a better one." He smirks. Cocky bastard.

"Alright, if you put it that way, I accept. I loved that car, and I'm sure I will like this one."

The guy comes back, and he smiles at Relic. "So, brother, *le gusto?*"

Relic smiles in my direction. "*Si, le gusta, hermano.*" I have no idea what he is saying, but I'm sure he is telling him I like the car.

"*Estás enamorado, hermano?*"

I watch as Relic shrugs. "*No, le caigo bien.*"

The guy laughs and I know they're talking about me. "*Ella está loca para que le des un beso.*"

"What are you two laughing about?"

The guy walks away to get the keys, but he turns around. "Hey, King!" Relic turns to look at him. "Go for it!"

I'm already out of the car and I walk behind him, trying to understand what they are saying, but I only understand kiss. Relic turns around smiling, walking me back when my back hits the car gently. He lowers his head. Is he going to kiss me? My body freezes and I can smell mint and the scent of his cologne as he inches closer to my lips, making me dizzy.

"Are you dying for me to kiss you, Selena?" he whispers against my lips. I close my eyes as I clench my thighs together. "My friend seems to think you are dying for me to do this." He swoops in like a hawk, capturing my lips.

I grab his hoodie, pulling him closer, so he can devour my mouth with his lips and tongue. God, he can kiss. It feels like I'm floating and weightless, lost to the scent and feel of him. He tastes of spearmint, and the scent of him brings all the feelings I have locked away to the surface.

He places his hands on my hips, caressing my slightly exposed stomach with his thumbs. He sucks my top and then my bottom lip, ending the seduction with tender pecks on my lips, his stubble leaving red marks on my skin as a reminder of his kiss. Reminding me it happened.

He steps away and guides me to the small office. He smiles at his friend, who is sitting at his desk getting the papers ready. "You were right, *carnal*."

"I could see it when you came in, *ese*." His eyes twinkle in my direction. "Do you like the car?" he asks.

"Yes, it's beautiful," I reply.

He looks at Relic. "Alright, here are your keys, and the car is in her name, as you requested. Money is in the bank, so we're all set. Now take your girl out to eat."

"I am not his gir—"

"Yeah, whatever." He chuckles. "You are more than just his girl, sweetheart." He fist-bumps with Relic. "*Hermano*, until next time."

"Catch you later, Manny."

Relic gives me the keys, and I back the car out while he waits for me. I feel giddy and smile to myself. *How are you, my black nemesis?*

I am going to call her Nemesis. God, it sounds beautiful when I rev the engine. I turn the music up, and the bass is louder and more powerful, almost like the red Urus on steroids. I am in heaven as I follow Relic back to his house and park next to his Maclaren.

Chapter Fifty

We enter the house and I notice the housekeeper in the kitchen. Relic should be here shortly.

"Oh, hello, Selena. Mr. King informed me you will be staying here with your cousin for a bit."

My cousin? Oh, Yan. Right, it's not like he can say he's a yakuza. "Yes, thank you. Did he tell you which room?"

"Oh, yes. The one closest to his."

Great. He is going to torment me when I am trying to sleep, and I will probably hear him moving around in his room.

She shows me to the room that I will inhabit for the time being.

"Your cousin is in the room on the other side of the house." She winks at me when she says *cousin*. I don't look Asian enough for Yan to be related, and I can tell she is not stupid.

"Thank you," I reply.

She leaves, and I turn around and take in the room with its own en suite. I open the closet and all my things are neatly hung and organized.

When I walk into the bathroom, the tub calls for me to get in it. My makeup and toiletries are laid out on the counter and there are soaps of all kinds.

I select my favorite lavender shampoo with conditioner and turn the water on so I can make bubbles. I haven't had a bath in a bit and would love to relax.

I get in the tub and soak, closing my eyes, before holding my breath and going under. When I come up for air, I see someone standing there, and I reach out, ready to punch them in the leg.

A large hand moves like lightning and holds me as I struggle, water going everywhere. "Shhh... Selena, it's me."

I wipe my face and can finally see clearly that it's Relic standing there. He takes his hoodie off, now soaked, revealing his muscular arms in a white T-shirt. "What the hell, Relic? Creepy much."

He smirks. "I knocked, and you didn't answer. I was making sure you were okay." He looks down at my breasts dripping with soapy water and I quickly sink under so I'm hidden under the bubbles up to my neck.

"What do you need? I am alive and breathing."

"Get ready."

"Why?"

"I'm taking you somewhere. Stop asking so many questions and trust me."

I sigh. "Fine."

He walks out, and I finish taking a bath and get dressed in a keyhole sweater, skinny jeans, and black thigh-high red-bottom boots. I leave my hair loose down my back and apply black eyeliner and use a nude color palette for my makeup.

I grab my small handbag, tuck my knives in my boots, and check my wounds. There is a knock on the door, and I quickly spray perfume.

I open the door, and Relic is standing there in jeans and a fitted three-quarter-sleeve sweater. His eyes scan my outfit and stop at my breasts, peeking out from the keyhole design of my sweater. I don't have overly large breasts, but they are a little more than a handful.

He walks into the room and stands by the floor-to-wall mirror I am particularly grateful for. "Come stand in front of the mirror, Selena."

I look at him curiously but do as he asks. I stand in front of the mirror, and he stands behind me. He slowly moves my hair to one side and slides a choker necklace around my neck. It has a crown with diamonds and red rubies on each tip. I stare at it in the mirror and run my finger across it, feeling the diamonds.

"Is that too tight?"

"No, it's perfect."

"Do you like it?"

I breathe in deeply and smile. "It's beautiful." I turn around and kiss his cheek. "Thank you," I whisper.

He looks down at me with a smile. "I didn't want you to have to choose between the necklace Jiro gave you and the one I wanted to give you. I wanted you to wear this one almost all the time and try not to take it off." I notice the crown looks like the one tattooed on his neck.

"How are your wounds? Do you need anything?"

"No, they're fine. They're not that bad."

"Selena." He takes a deep breath.

"Yes?"

"I'm sorry for everything." He slides the back of his hand on my cheek.

"Me too," I say.

"You mean a lot to me, Selena, more than you'll ever know. Let's go," he says, giving me a soft peck on the cheek that has my insides battling to set my emotions free.

I take one last look at the glittering diamonds and follow him into the hallway. He slides his fingers through mine and we walk to the garage. We get in the Aventador.

He opens the garage door, and we take off.

We arrive at a very busy restaurant, and of course, he has a table waiting. "Hello, Mr. King. Your party is waiting."

I'm confused about why we are here as we're guided to a large table. Everyone is there: Liam, Deacon, Mia, Yan, and two other men I have seen at the VIP tables at the club. I smile, and Mia eyes me curiously, her eyes trained on the necklace.

I take a seat to Relic's right, in front of Mia. She motions to her phone.

I pick mine up and silence it so that no one can hear the ding of the incoming messages.

Selena: What's wrong?

Mia: Your neck.

Selena: What about it?

Mia: You belong to him now.

I keep rereading the last message Mia sent, not following.

I glance at her, and she's smirking at me. I look to my left and see Relic lost in conversation with Liam. My fingers fly across the keyboard.

Selena: What do you mean?

Mia: The way he brought you in here and sat you next to him. The necklace he gave you is the same crown tattooed on his neck. He wants everyone to know you're his.

I move to put my phone away and stick my tongue out at Mia. She smiles back, winking at me.

"What's so funny?" Mia and I both look at Relic like we were just caught with our hands in the cookie jar.

Mia is the first to speak up. "Nothing. I was just admiring her new necklace." She grins and my eyes widen. I'm going to kill her.

A mask falls in place and his tone changes. "It's not what you think. It's what I want everyone else to think. For now."

What the hell does he mean by that? I stay silent and look away, not meeting his eyes, trying to hide the confusion that must be written on my face.

The waiter brings the drinks and food that was previously ordered. It's a Chilean sea bass paired with wine, and I suddenly lose my appetite, craving shrimp tempura. It grew on me when I was in Japan.

I wonder who ordered this as I separate my food like a child that doesn't want to eat their dinner and remain silent. When I go back to Relic's house, I'll ask Yan to go with me to get food.

"You don't like it?" I look up at the sound of Relic's voice and meet his gold eyes, searching for what exactly I don't know.

Maybe I want normal.

Maybe I just want to be alone.

I know one thing. I want to find a safe haven. I thought I could have that with Jiro on some level, but it's clear I have to serve a purpose in running Elysium. Jiro has his purpose as the head of the yakuza, and there is no room for fairy tales and a happily ever after with a family. He will always be my childhood friend and a loyal ally and I will always love him.

But my fire and desire are staring into my eyes, and honestly, he scares me. His golden eyes are the window to his soul. A soul I can see that is powerful and dangerous.

"Um..." I take a deep breath and sigh. "It's good. I'm just not that hungry."

"You don't have to eat it, Selena. I am sorry."

"It's okay, really. No big deal."

I am mortified and embarrassed. He motions for the waiter to take my plate before he gets up and grabs my hand, motioning me to get up from the table.

Everyone looks at us curiously as I stand.

He leans next to me and whispers, "Get your purse. We are leaving. Just follow me."

I nod and follow him quietly with my hand in his, not understanding why we are leaving so suddenly.

He opens the door, and I slide into his powerful car. He takes off his sweater and is in his white V-neck T-shirt, molded to his muscular body. You can see the outlines of all his ink, and if I'm going to be honest, my insides flutter and heat pools between my thighs.

He gets in the car and pulls out into the street. He rubs his thumb over the top of my hand, and electricity zaps right to my heart at the simple gesture.

"What do you really want to eat, Selena? Whatever it is, tell me."

I rub my index finger over his thumb, and he links his fingers with mine. Butterflies dance in my stomach and I let out a shaky breath.

"Shrimp tempura," I say quietly.

"I know just the place."

I smile. He noticed I didn't like the food. I guess whoever ordered it thought I would like it. I still have no idea who that was, but I know it wasn't Relic. "Thank you."

"My pleasure."

We drive to a quaint Japanese restaurant, and he holds my hand on the way inside. I love this side of Relic. He has shown me glimpses, but the monster attitude always takes over again, eliminating every sweet touch he makes.

We enter, and a small older man greets us. Relic smiles and speaks Japanese, exchanging pleasantries. My eyebrows rise briefly, shocked that he is fluent. I keep my surprise hidden, and the man escorts us to a small table in the back with a view of a small pond of Koi fish.

It's honestly beautiful and perfect. Looking down at the menu, I grin when I see my shrimp tempura. I order my meal, and surprisingly, he orders as well.

"You didn't like your food either?"

"Actually, I wanted to be alone with you, to be honest. I lost my appetite when I saw you weren't eating."

"How do you know Japanese? You speak it fluently."

He leans back in his chair, and I drink him in. He has put on more muscle since the last time, but when he looks at me, there is something different I didn't see before. Sure, he is attractive, but there is more. It's like he deeply cares what I like or dislike.

"You like what you see?"

"Don't flatter yourself." I roll my eyes, teasing him.

His lips curl in a white-toothed grin. Making the heat between my thighs wetter by the minute but I cannot let down my guard with him. I already did, and I got burned. Burns hurt, and then leave irreparable scars. And I learned my lesson the first time.

"You are not the only one that has to own up to their birthright. My father made sure I owned up to mine. Like you, I had to train and learn the business, and I was not left with much of a choice. My father knows Jiro's father, and they decided it was best to send me to train in Japan. My father made sure I learned other languages that are beneficial for our other line of work."

"I see. How long have you known Jiro?"

"Since I was fifteen. We became friends immediately, but when I came back and took over for my father and he took over for his father, we just got caught up in our family responsibilities and were not as close as we used to be, but we have much respect for each other when we have business dealings. Loyalty above all else. He talked about a girl once, about a childhood friend. A girl that was special and had to move away once she was offered an academic scholarship to a college. I have now come to realize that girl was you."

"Some of his friends used to tease him when we were younger. In the summers when I was over there, he would beat up anyone that said mean things to me. I was from America, an outsider, according to some of them. I didn't look Asian enough, but Jiro was always there, protecting me. I called him my warrior when I was little." I smile.

Relic stays silent, studying me. I am not used to opening up to him, and I don't trust myself around him. I kind of got ahead of myself, revealing a little too much for my peace of mind.

"I can see why. I would have done the same."

I decide to change the subject and get more clarity being around him. "Look, I have been meaning to talk about what happened in the shower." I sigh and look down. "I was in another place after I––"

He interrupts me. "Selena. It was my pleasure, and it will always be a pleasure. Whatever happens, just let it happen." I look up, watching him intently. "Promise me."

"Okay."

The food arrives and we eat. I am in heaven because the food tastes so good. "Thank you for taking me here. The food is delicious."

"Anything for you, *preciosa*."

Chapter Fifty-Three

The next morning, I get ready and make my way to the Elysium building with Yan. I didn't see Relic this morning. He drove us back to the house after having dinner at the Japanese restaurant, and I immediately said good night and went to my room.

I had a great time with him and love this side of him, but I know he can easily switch to the cold monster underneath.

We make it to the office, and as I walk out of the elevator, I am greeted immediately by a woman at a desk who looks like she is in her midfifties with a petite form and glasses. "Hi, you must be Selena. My name is Sue. I am your secretary and will handle any paperwork or anything else you might need."

"Thank you, Sue. I will let you know if I need anything. I assume my schedule is listed in my Outlook?"

"Yes." She smiles, and I instantly like her demeanor and the fact she speaks fluent English and Japanese, based on her employee file.

Yan follows me into the same office that my world shifted in and I'm met with the same minimalistic decor and desk.

"Selena, I will be on the third floor if you need me. Don't forget after lunch, you will be escorted to the Kings' building. I think the agreement is for you to help them over there with the missing ship-ments and to see if you can offer them any insight."

"Okay. I better get to work here then, catch Elysium up with imports and exports. I have to run some data analytics and see where we need improvements."

"Jiro said you were smart." He smiles as he turns to leave, closing the door behind him.

I get to work and don't stop until it's way past lunchtime. I completely forgot about lunch and had to rush to make it to the Kings' building. I got so caught up in learning everything that I lost track of time.

Someone knocks, and I glance at the door. "Come in!"

The door swings open, and Relic walks through the threshold. My breathing speeds up, and my eyes go wide in surprise. His dress shirt is untucked over his gray slacks, and his sleeves are rolled up, exposing his arms.

His hair is disheveled as if he has been running his fingers through it multiple times. He looks sexy with an air of confidence.

I stand up, and his gaze drops to the swell of my breasts, where my blouse is unbuttoned. My hands move to close the buttons instinctively.

"I have seen all of you, there is no need on my account."

I quickly button the blouse to cover up. "Yeah, well, let's leave it in your memory. How can I help you? I'm surprised that you are here."

"I was concerned when you didn't make it."

"I actually just realized the time and was about to make my way over there."

"Okay. Great. So, let's get going. I will take you. Yan can take your car and meet you at the house later."

"So, you just waltz in here and decide for me?"

He smirks. "Well, of course. I am to watch over you and make sure no one tries to hurt you."

If he only knew, the one he needs to worry about is himself.

"Let's go." I walk over so we can leave. I'm starving and want to get to work at the Kings' building.

I love my work and have worked hard to be qualified, at least academically. It keeps me grounded. He lingers so I can walk out first, but when I get to the door, he suddenly closes it and pushes me against the wood with his hands on both sides of my head, blocking me in.

"I don't want a memory of how you look or how you taste."

My legs squeeze together. He can smell my arousal, I'm sure of it.

His mouth inches closer to where the necklace he gave me is against my throat. He kisses softly against where my pulse is beating wildly before whispering in my ear. "You smell so good. I bet you are so wet right now. When you wear my necklace, it turns me the fuck on to know that you belong to me."

I glare at him. "Are you sure? Let's get this straight. Just because we fucked doesn't mean I belong to you. If that's the case, then you must have a harem of women and I don't like crowds. I am not an object that you can claim. Now, get off me."

He thinks he can just claim me like some toy. If some Polish assholes weren't after me, I wouldn't even be in his house. My feelings for him have not changed, not after a year and not after Jiro. But I always fall for his charm, and then the monster inside him comes out to play.

He pulls away, and right when his hands are off the wall, he grabs my face and kisses me. The kiss is brutal. His tongue ravages my mouth, searching, sucking, and devouring me.

Then he softens the kiss and I'm breathless. My hands slide up his chest. I can't help the feelings that he stirs inside me, and I kiss him back. Our tongues swirl and explore until he finally lets me up so I can breathe. He drops his forehead to mine and I close my eyes.

"Why do you do this to me?" I whisper, trying to catch my breath.

He angles his head near my ear and whispers, "Because I want you to know that you're mine and I'm yours. Do you want me, Selena? I can feel it, but I need you to say it."

I open my eyes and rub my thumb on his lower lip. "I've wanted you since the first time you touched me." I feel like I'm betraying Jiro's love.

His eyes light up with possessiveness. "Let's go. Your secretary is back."

He releases me, and I touch my kiss-swollen lips. I am on fire inside. I can't believe I told him how I feel.

After I compose myself, he opens the door. Sue looks up, surprised to see him. She stares as we walk out into the hallway.

"I am sorry. I did not know Miss Tenaka was expecting anyone."

"That's okay, Sue," I chime in. "I was on my way out."

Relic smiles at Sue. "Hello, Sue, my name is Relic King, and I'm here to pick up Selena."

Sue looks between us. "Are you Relic King, the CEO of King Enterprises?"

"One and the same."

"Oh, my. It is nice to meet you," she says.

"Have a nice rest of your day. Selena is lucky to have you." He places his hand on the small of my back.

"Oh, thank you, sir. Miss Tenaka, if there is anything you need from me, please call me, and I will get it for you."

I smile. "Thank you for everything, Sue. Relic is right. Elysium is lucky to have you on board with us. I will call you if I need anything. I'll see you tomorrow."

We walk toward the elevator, and his hand remains on the small of my back, burning me with his touch.

Once outside, there is a driver waiting in a black Rolls Royce. Relic opens the door and slides in after me, placing his hand on my thigh.

"We will eat before heading to my office. I have some files I need you to look over."

"Okay. Sounds good." I try to move out of his grasp, but he increases the pressure, holding my thigh in place.

His gaze travels up my thigh-high stockings, and he glides his thumb just below the hem of my skater skirt. I clench my knees together, hoping I don't drip all over the back seat of the car. When I look up, his expression is filled with desire.

But I can't give in to him. If he could just want me for the right reasons and that want might turn into love, I would let him take me right here in the back seat of this car. My eyes fill with unshed tears because sex is empty without love. Before, I was just a girl that graduated from college, wanting to find a good job, marry for love, and have a family. Now, I am just a woman that has to fulfill a legacy without all the things a normal girl craves out of life.

He frowns and removes his hand as if he has been burned. "Is everything okay?"

"Everything is fine."

If he only knew how torn I am. I'm torn because I can't want any of that with him without Jiro. And it is killing me inside.

His demeanor changes when we pull up in front of an Italian restaurant, and the driver opens the door to let us out. We are greeted by the host and shown to an intimate table in the back corner.

"Mr. King, if there is anything you need or require, please do not hesitate to ask."

"Thank you, Tomas. I think the lady would like some of your finest white wine."

"Absolutely."

The wine is placed on the table, and the waiter pours me a glass. Relic gets a whiskey neat.

"I really shouldn't be drinking if we have to go back to work," I say.

He looks up from scrolling through his phone. "A little wine and a whiskey are fine, and we are not driving. If not, there is always tomorrow."

"I guess."

My phone dings and I pick it up.

Relic: I want you to get to know me. The real me.

Selena: Why is that?

Relic: Because for the first time, I am interested in a woman and that woman is you.

Selena: Okay. Thank you for taking me out to lunch, and why are we texting each other if we are right here?

Relic: I wanted you to have my words written in case you forget.

I put my phone down and smile. He does the same.

"So, who is the real Relic King?"

"You are going to find out."

Chapter Fifty-Four

SELENA

We make it to the offices of King Enterprises, and most of the employees that were here when I started still work in their respective positions. They look at me curiously when I arrive with Relic, but no one dares to ask why I am back here.

Some smile when he isn't looking and wave. He walks us into the boardroom and Deacon, Mia, and Liam are seated at the table, along with Relic's mother and father.

I wonder what this is all about. His mother eyes me and then her nude-colored lips tip up into a smile. Relic takes his place at the head of the table and Mia smiles, her eyes full of excitement. I smile back, relieved that she is here.

"I called this meeting so there is no confusion about Selena's presence here at King Enterprises. If anyone asks questions, she's a consultant. She will also stay with me at my home for protection as an attempt on her life has already been made. I know you may have wondered why she did not let everyone know she was to take over Elysium and who her grandfather was, but she was sworn to not say a word for her safety. I know she can handle herself, but one person cannot fight an entire army of the most ruthless families in the world that have ties to world leaders." His father nods in understanding but glances at me curiously. "I will protect Selena at all costs," Relic says,

I feel giddy hearing those words from him, even if they are out of duty and loyalty.

Deacon and Liam all smile. Relic's mother, Victoria, notices the necklace I subconsciously touch when I am nervous. I think it's because it's new and I am not used to having it on.

"That is an interesting piece, Selena."

Relic interjects. "I had it custom made for her."

His mother smiles. "Finally, my son is in love. You are a very lucky girl to have the attention of a King. You will have enemies both powerful and of the lady variety, but I think if the rumors are true, you won't have any issues in that department."

My heart races at the mention of Relic being in love with me. "I guess so."

I glance at Mia, and she grins.

Relic speaks up. "I guess everything is clear, and I am glad everyone is on the same page. So, let's get to work. Selena, my office."

I get up. "Okay."

I give a hug to everyone, including his father. "A Tenaka, huh? This is going to be interesting. I wonder if my son can win your heart, or does someone already have it?"

I glance at him, noticing he looks very much like Relic. "Honestly, I'm not sure my heart is what your son is truly after." I turn and walk away, certain he was referring to Jiro.

He knows my grandfather and Jiro's father, so of course, he made the connection. I realize that Relic's father wants to make an alliance and his goal is for Relic to marry into the right family, but my heart is split in two. I don't think of marriage as an alliance but of love between two people. The problem I have is that my heart is torn. I love Jiro, but I'm also in love with Relic.

Relic's secretary smiles at me as I follow him toward his office. "I knew he would bring you back. How are you, Selena?"

"I'm great."

"I am glad you're back. If there is anything you need, refreshments or the like, let me know. Looks like it will be an all-nighter for you both."

"I guess so."

I walk inside his office, and Relic closes the door, but I notice there is a chair right next to his. I assume it's for me and notice the files he mentioned sitting on the desk.

How cozy. I wonder how I will concentrate with him so close. I can be a professional and do this, so I take the seat next to his and open the files, getting to work on my analysis of acquisitions his company has proposed. He wants me to see which ones are more profitable, and Elysium will get a percentage. It's a win for both companies.

When his phone rings, he answers, taking a seat. I can hear a woman's voice. He gets up and walks toward the floor-to-ceiling windows overlooking the city below. I stop what I am doing, and I get up to leave so he can have privacy.

He doesn't even notice I can hear his hushed tone. "I can't right now. I am in the middle of a meeting. My answer is still no."

My stomach sinks and I leave his office, not wanting to hear anything further. What did I expect? Maybe it's just better this way.

I just need to keep myself in check and not think too much about it. I'm walking toward the elevator, needing some space from my feelings. Hopefully, they fade in time. It's getting late, so I look for a lounge on this floor so I can get a coffee or something.

Passing an office door, I see Deacon sitting at his desk.

"Selena, wait. I was just going to call Relic."

I stop just outside his office door and notice it's the same size as Relic's without the view. I notice a picture frame on his desk of him and Mia.

I respect him for his love for my best friend and wish Relic was like him. "What's up, Deacon? Relic had to take a call, and I slipped out to give him privacy."

He eyes me warily, sensing I'm bothered by something. "You know what? Serves him right."

I look at Deacon, confused. "I am not following. What do you mean serves him right?"

"Look, I was going to tell the asshole Russian no, but I want to ask you first. You don't have to say yes, but hear me out. The Bratva contacted me." I step into his office and he moves to close the door behind me so no one can hear our conversation. I move to sit in a chair and listen to him intently. "The son of the head of the Bratva, Dimitri, wants to call a truce with you. He is overlooking the fact you slit his distant cousin's throat but is aware of his business dealings with the Polish Mob and will overlook it. The business dealings were not agreed upon with the Bratva, and they would have killed him anyway."

"What does he want with me?"

Deacon looks at me with a serious face, contemplating his next words. "He wants you to go out with him. A date to call a truce."

"How do we know it's not a trap?"

Deacon takes a deep breath. "It's not a trap because he will go to war with the Polish on your behalf. He knows who you are, and he would have tried by now. He doesn't need to go on a date to kill you. He is requesting that you consider this and give him your answer by Friday."

I sit in the chair, deciding if I want to live on the edge. How bad could the son of a Russian be? Without thinking any more about it, I tell him, "Fine. I'll do it."

The door behind me to the office opens. "You'll do what?" I look behind me, not realizing Relic has entered the office.

Deacon looks at him sternly. "Dimitri wants to go out with Selena to call a truce."

"Fuck no. That cocksucker doesn't get to go out with Selena because he wants to call a truce. He can call one without going anywhere near her."

I get up from the chair, pissed off that he gets to have a say in what and who I can go out with for a business meeting. A minute ago, he was on the phone excusing himself about going out with someone else. Fuck him. "I have already agreed. I will go to the business meeting and see what he wants."

Relic's eyes light with golden fire. His fists are clenched at his sides. "The only thing he wants is to stick his slimy Russian cock in your pussy, nothing more."

In his eyes, men only want me for one thing. I need to prove a point, and fast. "Regardless, I have already agreed. Now, you can go on a date and won't have an excuse not to go. Hurry and call her back."

I know I sound like some jealous, jilted girlfriend, but I'm tired of his games.

I turn around to leave, and Relic grabs me by the arm. "Where the fuck do you think you're going?" he asks through clenched teeth.

"I need to get home so I can plan my business meeting with the Russian, and you need to make plans for a special night with your girlfriend. Now get your hands off me."

W hat the fuck just happened? I wasn't prepared to take that call, and I told Katrina repeatedly I was not interested in her. I have only one interest and it's the woman that makes me act like a jealous psychopath. I had been seeing Katrina on and off before Selena. She recently came back to the states and obviously doesn't understand that I'm not interested. When Selena left the office, I told her the truth. I'm with someone else and I have no plans of letting her go.

I still can't believe I was stupid enough to answer the phone, but I feared the worst. Her showing up. It's like the woman has a sixth sense or something.

I look at Deacon, and he has his hands up in surrender. "I had to tell her before the guy contacted her himself. You know Dimitri is resourceful and very persuasive when he wants something, and brother, he wants Selena."

What the fuck? He wants Selena? Is my brother crazy? "That *pinchy puto* can't just demand that Selena go have a business meeting with him and get what he wants, *ese.*"

"Well, brother. She accepted the invitation. She is the head of Elysium, and it's her duty to——"

"No *mames*, Deacon. She accepted to piss me off because she overheard me answering Katrina's call."

Deacon smirks. "So go out with Katrina. Like Selena said, you're free to go out on a date."

"Fuck you, *ese*. You know how I feel about Selena. I'm not interested in anyone but her. You know damn well I have been trying to figure out my feelings for her."

"Now you have the time to figure them out."

"Yeah, while the woman I really want is out with the son of the head of the Russian Bratva."

"We will send people to tail them. It's not like we were going to let her go alone, *ese*."

I run my fingers through my hair, frustrated. "Yeah, where did Selena run off to?"

"You want to head to the gym?" My brother glances at his phone. "According to your driver, she is at the gym."

"I guess I'm heading to the gym."

"Yeah, yeah. Let's go, *cabrón*, before you do something stupid."

We leave the office and I am sitting in Deacon's car, trying to figure out how to win Selena back. When I think I am getting close, everything turns to shit. I had the necklace made for her as a token of my feelings for her. I wanted to remind her when she looked in the mirror that she means more to me than any other woman in my life.

Multiple times since day one, I have treated her like shit. Now I have to sit here and accept the fact that she is going out with one of the most notorious sons of the head of the Russian Bratva. The worst part, he looks like a Russian model. I have no beef with Dimitri, but he will try to seduce Selena at the same time to test her, and I can't let that happen. I'm insecure because of my own stupidity when it comes to Selena.

We arrive at the gym, and I see there is a small crowd watching one of the private rooms we have for members to use. Deacon follows me up the stairs to see what has everyone so captivated.

Sure enough, Selena is with a katana sword in a warrior stance, practicing. She begins with vertical overhead strikes that bring the sword perfectly level, she then swings the sword down, reaching its intended target. An imaginary target but one all the same.

"Yo, Selena is badass, brother," Deacon says.

I stay silent, knowing what my brother is saying is true. Selena is a beautiful woman with a uniqueness like no other. She is one of the most beautiful women I have ever laid eyes on.

I know she was lying in her office earlier this afternoon about us just having sex and that it meant nothing more. We both know I made love to her. It was more. I didn't realize it then, but I realized it when I saw her asleep with Jiro.

I was jealous and scared that I had lost her. When Selena fell asleep in my bed, she slept with her beautiful hair lying across my pillow with our limbs entwined as if we were making love in our sleep.

It was different, and it will always be different with her. I can hear music playing inside, and it's not a traditional Japanese song. It's Halsey playing through the speakers.

I decide to go inside and practice with her and walk to the private lockers we have set up just for us Kings to change.

She sees me coming up behind her and keeps the sword at a safe distance. I stand behind her, wearing sweatpants with no shirt.

I lean down and kiss her cheek, dying to taste her. She just doesn't know it yet, but I will taste her. I will have her, and she will be mine as much as she is his.

I place my hand over hers on the handle of the sword. "Horizontal strike and we finish with a kata," I instruct her.

She nods and we execute the movement in sync together, mirroring each other's movement as if we have been training for years together. Each movement is executed from memory, and it's beautiful to know she can mirror every technique with each movement.

When we are done, I'm reminded there's a small crowd of gym members as we hear them clap. We both smile and turn to bow to our audience.

"Let's go home," I tell her.

"I'm still mad at you."

I never expected him to show up at the gym. I needed to practice and blow off steam. My emotions were all over the place, and I lashed out. It hurt me, the thought of him going out with someone else, and secretly, I wanted to hurt him just as much. I never thought he would follow me inside the private room at the gym.

As soon as he entered the room, I could feel his presence. The air suddenly became charged like an electric current.

When I noticed he wasn't wearing a shirt, I almost dropped the sword. I didn't have the will to turn him away. When I felt him behind me and he kissed my cheek, goose bumps broke out all over my body, and I secretly wanted to melt against him. It was amazing how we were in tune with each movement. It was a connection. A connection that I felt inside me. Our cultures bonding as one. An understanding that we can coexist. That he understands.

We're on our way to Relic's home after Deacon dropped us off at the office. He is sitting next to me, looking at his phone as we sit silently in the back of his car while his driver pulls into the driveway.

When we reach his house and go inside, he turns to look at me. "Follow me."

"Why?"

"Please?"

"Fine," I quip.

"Yan has already retired for the night."

"Thank you for letting me know. Where are you taking me?"

He sighs. "Just trust me, please, Selena."

I follow him just inside my room and he places my sword case on the dresser. He grabs my hand and guides me toward his bedroom.

I tense, and I'm about to protest, but he pleads, "Selena, trust me, please."

I let go of the tension in my hand and give in. He ushers me to his bathroom and turns on the shower. He closes the door as the steam begins to fog the bathroom and he walks up to me slowly.

He takes off my gym clothes, his gaze never leaving my eyes, and I get lost in the feeling of having him close to me. It reminds me of the first time I was in here with him. I remember the butterflies in my stomach when he chose me to be with him that night at the party. The longing I felt just to be with him.

When I am standing naked in front of him, he takes off his clothes and walks us both under the spray of the shower. I release my hair from the ponytail, closing my eyes as the spray of hot water consumes us both. He washes me, and I turn around with my back against him. His soapy hands rub my breasts, running down like the water to the apex between my thighs.

I can feel his erection on my lower back, and I clench my thighs together. He washes my hair, and it's the most delicious thing I have ever felt. His fingers massage my scalp, and at the same time, the evidence of his arousal pokes me on my lower back.

Turning around, I return the favor by washing his beautiful body, sliding my hands between his muscles. I can sense he is struggling because he turns around and puts his hands on the cold tiles, leaning on them like they're the only thing keeping him up. I continue to wash his back, following the planes of his muscles, savoring the feel of his skin, tracing the intricate swirls of color from his ink.

"Relic?"

"Yeah?"

"Are you okay?"

"No."

"Do you want me to leave?"

He pushes off the tile and turns to look at me.

"Never. I don't want you to leave. I want you to stay with me here in my bed." I swallow at his words. I think hard and know I feel the same way. I want to stay here with him just as much.

"I'll stay."

"I'll never force you, Selena. I want you to want to stay with me, but I'll never force you."

He moves his hands and cups my face, leaning in and kissing me deeply. I kiss him back, sliding my hands up his chest. He picks me up and holds me against the shower wall. I instinctively wrap my legs around his waist. He trails kisses down my throat as I tilt my head back, allowing him access to my body.

"I only want you, Selena."

I breathe him in, listening to his words. Words I have secretly wanted to hear from his lips. He guides the tip of his cock inside me, stretching me. My pussy grips him in a vise.

"You're so tight," he whispers in my ear before he bites my neck.

I moan as he slides in and out of me, my orgasm building inside of me, waiting to release.

"Even in the shower, you are so wet for me."

I moan and plead, "Deeper, Relic. I want more."

"Hold on."

I hold on to him with my arms wrapped tight around his shoulders. He lifts my legs, holding them with both of his arms while he pins my back against the tiles. He begins to thrust harder into me.

I see stars as he pounds into me so deep that my orgasm comes rushing through me. I moan his name as his eyes watch me come undone. He thrusts hard two more times and stills on a grunt, pulsing inside of me with his face in the crook of my neck.

He kisses me one last time and releases my legs gently, careful my knees don't buckle. He holds on to me until he is sure I can stand.

He turns the water off and walks out of the shower and grabs two towels. He wraps me in one before carrying me to his bed. I lie there silently, loving the warmth his body is giving me.

"I know I haven't treated you like you deserve. That woman I was talking to on the phone, I ended it with her. And I haven't seen or met with her since you have been back. I just want you to know that."

It is really what I want to hear, but I am torn. Should I want him? I know deep down I do. But I also love Jiro and I can't help feeling guilty.

One thing I'm sure of is what I feel for Relic when we're together makes everything melt away around me.

"Will you still give me a chance and get to know the real me, Selena?"

"I thought that was what we were doing?"

He chuckles and slides his hand up the side of my hip, giving me goose bumps all over my skin. I look into his eyes, and his lips lift into a grin. "I hope you're ready to see who I am with those beautiful eyes of yours."

"Who are you, Relic King?"

"I'm your king."

He makes love to me throughout the night. That's what you call it when a man gives you the most mind-blowing sex, the tenderest of touches, and watches you come repeatedly.

I don't remember falling asleep in his arms, but when I wake, it's with a sense of loss. I'm alone in the bed, in a tangle of sheets from our lovemaking. It's like a dream I don't want to wake up from, but I know I'm missing something or, rather, someone.

I hear the shower running, so I slide out of bed and wrap the sheet around me to head to my room.

When I step out of the room, I see Yan at the end of the hallway, walking over to this side of the house, no doubt looking for me to get to work.

He arches his brow at me. "Rough night?"

I roll my eyes dramatically, giving him the middle finger. "Don't start."

He holds his hands up in surrender. "I'm not judging."

"Give me a minute."

I hurry into my room, quickly shower and get dressed. When I walk out of the bathroom, Relic is waiting for me in his suit, looking very much the CEO. "Ready?" He asks.

"Yes, I thought you would be gone by the time I was ready to leave. Yan is waiting for me."

"I know, and he is coming along. He will follow us in your car."

I honestly didn't expect this change from Relic.

"Won't taking me make you late?"

"Selena, I own the company. I think it will be fine."

We get in his Aventador, and Yan follows behind us in the Urus. I can't believe he is taking me to work like we are a couple.

We get to the Elysium building, and he lets me out in front and says, "I will pick you up at lunchtime."

"Okay." I move to leave, but he grabs my wrist and pulls me in for a kiss.

"I'll see you in a little while."

I straighten my pencil skirt and blouse and grab my designer handbag and head into the building, smiling. Yan is already at the elevator and ushers me inside with a grin on his face.

"What?"

"All I am going to say is, I never thought anyone could do it."

"Do what?"

"Bring Relic King to his knees."

I snort. "Yeah. Right. Until he gets bored."

Yan shakes his head from side to side. "I don't think he could ever get bored with you."

The elevator dings signaling that we have arrived at my floor. Immediately, when we get out of the elevator, Sue greets us.

"Good morning, Miss Tenaka. Yan."

"Good morning, Sue."

"You have two messages. One from Mr. King. He wants me to remind you that your breakfast is at your desk and that he will be here at lunch." I turn to look at a smirking Yan. "The second message is from a man named Dimitri. I left the note on your desk. Let me know if you need anything or if you want me to send a message. Also, here are the reports you requested." She hands them to me.

"Thank you, Sue."

"I will be next door," Yan says. "I need to make a couple of phone calls."

His face got all serious when he heard Dimitri's name. I know he will call Jiro. I need to text Jiro. I should have told him sooner about my meeting with the Russian.

I head to my office, and just as Relic promised, my breakfast is on my desk. I pick at it while I take out my phone and text Jiro.

Selena: We need to talk.

Jiro: What took you so long to let me know?

Selena: I've been busy.

Jiro: Yep.

Selena: I wasn't thinking, and I accepted a meeting with Dimitri. My purpose is to get information on what he really wants.

Jiro: You know what he wants.

Selena: Very funny.

Jiro: You're not going alone, Selena. Get your intel and leave. The Bratva hasn't fucked us in the past, but right now we can't trust them.

Selena: Fine, Yan can come along.

Jiro: Wherever you meet this asshole will be in King territory.

Selena: Fine, that makes sense.

Jiro: Be careful, Selena. I will be there soon. I am taking care of this thing over here. It's almost over.

Selena: Okay. I miss you.

Jiro: I'll be there, beautiful.

I look at the note on my desk from Dimitri. It says to reply to a text message that I will receive to accept his invitation personally to let him know a time and place. I look at my phone and I have not received a message. I get to work looking at the manifests and making sure we are getting payments.

Before I know it, lunch is almost here, and I've only picked at my breakfast because I'm a little nervous about Friday. I shouldn't have accepted, and I wasn't thinking clearly because of my jealousy.

There is a knock on my door while I'm adding up the amounts.

"Yeah?" I call out.

The door opens and Relic appears. He closes the door behind him and walks over.

I take in his hard expression as he walks around my desk, not expecting him to lift me and plop me atop the papers on my desk. My breakfast falls over, the fruit scattering to the floor.

He pushes my skirt forcefully up my thighs and forces my legs open so he can look at my panties. I'm already dripping.

He undoes his belt. "Beautiful and already wet for me. What am I going to do with you, Selena?"

He moves my panties aside and pushes his finger inside the wet folds of my slit. I gasp out a moan, my head tilting back at how wet and slick my pussy is while he slides his finger in and out. He pulls out and brings his finger to his mouth and sucks my arousal right off.

He leans down to kiss me so I can taste myself on his lips while his tongue devours my mouth. My breathing picks up and I open my legs wider, giving him access so he can slide his deliciously thick cock inside my pussy. I yearn for him to be deep inside me and I lean back on my hands so I can watch him fuck me on my desk.

"I am sorry. I couldn't wait. You are all I think about," he says breathlessly.

He thrusts in and out slowly before he picks up the pace, and I moan his name.

"Fuck, Selena. I am going to be inside you everywhere. You're mine," he rasps on the skin by my ear. His nose rubs against my cheek. "Look at me." I gaze at him as he slows his pace and slides in balls deep, cupping my face in his hands. I get lost in his eyes, feeling him deep inside me. "This is mine."

I've fallen hard, and I know he senses it. The way my body responds to him is enough for him to know. He means more to me than any word from my lips can deliver.

I nod and kiss him fiercely, and he moves inside me faster. I fall deeper when my orgasm hits me in full force and I come.

He suddenly stiffens and grunts, coming inside of me, not breaking our kiss until we are both spent. We dress quickly, realizing that we didn't even think of someone hearing us.

"Let's go eat. I have lunch being delivered to my office. It's your favorite, shrimp tempura."

My eyes light up at the mention of my favorite dish. "Thank you." I'm getting to like this thoughtful side of Relic, a side I never knew he possessed.

"You scared me," I say. "What's not to like? There must be thousands of dollars' worth of clothes in here. You didn't have to do this," I say, running my fingers over the soft fabrics. "Don't get me wrong, I love all the clothes and shoes, but––"

"I wanted you here with me in my room and in my bed." He comes closer as I swallow nervously. "Do you want to stay with me, Selena?"

"Yes," I whisper.

"Good. Now turn around." I turn around and drop the bag containing my outfit, and he removes my clothes down to just my underwear. He removes his shirt, and I can hear "Might Not" from Belly and the Weeknd playing from the built-in speakers in his room. "Bend over and place your face on the chaise."

He holds my hands behind my back with one of his as I comply with his demands. My ass is exposed with just a thread of lace, keeping him from sliding his cock inside. "Have you ever been fucked here?" he asks as he slides his finger to remove my thong.

His finger swipes from my clit to my ass, swirling my juices around the entrance. "No, never." I breathe.

"Hmm. Can I have this part of you?"

I am breathing fast as he slides his index finger into my pussy and swirls his thumb on the rim of my ass again. He maintains a rhythm with his index finger swirling over my clit and slipping inside. I'm so wet, I'm dripping onto his hands. I feel like I am going to come when he slips his thumb inside my hole.

My knees almost buckle as he keeps my hands locked behind my back. I feel so full. I hear him unbutton his pants and feel the heat of his cock on my ass cheek. He slips his cock fast inside me, balls deep inside my pussy while his thumb is still inside, and I mewl his name. "Please don't stop, Relic. Fuck," I whisper loud enough for him to hear.

"You like me inside you, Selena? Do you like my fat cock inside you?"

"Yes."

He removes his cock from my pussy, and his cock pushes slowly inside my ass. The pressure feels so intense. He releases my arms from behind my back, and I hold myself in place on the chaise.

His cock inches deeper. I can hear him breathing deep and hard. I feel fuller as he moves in and out slowly, and my pussy gets so wet I'm on the brink of coming.

I fist my hands on the chaise, and he grabs my ass cheeks in his hands. We are both sweating, our bodies slick and heated.

"Selena, your pussy and ass are mine. I'm going to come inside you."

He thrusts harder and harder and my pussy pulses on the brink of an orgasm. "I'm coming! Don't stop, baby. Please!"

He keeps thrusting, not letting up, faster and harder. His thighs slap against my ass. He groans when he comes inside my ass. We are both panting, and I can't believe how good that was with the feel of both our juices leaking out of me everywhere.

He picks me up and carries me to the bathroom, placing me in front of the tub. "High for This" by The Weeknd plays while he runs the bath.

I step inside the tub and he slides in behind me. As the hot water fills the tub, I lean my head back against him. He pours my lavender soap inside the tub, and it smells nice and relaxing. I close my eyes and think I drift off to sleep because I wake up to soft kisses and whispers of, "I love you, Selena."

My eyes flutter open.

"I have never meant those words so much in my life, and I have never uttered those words to any woman besides my mother. I love you, Selena. I don't want anyone else. I only want you. If you don't love me yet, I will wait until you do."

He caresses my face tenderly, and I am not sure if I should tell him I am in love with him the same way, but I need to say it. I need him to hear it because I'm not promised tomorrow.

"I love you too," I whisper.

He kisses me and says softly, "I will never let anyone hurt you. I'm your king, and you, Selena, are my queen. I will live my life to make you happy."

SELENA

I wake up knowing today is the dreadful day of the date with the Russian. I work until noon, with Relic dropping me off and picking me up while Yan follows behind us.

I arrive back at the house to get ready, but I decide to take a nap and wake up before Relic gets back. My phone vibrates from an incoming text.

Relic: I will pick you up early so we can eat dinner before going to see this pinchy pendejo.

Selena: LOL. I will be ready at 6:30 p.m., okay?

Relic: I love you. Te amo, mi reina.

Selena: I love you too, my king.

I smile, looking at the text, realizing I'm not dreaming. My mood is suddenly better now that we are having dinner together. I take my time getting ready, making sure I look perfect for Relic, not for the Russian.

I wear my hair clip on the side with my hair down, and it matches perfectly with the red minidress. I've got my set of small knives on my inner thigh, encased in a thin holster for protection. My makeup is light on foundation but heavy on the eyes with winged eyeliner and shadow.

My coat is black with a satin lining, matching perfectly with the red Herve Leger dress.

A knock sounds on the bedroom door. I open it and find the housekeeper.

"Miss Selena!" Her eyes are alight with excitement. "He is waiting for you in the car out front. You look gorgeous, dear. *Que hermosa*. I love the coat."

I smile and open the coat so she can see the dress, and she gasps. "Wow!"

"You think it's too much?"

"Absolutely not. I think it's sexy and chic." She smiles.

"Thank you, I better get going," I say, spraying some expensive designer perfume Mia made me buy. She smiles, giving me a knowing look as I make my way out of the bedroom to the front door.

When I slide into the leather seat of the Wraith, Relic smiles. "You look beautiful. I hope you like dinner tonight."

"I know I will. It's after dinner I am not so sure about."

His face turns serious and he clears his throat. "Don't worry about it. It will be over soon."

I want to kick myself for messing up his mood. I should have kept my mouth shut. It's probably because I am anxious about things tonight. One thing is for sure, I'm ready for whatever the night brings.

Relic broods in silence on the drive and doesn't utter a word or hold my hand. Feeling a sense of loss, I hug my coat tighter around me, crossing my arms across my chest.

Once we reach the parking lot of the restaurant, there is a long line of cars waiting for valet parking.

When it's our turn to leave the vehicle, Relic gets out first but doesn't hold my hand to help me out. I know he is upset, and I get it. I'm dressed to kill, and it is for another man to enjoy.

He just stands there and waits for me to get out, looking straight ahead to the man at the door. He still doesn't reach for my hand, so I decide to slide mine through his, but he quickly gives the man at the door a hug and shakes his hand, making me feel awkward that I was shrugged off. Maybe bad timing on my end. Feeling deflated, I just wait here while they talk.

"Hey, man. Thank you for the help with my sister's medical bills. There was no way I could pay them."

"No worries," Relic tells the guy. "I'm glad I could help your family out. They're treating you good here?"

"Of course, a King referred me." The guy looks over at me, expecting Relic to introduce me, but he has no intention of doing so.

Hiding my feelings of hurt, I look away. Not waiting until they show us to our table, I excuse myself to go to the restroom. The guy Relic is speaking to watches me, but Relic doesn't notice me slipping away. I reach the stall quickly and text Yan.

Selena: Yan, I am sending you a pin on my location. Come pick me up, please?

Yan: Be there in five, Selena. Everything okay?

Selena: No, I need to leave.

Yan: Okay. Two minutes. I'll be outside.

Selena: Thank you.

I make my way outside without Relic noticing because they've already seated him at a table. When I see the Urus, I head over and get inside.

"Floor it before he figures out that I'm gone. I have an hour and a half before I have to see that dick Dimitri and find out what he wants. Relic is treating me like I don't exist because I stupidly mentioned the meeting, and I know he is dreading it, but he didn't have to act like an ass."

"He is probably worried just as much as you."

"Don't make excuses for him, Yan. He didn't have to treat me like I was invisible. He spent time talking to someone inside, and he didn't hold my hand or introduce me. I tried to hold his, and he ignored me. Take me to get a burger, please."

"Sounds good, Selena. I think I'll join you if you don't mind?"

My phone goes off when we arrive at a burger joint. It's Relic. I keep ignoring his repetitive calls.

"Are you going to get that?"

"No. He needs to leave me alone. I have something important to do and don't have time for his hot and cold tantrums. I have to see what Dimitri really wants so I can have my life back."

"I get it and I don't blame you."

After we eat, I feel full and satisfied. "Ready?"

"Yeah, let's go."

I pay the bill up front, even though Yan insists on paying.

We arrive at Mayhem. Apparently, Dimitri made arrangements to rent out the entire upper section of the club facing the DJ. I make my way up toward the section, and I can't see his face but notice that he is a very large man with tattoos and blond hair.

The bodyguard motions me to remove my coat. When I remove my coat, his eyes roam my body. He motions for me to go ahead but stops Yan. "He stays. Dimitri is waiting for you."

Fuck. "Fine."

When I walk toward Dimitri, he stands and his light eyes undress me, making me feel like I'm a piece of meat in a meat locker. He opens his arms wide with a big smile on his face. "So, she arrives," he says in a deep Russian accent.

I am surprised that he is attractive. Good-looking but not my type at all. He is tall with a muscular build but does nothing for me in the looks department. He looks like a Russian model.

"I must say, Selena, you are fucking hot." He notices my necklace and chuckles. "So, you are the one with Relic's attention. I had to see you for myself." He pauses in thought, waving his finger. "You are... what do you call it here in America? Ah... a triple threat?" He laughs, but I don't smile or play into his jokes.

"What do you want, Dimitri?"

"I want to meet you and assure you I am no threat to you. The only threat I will make is to take you to my bed and make you mine." His eyes fill with lust as he gazes at my legs.

"Keep looking at her like that, Dimitri, and there will certainly be a problem." My head whips around, hearing Relic's voice. He comes over, placing his hand on my shoulder. I want to shrug it off, but I can't forget Dimitri will think I am not interested in Relic.

Dimitri smiles. "So, it's true."

"What is?" I hear Sophia say as she stands next to Relic. I look over, and her eyes look between Dimitri and me, and that's when I notice her necklace. He smiles and laughs. "Oh, this keeps getting better," he says, clapping his hands together.

I stiffen when I feel his hand gripping my shoulder tighter, but not tight enough to hurt me.

"Relic, it must be nice to have two women at once. I think I'm jealous."

I look over at Sophia and feel her stupid remark coming like sandpaper over my skin, and I secretly wish to slit her throat.

She sidles up to Relic and purrs, "I don't know about her, but I belong to Relic. Isn't that right, baby? She just needed protection?"

My pulse beats loudly, wanting to rip that smirk off her face. Dimitri looks at Sophia, not interested, and returns his gaze to me.

"Is that right, Selena? You really don't belong to a King?" He leans forward. "I honestly expected to have a nice time with you alone," he whispers. "So Selena is single, beautifully available, and a bit dangerous. She ticks all my boxes nicely."

I never saw it coming. Relic rips the necklace off Sophia's neck. She gasps. He throws it on the table and his hands go to her throat.

"Relic, what are you doing?" she pleads.

"Get the fuck out! I never want to see you again. Now!" he thunders in a rage.

She scrambles away in shock, almost falling, wearing a look of embarrassment as she leaves.

"She's mine, Dimitri, and if anyone touches what's mine, I will kill them."

Dimitri chuckles. "You must have a pussy like gold to have Relic King claim you in front of me. Not to mention, I have heard the head of the yakuza is smitten with you. I have connections everywhere, but now for the good part. I want to... get rid of this Polish problem. It's not good for business." He sits on the red velvet sofa, casually crossing his legs.

I sit on the couch. "I agree. What do you suggest?" I ask, my insides singing at the way Relic tossed Sophia out.

He looks at me and gives me a predatory smile. "Jiro has taken out most of them already. That man is very loyal to you to be killing in your name, but I hear there is a threat coming your way soon. I'm here to warn you that you should lie low or go on vacation." He leans forward to pick up his drink. It's probably vodka.

Relic sits next to me with his arm draped behind me on the couch and orders a scotch. He offers me a Moscow mule, and I accept, needing the alcohol.

"I will send some men to deplete as many as I can to weaken them as much as possible, and I think it's best we eliminate them completely."

"I need you to shut down all their business dealings. They're into human trafficking," Relic adds.

"I asked you to come here with me to make sure you had someone or somewhere to go with you on this vacation I am suggesting. But, obviously, you belong to this asshole," he says, giving me a grin.

I smile at his comment, realizing he is trying to get under Relic's skin. Relic rubs my lips with his thumb. "She belongs to me. All of her," he says.

"Well then, have fun tonight and drink with me."

"Lost in the Fire" by Gesaffelstein is playing in the club, and not wanting to be rude since Dimitri came to warn me, we decide to stay awhile.

I move to the rail and Relic comes up behind me, holding my hands behind my back like he did in his closet.

He pushes my hair to the side so he can whisper in my ear. "You thought I was going to let that bitch get away with what she said about you, possibly putting you in danger?"

I shrug my shoulders, not knowing what to say.

"I'm sorry about earlier. You had every right to leave my ass there alone. Don't you ever forget that I love you, Selena." He kisses my neck and turns me around, putting my back against the rail. I raise my hands to wrap them behind his neck. "You look fucking hot in that dress. I want to slide your dress up and slide my cock inside you and watch you come all over me."

I arch into him because I want the same. I want him to take me right here. "Then do it."

His eyes darken, and he drags me toward a back room to the right. It's the perks of renting this side of the club. He takes me in and lifts me against the wall, pulls the shoulders of my dress down, and reveals my breasts. My legs wrap around his waist, and his tattooed hands hold me in place against the padding of the red velvet wall.

Anyone passing by the open door can see us, including Dimitri, but I could not care less. My head falls back against the wall as he slides his hard cock inside me.

He smiles when he feels the holster holding my mini collection of knives. "Naughty girl, I like it."

He thrusts inside me faster while he sucks a nipple into his mouth and then the other, trailing his tongue up my neck to meet my mouth. His stubble is turning into a beard, leaving red marks on my skin.

My breasts are exposed, glistening in the light of the red room while my pussy is drenched, taking him in. When he thrusts in deep, I push the heel of my spiked pumps into his ass, letting him know to go deeper.

"More."

"More, Selena? You want to give me that ass here in front of everyone?"

"I don't care. I want more," I breathe.

He slides me down the wall, and the tips of my pumps reach the floor. I bend over the couch and I watch in the mirrors on the wall.

He slides my panties to the side and slips his cock inside my ass while fingering my pussy and the sensation is too much. I come in seconds while he pounds into me, watching us in the mirror. He thrusts deep inside me and groans my name as I clench around his fingers.

He turns me back around and eats my pussy, sucking all of me clean. I fist my hands in his hair, whimpering his name. His beard feels amazing as he eats me, the rough sensation making me climax again.

"Fuck. I'm coming again."

When I finally come down from my high, I slip my dress back in place and fix my hair, waiting for Relic. He disappears into the restroom and brings me a wet towel to clean up and whispers softly, "I love you."

He looks up and kisses me. "Me too. Let's get home to bed."

Dimitri was watching us fuck from the couch, making sure no one could witness us, his erection tenting his pants. I glance at him with an arched brow.

"Oh, *malysh*, no wonder he's in love with you." He kisses his fingers. "I'm about to come in my pants just looking at you."

"Watch it, Dimitri," Relic scolds.

"Okay, King. I will respect your woman. It was nice, and if he fucks up, you can call me anytime, Selena."

"Not going to happen," Relic snaps.

"It was a pleasure, beautiful." He chuckles.

"Thanks for the heads-up, Dimitri."

"Always, Relic."

I kind of find him funny, but danger lurks in between his banter, but he does it to get a person's guard down before he strikes and kills you. When we are finally outside of the club, Relic motions for Yan to follow in the Urus back to the house. We wait in the valet area and I'm looking for Relic's car, but I am surprised to find Liam waiting for us in his GT-R.

I get in the back, and he smiles. "What are you doing here?"

"*Tu saves*. My big brother called for reinforcements in case shit went south. Besides, you both have been drinking, and he wants two cars instead of one. Just in case they are looking for you in a Urus."

"Yeah, yeah, I get it. It's smart."

"I heard you two were fucking like porn stars in the private room in front of Dimitri."

I smile. "Oh, come now, Liam. You know you can't believe everything you hear."

"So, is it true? Did I miss it?"

Relics slides into the front passenger seat and the door closes with a thud. "Fuck off, *cabrón*," Relic says playfully.

"I'm glad though," he says.

I look at him through the mirror in confusion. "About?"

"My brother falling in love with you. For officially having a girl like you."

I blush. "That is so sweet, Liam. I hope you find your queen soon."

He grins. "I don't know, maybe queens, plural. *Hynas*," he says, emphasizing the *s*.

After the twenty-minute drive, Relic and I walk into the house to the master bedroom and he continues to make love to me all night, holding me, reminding me that he will protect me.

My fear is losing myself to the darkness that consumes me after each kill, each life I must take to protect my own,

Chapter Sixty-One

RELIC

I make love to her throughout the night, whispering sweet nothings in her ear. If she only knew the things I have had to do for her. The Polish fucks that have threatened her. She probably thinks it's Jiro always protecting her, oblivious that I have had men infiltrating them since the night I told her to leave my house in a fit of jealousy and they attacked her. I sent them to assist Jiro.

They came here to find her, and my sources led me to their hideout. Liam, Deacon, and I found them with the Hillside Kings and slaughtered them.

They were here to rape and torture her, but I got one of them to speak after cutting off his fingers one by one. In agony, he told me their plan, and I saw red. Liam and Deacon knew right then how much I loved Selena, and how far I would go to protect her.

I watch her sleeping at my side peacefully, her hair sprawled on my pillow, her plump lips swollen from all the lovemaking. I took her in every position until she couldn't come anymore, her last moan on her lips when she fell asleep exhausted.

Jiro is meeting me in my office at the house. She has no idea that he's coming here. We need to discuss our next move with the Polish and eliminate the impending threat. The Polish will not relent until she is taken, and that will never happen. I will kill and slaughter anyone that touches her.

I have to put my jealousy aside and hope our love is strong enough for her to choose me because my fear is that her love for him will always be greater.

I've messed up many times with Selena because of my temper and fits of jealousy. I'll give her anything she wants, even my soul if she asks for it.

My phone buzzes on my nightstand, and I reach for it. Jiro is here, and I haven't even left the bed.

I get up quietly, trying not to wake her, reluctant to leave the warm bed with Selena entwined in the sheets from our lovemaking.

After I brush my teeth, I make my way to the front door and open it. Jiro is in his suit the yakuza wear. Every bit the leader with his shades.

"Hey, let's talk in my office," I say.

"Sure, where's Selena? Is she up already?"

"Err, no. She is tired and I didn't wake her. She doesn't know that you're here."

He follows me and when we reach my office, I sit down behind my desk and motion for Jiro to take a seat in the chair. We are going to discuss Selena and what information Jiro has found regarding the Polish and the threat against the head of Elysium.

They want to take control of the cartel and use their contacts to continue to smuggle women and children into their sick and twisted sex trade. That is never going to happen. My family is the cartel, and I have conducted business with my family since my father began running the business. They're in agreement to eliminate them and will do so at my say so. It would be the last card up my sleeve if Jiro turned out to be unsuccessful.

"Would you like something to drink?" I ask.

"No, I'm fine. Thanks, brother."

Jiro takes his yakuza hat off when he is around my brothers or me. We respect each other's culture and involvement in our families.

He sighs. "Everything is taken care of. The entire Polish family has been eliminated. There were no children, so that part was easy. She is safe for now until another asshole thinks they can succeed because they think she's vulnerable."

"Good, they don't know her skill or position or the fact that she has both of us willing to do anything for her." I am relieved that he took care of everything and that she will be safe with no one to harm her. The only thing that is going to bother me is that she doesn't have to stay here anymore. She can decide to go back to her apartment and her work. I don't want her to leave my house, not after I have fallen in love with her.

I want her to stay here with me, so I can protect her and make love to her when I come home.

"I have talked to Yan, and he agreed to stay here with her and work for Elysium and be her personal bodyguard. They get along, and he has proven that he can protect her. He will report to us both if he hears or sees anything. Especially when she gets in her moods and runs off alone," he says, making a point.

"Yeah, she can become a little firecracker when the mood strikes. I will try not to piss her off. I appreciate everything you have done for the Kings and Selena."

"I will always protect Selena even if I can't be with her, Relic. I told you, ever since we were kids, I have loved her and will always love her, even if that makes me sound weak and pathetic."

I am not going to lie and say I am not jealous of his love for her. She loves him and I know that. But if he loves her, I love her harder, so I will not ask her to choose.

"I think it best we both tell her everything. Lay everything out on the table and let her know everything that has been going on that she doesn't know."

"All right."

There is a knock on the door, and I draw my eyebrows together, not expecting anyone since I gave the housekeeper the night off. Yan isn't here yet, so it must be Selena, and honestly, I am nervous about her seeing Jiro. Will she forget about me and run to him?

"Come in," I say in a firm voice. I am trying not to show that I'm worried when the door handle turns.

Once the door opens, Selena is standing in a kimono robe that doesn't hide the fact she is naked underneath. Her nipples are visible, and my cock instantly hardens, straining my shorts.

Once she spots Jiro, her eyes go wide with shock.

"Jirosan?" she says. "What are you doing here? How did you..." she trails off once her gaze locks on mine. She walks inside and closes the door behind her.

"Good morning, beautiful," I say.

Her cheeks turn bright pink at my endearment. She looks like a woman who has been thoroughly fucked all night and has woken up to find herself alone and is looking for her lover. I'm pleased she woke up seeking my warmth in the bed.

"Good morning."

She is nervous, I can tell. Having both of the men you love in the same room can make a woman a little nervous when she doesn't know what will go down.

Jiro smiles. "Selena, you look beautiful. I am happy to see you. Please sit down. We need to discuss a few things with you."

She nods and moves to sit on the small couch. When she sits, the robe opens slightly, and you can see the swell of her breast and the outline of her nipple through the silk as she tries to adjust it.

Jiro swallows, and his eyes don't hide his want and need for her. He wants her just as much as I do. He tells her she is safe and all the details about the retaliation. She nods, understanding when Jiro says she doesn't need to stay here any longer but will still have Yan.

When it is my turn to speak, I look at her and smile. "I know this is a lot to take in, but I am glad we are telling you together with no interruptions. When you were in Japan, I knew you were upset at me, and at first, I was upset that you never told me who you were. But under the circumstances and after the way I treated you, I understood. I didn't want to admit my feelings for you because I had a duty to the Kings. Whether or not you were mine, I realized I fell in love with you. I was angry that I had to let you go, but I want you to know I never slept with Sophia after you left. I never chose her over you because when I saw the look on your face when you left, it ripped me apart to hurt you, and I had to figure out a way out of it. Please forgive me for being a coward and not fighting for you, Selena."

She stays silent and then looks at Jiro. He nods.

"I want to stay here. I don't want to go back to my apartment," she says.

The relief that floods through me is ecstasy in my soul. She wants me, but I can also see the torment in her eyes regarding Jiro. She is choosing me, choosing us. But...

"Selena, come here."

She doesn't hesitate and moves from the couch toward me, and I grab her hand and motion for her to sit in my lap, facing Jiro.

Jiro smiles at her, and she looks between us, confused.

"I'm going to ask you to marry me, Selena, but I want you to be sure that I'm the one you want as your husband," I say. "If you say no, I will understand. I know I have been a complete asshole, but I'm in love with you."

She looks at me with tears in her eyes and then back at Jiro.

"Say yes, Selena," he says. "I've known you almost all your life, and you love him. I can't offer you what you deserve, Selena. Even if I have to see you married to someone else, I will still love you and protect you. I love you that much. But there is a way to have us both."

"Yes. But what do you mean?" she says through her tears, and I hug her close to my chest.

"I love you," I tell her, kissing her eyes where her tears are pooling. I reach in the pocket of my sweatpants and pull out a black velvet box. "Jiro helped me get this because it had to be special."

I stare at the black velvet box and look between them. My heart is beating wildly in my chest, not believing that Jiro helped him choose the ring he planned on proposing to me with. Jiro smiles at me with happiness and love in his eyes.

Relic holds my hand. "Selena, will you do me the honor of being my wife? I promise to protect you and love you." He opens the box to reveal a huge red diamond ring with five rows of diamonds along the band. I inhale at how beautiful and rare the red diamond is as he slides it slowly on my finger.

"Yes," I say, sniffing back the tears of happiness.

"I know your favorite color is red, and your warrior over there knew where I could get a red diamond."

Happy tears slide down my cheeks. "Thank you, both of you. It's beautiful."

I get up from Relic's lap and give Jiro a hug. "Thank you for being there for me," I whisper.

"I'll always be here for you and by your side. Someone has to make sure your husband treats you right. But from time to time, I'll treat you better," he says, giving me a playful wink.

I giggle and his eyes connect with Relic's. Relic gives him a nod and I gasp when Jiro lifts me and sets me on the desk. He slides the robe off my shoulders, and it falls to my waist.

Jiro steps back and grins. My eyes are wide. What is happening?

"Will you come for us, Selena?"

"Okay, you two. Stop it." I laugh nervously.

Relic gets up from his chair and he isn't laughing, and neither is Jiro. My head whips back and forth between them both, and all I see is fire and lust in their gazes. Acceptance.

In a split second, they both pounce on me. Relic removes my robe, dropping it to the floor and I'm left completely naked and at their mercy. Relic grips my chin and tilts my head and takes my mouth to assure me he is okay with this. Our tongues meet and then I feel Jiro's hot mouth and wicked tongue between my thighs, and I whimper in Relic's mouth.

"I love you, Selena. We both love you. You can have us both," he says against my lips, and I'm lost. I'm complete. I belong.

I lift my hips, seeking more from Jiro's tongue.

"Heaven," Jiro says against my lips below. "I love you, Selena. I always have and always will love you."

"I want you both inside me."

Relic grips my throat. "Ready to take us both, *preciosa*?" He lowers his voice near my ear. "You're ready. We are going to take you and fill you."

That is why he took me from the back. He knew the whole time. "Mmm...fill me."

Jiro picks me up and Relic walks to the couch and lies back, sliding down his pants to fist his cock. Jiro allows my legs to slide down his body until I'm standing. He lifts my chin and kisses me passionately.

I turn and hover over Relic, impaling myself on his cock. I close my eyes as Jiro settles behind me. He spits on his cock as I lean forward to give him access.

He pushes the tip against my entrance, and I arch my back as we move in sync.

I moan. "God, yes."

Jiro slides his hand down my back and grips my ass. "Beautiful. She's ours."

He thrusts into me and I hold on to Relic's chest.

"She's gorgeous," Relic says, watching me grind on his cock while Jiro pounds me from behind.

"Fuck, she's tight. I'm not going to last," Jiro says.

Relic pinches my nipples and it pushes me over the edge.

"I'm coming!" I scream.

"Shit, I'm coming," Jiro grunts out and groans.

I grind on Relic, feeling him coming inside me. Jiro kisses my back, not yet pulling out of me.

"I love both of you. I will always love you both the same."

Epilogue

SELENA

SIX MONTHS LATER

Everyone is seated at the table in our home, including my grandfather and both our parents, to celebrate our wedding as Mr. and Mrs. King. I couldn't be happier to have my entire family and close friends together, including my warrior. My family is happy that I got married to Relic and know that I will be happy and safe.

Relic and Jiro have made me the happiest woman on earth. He showers me with love and respect, making sure I never have doubts about us, and I never stop showing him how much I love him. Jiro will always be my childhood friend and close protector. I will always love and respect him for helping me find who I am and making me fierce enough to fulfill my family tradition.

His loyalty to the yakuza means everything to him and his protection of me even more. It also means that Jiro will always be devoted to me. Relic and I have a strong bond as husband and wife, but I also have a bond with Jiro.

It is full of love and respect for each other. We have formed a tight allegiance in our underworld.

"Relic, what are your plans for you and Selena?" my grandfather asks.

Relic gazes into my eyes as he replies, "Sir, I plan on making you a great-grandfather and our parents' grandparents," he says mischievously.

"Selena, you picked good men. They have the right idea."

I smile at Mia, my face reddening by the second.

"So, when are you two going to make me an aunt?" I ask, pointing to Mia.

Deacon grins and Mia smiles. They got married two weeks before Relic and me and are very much in love.

"I'm working on it," Deacons says with a wink, and we all start laughing.

"Do you want to start now?" Relic whispers in my ear.

Turning my head into the crook of his neck, I whisper, "What about our parents?"

"I don't think they would mind," he says.

I have a secret. I don't think Relic has realized that Jiro has been careful. He doesn't want children because of his duty to the yakuza. He fears they would be a target, and traveling back and forth, he says he wouldn't be a good father.

"I have a secret." His eyebrow rises with curiosity. "I was going to wait, but since we are on the subject... I'm pregnant."

Relic's eyes widen and he drops his phone.

"Relic, are you okay?" I ask, worried and looking at Jiro.

"I have been careful," Jiro says, giving me a wink.

"Really?" Relic asks with a smile, happiness radiating from him.

I nod my head, confirming.

"When? How long?" he asks.

Mia grins knowingly. She's been hiding my secret for three months already, and I have been giving her crap about having kids. She knows Jiro has been careful. He doesn't want children. Everyone stops in midconversation with happiness dancing in their eyes. Our parents are hugging each other, and my grandfather sports a grin of approval.

"I'm sorry I have kept it from you all, but I had to wait because I didn't know until recently why I wasn't feeling well. I'm three months pregnant with twins," I say proudly.

Everyone congratulates us and hugs each other. Relic picks me up from my chair and twirls me, giving me a hug. He sets me down and caresses my stomach, knowing his babies are in there. He makes calls on his phone, giving orders.

"What are you doing?" I ask.

"What do you think I'm doing? Getting everything arranged. You will not lift a finger. My wife will not be stressed, and she needs the best of everything."

"I already have the best of everything, including both of you."

"I love you, our queen."

"I love you, my king." My head turns to glance at my warrior. "I love you, my warrior."

"I love you, my queen. Near or far. Together or not. Forever."

The End

I would like to thank my editors, beta readers, bloggers, ARC readers, and IndiesagePr, Thank you for everything. I also want to thank my editors Paula, Ellie Mclove, and Rosa for making my words shine.

Carmen Rosales is an emerging Latinx author of Steamy, and Dark Romance. Join her VIP list- www.carmenrosales.com

She loves spending time with her family. When she is not writing, she is reading. She is an Army veteran and is currently completing her Doctorate Degree in Business and has the love and support of her husband and five children. Follower her on social media, she loves to see a review and interact with her readers.

Scan the QR code to follow her on Social Media and sign up for her Newsletter:

www.ingramcontent.com/pod-product-compliance
Lightning Source LLC
Chambersburg PA
CBHW051120190726
48290CB00006B/1617